FABLED REMAINS

by

R. E. Busby

Copyright © R. E. Busby 2017

All rights reserved

Table of Contents

Preface

As the breath of life, that is common to all, is remorselessly drawn from the Earth, the Earth, left more and more uneasy at each near fatal blow, begins to rumble and roar as its shifting gaze seeks out a way to restore the balance between itself and humankind, humankind who plunder, ever remorselessly, its riches. Hopes of a peaceful resolution are failing, have failed, and there are growing signs, for those who wish to see them, of an uprising taking place under our very feet.

In nooks and crannies; hidden from the eyes of humans; peoples, fictionalised and forgotten, are awakened to time-worn portents. Portents, which some see as hope in the promise of reunion and reconciliation, others as the sign of a renewed ascendency and dominance. Each wait patiently as humankind, blinded by, and fettered to, their finite view of the empirical, blunders on towards their inevitable demise.

How far they fall, however, lies not in the hands of those who wait, or even in the insurgent earth itself, but in the hands of an ancient heritage; which one young woman is about to discover can lie dormant in the most ordinary of us, inherent in the very clay from which we sprang.

CHAPTER ONE

Facing Up to Fate

"I'm going to the Lake District and I'm not even sure where it is."

"It's in England."

"I know that! . . . Here in the north . . . right?"

The raise of Sarah's eyebrows said it all. Naomi had come flying into the staff room with the above exclamation and a complete look of alarm written on her face.

"I hate the countryside, the closest I ever get to nature is an apricot facial scrub. I'm the only person in my apartment block who doesn't have flower tubs on their terrace. Why did Laura have to get sick just before the Year Six trip to the back of beyond?"

Naomi slumped into one of the staff room chairs and sighed. She had been teaching in Reception for five years now and she loved it. It was challenging dealing with thirty, four and five year olds, but she and her Teaching Assistant Eva had a great working relationship and Reception class was their little world. It was a world that Naomi was extremely comfortable in, thank you very much, and one which she did not appreciate being pulled away from. Why the head had chosen her to replace Laura, the Year Six teacher, on this outdoor adventure course she just had no idea. She could only think it must have been the mention of an outdoor course, on her CV, that she had gone on once. Someone had recommended that it might look good on her CV for teacher training college. Perhaps it had, however, it had been four of the worst days of her life. She had climbed, walked, canoed; well she didn't actually canoe as she just kept tipping the canoe over and the instructor eventually took pity on her and let her go back to the hostel to dry out; she also hadn't done much walking or climbing either, rather she'd fallen over things into things and come back exhausted, bruised and vowing never to put herself through anything like that ever again. Now though, it was looking like the whole experience had come back to haunt her.

"I could say I was sick, that I'd caught the same bug as Laura," she heard herself say out loud.

"Don't you dare," Sarah warned, "If you do that I'll be next in the firing line, and I've just booked a long weekend to Dublin . . . *Non Refundable*."

Naomi's head fell back on the chair, it seemed her second brush with nature was inevitable.

Abruptly, the staff room door opened, and several other staff members came chattering in.

"That's the second earthquake in three days, one in Manchester . . ." A tall blonde woman in her early thirties was quickly interrupted by a short, round, middle-aged woman.

"I felt that one, just as I was getting out of bed on Monday morning."

"And now one in Leeds *this* morning," the blonde woman continued

"Yes, and they were quite strong," a young man in his early twenties chimed in.

"It's not unusual though," the blonde woman carried on, as she picked up a can of soup and began preparing to put it in the microwave, "the expert they had on the news this morning said we often have earthquakes in Britain and don't even notice them."

"That's all well and good," replied the short, round woman, seating herself at the staff room table and unwrapping her sandwiches, "but we *did* feel *both* of these."

"Yes, and on the programme I was watching last night they said it was unusual to have two of a magnitude of between 4.5 and 4.9 so close together." The young man relayed this worrying piece of information while chewing on a beef sandwich that had been particularly well laden with mayonnaise. The blonde woman looked at him disapprovingly and passed him a paper towel to wipe his chin.

"That may be true," the blonde woman continued, "but the expert this morning said that, so far, there was no reason to worry in fact. . ."

"*So far*. That means . . ." the short round woman jumped in again, "they don't really know whether we should worry or not. In fact, it often means they're trying to hide something and they're only saying we shouldn't worry so they don't cause a panic."

The short, round women seemed determined to think the worst and before the blonde advocate for calm could refute her feelings of apprehension, Naomi, who had been sitting listening to this conversation with growing interest, spoke up.

"Moira, I think you could be right, I mean two earthquakes in two days, of unusual magnitudes, that sounds worrying to me. Who knows where the next one may strike?"

"In the Lake District, *perhaps*," Sarah said, sarcastically.

"It's possible," Naomi retorted.

"What makes you think that?" Moira exclaimed.

"I don't," Sarah said, "and neither does, Naomi. She's just trying to use it as an excuse to get out of going on the Year Six outdoor activities weekend."

Naomi eyed Sarah reproachfully.

"Well, it's the truth," Sarah said.

"Oh you got lumbered with that joyful little excursion did you?" the blonde woman asked.

"Holly it's just awful, I don't know why the head didn't ask you or Keith. I mean you both work in Key Stage 2. I haven't worked with the juniors since my training six years ago."

"I think that's probably the point. You know how Neil doesn't like any of us to get *too* comfortable. He's always moving us around, giving us new initiatives to keep us on our toes. It's just your turn for a shake up."

Naomi knew Holly was right, she was just going to have to bite the bullet and get on with it.

"I could help you with advice on the sort of kit you'll need," Keith added helpfully.

Naomi answered him with a resigned. "Thanks."

Before he could begin his advice, the bell rang for the end of infants' dinner and Naomi and Sarah had to make their way back to their classrooms.

At the end of the day Neil Layton, the head, came to Naomi's classroom, just as the last child was leaving, to discuss the fated weekend. They both sat down at one of the class tables and Neil opened a folder and began.

"I've got a copy of the risk assessment here for you, and even though all of the children will be together most of the time, there will be occasions when they will be put in groups. There'll be three groups shared between me, Tracey and yourself (Tracey was the Year Six Teaching Assistant.) All of Year Six are attending so we will have ten children each. Here's your list."

Neil handed her a list of names. As she scanned them, her gaze was stopped short by one name, Elliott Freeman. Her heart sank. Elliott was one of those children whose name everyone learns very quickly because they have to say it so often. Elliott was one of the 'naughty' children. He had been difficult from day one, he didn't like to work and often talked back. Naomi had been thankful in the past that she had never had to teach him. He was in year one when she started teaching in Reception. He had become even more difficult in the past year. She had often seen him sitting outside the headmaster's office because of his behaviour towards his teacher or the other children in his class.

"We'll be staying in a hostel for the weekend except for one night when we'll be camping by the lake," Neil continued.

Camping! The word filled Naomi with dread, she immediately had visions of tossing and turning in a smelly sleeping bag on the hard ground, listening to the rain and wind batter the sides of the tent, while children afraid of the dark or storm, and others who had somehow managed to soak the bottom of their tents, cried and complained all around her. The thought of this trip just got better and better, she sighed inwardly.

"You'll need a good pair of walking boots . . ." Neil advised. "Naomi? Naomi!"

Neil called Naomi back from her miserable musings.

"What?"

"You'll need a good pair of walking boots," he repeated.

"Oh yes . . . Where will I get them?"

"There's a good outdoor supply shop in the market in town, reasonable prices. You should be able to pick up a good pair of boots there. Your sleeping bag, tent and outdoor equipment will all be supplied by the centre."

"Right."

"Naomi are you okay? You seem distracted."

"Oh no, I'm fine, just trying to take it all in. Don't want to miss any important information," she lied.

Forcing herself to focus on what Neil had to tell her, half an hour later, armed with a folder full of information and advice, she made her way home, resigned to her fate.

CHAPTER TWO

An Awkward Pause

The fateful day came all too quickly, teachers, children, parents and grandparents met in the school hall. Naomi entered the hall and was greeted by the noise of excited children. As she walked through the hall, smiling and greeting parents and children, she heard parents advising their apprehensive offspring that 'everything was going to be okay;' 'it was only for a few days;' 'they would be back before they knew it;' 'once they got there, they would be fine.' Naomi found herself trying to take comfort from these and other such reassuring comments.

Many of the children stood in groups discussing all the things they hoped to get up to on the visit, such as late-night feasts, and staying up all night talking. Passing one particular group of giggling girls Naomi gave a little shiver as she overheard them imagining themselves falling in the lake whilst canoeing. The image of her own such experience ran through her mind once more, her scrambling about, gasping for breath underneath a canoe in freezing cold water. Mentally shaking this disturbing vision off, she continued her way around the room, until she was stopped by Mr Layton who asked her, hurriedly.

"Have you got the lists of children, activities, risk assessment . . .?" he stopped short and raised his eyebrows, waiting for an answer.

"Yes. They're in my bag," Naomi said, tapping the blue satchel hanging from her shoulder.

"Good, good. Well, see you on the bus," he said, rushing off in the direction of Tracey to no doubt obtain a similar confirmation that all was in order.

Naomi glanced around the room. Her gaze fell on two figures who stood, strangely still, amidst all the commotion. It was Elliott Freeman, with a woman Naomi presumed was his mother, although they seemed oddly detached from one another as they stood in silence perusing the room. Naomi made her way towards them, with the intention of introducing herself and hoping to start off on the right foot with Elliott, but just before she reached them a smiling, round faced boy ran up to Elliott, breathing heavily.

"Hiya! Thought I wasn't going to make it, dad was late getting up as usual," he said, looking back at a man a little taller than himself, but twice as round, with a sullen look on his face. "Then we had trouble starting the car, it's a heap of junk really, couldn't find a bag for my stuff, was a last-minute rush last night to get everything together . . ." As the round-faced boy continued this tirade, Elliott and his mother listened passively.

"Hello, Elliott, Luke," Naomi interrupted.

"Oh hi, Miss," Luke replied, happily.

"Miss." Elliott said, giving Naomi a half glance.

Naomi turned to the woman next to him.

"And you must be Mrs Freeman?"

The young woman looked confused for a moment.

"Erm no, I'm . . . Elliott's carer," she said.

"Oh, I see," Naomi said, quickly feeling the awkwardness of the situation.

"Come on, Elliott," Luke cried. "Let's see if the bus has arrived." Grabbing Elliott's arm Luke pulled him off towards the hall doors. Naomi felt a rush of warmth towards Luke for rescuing his friend from the tense situation.

"I'm so sorry," Naomi said to Elliott's carer. "I don't know the children in Year Six very well, I teach the Reception Class. I had no idea there had been a change in Elliott's home circumstances."

"Yes, his parents split up a few months ago and neither of them is capable at the moment of taking care of him, so he's been placed in a communal home," the carer explained, shortly.

"Right, I see . . . erm, well thanks for letting me know."

After a short, awkward pause Naomi made her excuses to Elliott's carer and went over to Luke's father and introduced herself.

"Mr Adams. Hi. I'm Miss Kelly, Luke will be in my group on the trip. He seems to be really looking forward to it."

"Yes."

"Well . . . we'll take good care of him."

Mr Adams merely gave her a half nod and continued to stare sullenly straight ahead of him, so after another awkward silence, Naomi excused herself again.

As she made her way back to the middle of the room, she was accosted by two of the Year Six girls.

"Miss, Miss, Miss!" a tall frightened looking girl with long, lank, black hair, and a slightly shorter blonde girl, ran towards Naomi, smiling excitedly. "Miss, I'm so nervous I don't know if I'm going to be able to cope," the tall frightened looking girl cried. "What if I fall off a mountain, or drown in the lake, or get lost on the walk, or get sick in the night? Anything could happen, Miss. My mum and dad say everything will be all right, but I just don't know." The dark-haired girl covered her cheeks with her hands and stared at Naomi with eyes wide open. Naomi had to suppress a smile at this comical look of horror.

"Your parents are right Ruth, you'll be fine. Hannah . . ." Naomi gave a quick smile, by way of greeting, to the blonde girl, "will be in your room and they have qualified instructors and all the best safety equipment, you'll have a great time when you get there." Naomi did her best to sound convincing, and it seemed to work as Ruth managed a half smile.

"Miss, will you be in charge of our dorm?" Hannah asked.

"Miss Lock and I will be, yes," Naomi replied.

"But, Miss, if we get scared in the night can we come to you?" Ruth pleaded.

"Of course, you can."

The girls gave Naomi a quick hug before they hurried back to their parents. Naomi was surprised, but also pleased, by this spontaneous burst of affection from the girls towards her. It left her with a feeling that, maybe this trip wasn't going to be too bad after all. The next moment, Luke and Elliott came rushing in, closely followed by the Head to 'inform' everyone that the bus had arrived. This caused a sudden rush to pick up coats and bags. Once outside, there were some tears, lots of hugs and kisses and more reassuring words, all culminating in a flurry of frantic waving as the bus pulled away from the school gates.

CHAPTER THREE

A Brush with Nature

After a noisy bus trip, filled with the boisterous singing of half remembered chart songs and excited shouting and laughter, they arrived at the outdoor centre. Naomi was pleasantly surprised by the scene that greeted her. The centre was set in a couple of acres of very pretty countryside and the rooms, although they were fairly small, were clean and functional, with a bed, cupboard and a more than adequate en-suite. She, Tracey and Neil had their own rooms. The children shared between four and eight to a room. Hannah and Ruth had begged to be in a room as near to Naomi's as possible. Luckily, it turned out there was a room for four just next to Naomi's and as most of the other girls wanted to be in a room for six or eight, so as many of them could be together as possible, they were able to share that room. Unfortunately, the two girls who ended up sharing with Ruth and Hannah didn't seem too pleased at the prospect and complained that they couldn't be with their friends. Naomi explained that they would all be able to spend time in each other's rooms, and that they would spend all day together. This placated the girls somewhat, although they still made their way to their room with sullen looks on their faces. Even though Naomi understood their being upset, at what they perceived as an injustice, she couldn't help feeling annoyed with them for their total lack of thought for Hannah and Ruth's feelings as they made it quite clear that they were the last people on earth they wanted to share a room with. Hannah and Ruth, however, didn't seem that bothered by their classmate's reaction to them, they appeared to be used to it and didn't let it spoil their excitement at sharing together. Nonetheless, despite their seeming lack of concern at being rejected by their classmates, Naomi decided she would keep a special eye on them both. Hannah and Ruth made this easy for her, as they very rarely left her side when they were outside and always insisted on being in her group.

Despite Naomi's deep reservations about the trip, she found herself enjoying it much more than she had expected. The weather was warm and sunny, which made all the activities much more pleasant experiences. Even the canoeing, which she had been dreading, wasn't too bad, she had managed to stay upright at least. She didn't get lost during orienteering either, indeed her group managed, by some miracle, to get back to base first. She even discovered she had a penchant for archery, winning her the accolade of the whole class, raising her street cred amongst them massively. She had thankfully managed to get out of abseiling, as Ruth, who she soon discovered liked the outdoors even less than she did, had become hysterical just at being *asked* to make her way down a high wall, hanging by a rope, with no other visible means of support. Seizing her opportunity, Naomi had offered to give up her turn and stay with Ruth, taking her for a short walk to help calm her down.

A three-mile hike was planned for the last morning of their stay followed by a night camping by the lake. Naomi spent most of the night before it, reassuring Ruth that there were no poisonous spiders or snakes or plants in England capable of rendering her lifeless in an instant, and that they were not likely to be attacked by any large wild animals. Fortunately, when the morning did arrive it was another pleasant day weather wise, which did a lot to alleviate Ruth's apprehensions regarding the trip. It also meant that she could put to rest her nightmare, that they had all got lost on the mountain during a terrible storm, which had culminated in three girls being disintegrated by random bolts of lightning. On hearing this night terror Naomi couldn't help wondering if the three girls who met their doom, so decisively, were the three girls who always made it their business to laugh the loudest whenever Ruth's fears got the better of her.

They set off at ten o'clock making their way up a slight incline with a light breeze in their faces.

As the walk progressed Naomi found herself at the back with the stragglers made up of, Ruth because she seemed to find each step torturous, Hannah because she wouldn't leave Ruth, Luke because he just couldn't keep up, and Elliott, who, although he said he hated walking, Naomi felt sure was holding back for Luke's sake. Luke had taken some flak over the weekend from the other boys because he had struggled with some of the activities and Elliott had acted like a sort of bodyguard, deflecting their cruel comments with a few choice words of his own. They were an odd couple, Elliott so lanky, sullen and brooding and Luke short and stocky always smiling and chatty. Naomi supposed that it was the fact that they were both 'different' that drew them together.

Naomi wasn't unhappy about her predicament, their pace suited her and gave her the excuse she needed to take the climb at a more leisurely pace, as the Head led his more able troops on ahead. There was another reason though, a more personal one, why Naomi, if truth be told, had taken these particular children under her wing and perhaps even taken the time to seek them out. She, like them, had always felt a little different, a little out of the 'mix.' As an only child and moving around a lot for her father's job she had found it difficult to make friends. Her parents were kind but distant. At eighteen she left home for university and rarely went back, throwing herself into her work and into achieving her goal of becoming a teacher. All these experiences and feelings gave her a silent shared sensibility with her little troop, and meant she was comfortable in their company, and it appeared they were equally relaxed with her. She and her little band of misfits made their way along the uneven path before them in a pleasantly relaxed manner chatting and encouraging one another. Even Elliott came out of himself a bit, revealing a love of the fells surrounding them that further belied his claim that he hated walking. The little group were really impressed by his knowledge and were full of questions, and as he answered them he further relaxed, there was even the hint of a smile threatening to emerge from his lips. His mini lecture also had the effect of calming Ruth, opening up to her the beauty that surrounded them as they climbed higher and higher up the fell.

They were enjoying themselves so much that it was some time before Naomi became aware that she could no longer see the rest of the group in front of them. Feeling a little apprehensive, at seeming to be alone on the mountain, she called on the children to speed up their pace a little.

"Come on we need to catch up with the others, Mr Layton will be wondering where we've got to."

The children immediately began to move forward with more focus on their actual destination. They had hardly made any headway, however, before they were stopped in their tracks by panicked screaming coming from up ahead. Before they had a chance to react, they felt it, the ground beneath them was moving and suddenly they too were screaming. Naomi fought to stay upright while, at the same time, trying to catch Ruth and Hannah, as they fell and lay scrambling on the ground near her. The rocks around them shook, uncontrollably, and conveyor belt like carried them down the incline. Elliott and Luke had also lost their footing, Naomi watched helplessly as they grabbed at rocks trying to stay their fall, only to have them come away uselessly in their hands. Finally, Naomi fell forward onto the rolling surface beneath her ... then ... nothing.

CHAPTER FOUR

A Tall Dark Stranger

The incline was getting steeper and steeper, Ruth and Hannah were becoming more and more anxious.

"Ruth, you take my hand and then you hold Hannah's hand, we'll be fine, just keep calm and follow me. Boys you. . ." Naomi stopped. Where were the boys? She looked about frantically for them.

"Luke, Elliott, where are you? Where are you?" There was no answer, the girls began to scream.

"Girls, it's all right, stop screaming." They paid no attention to her, they just kept on screaming. "Girls please, please, STOP!"

Naomi's eyes snapped open; she was breathing heavily. She closed her eyes and calmed her breathing. Slowly, she opened her eyes again and was startled by the face of a man leaning over her.

"How are you feeling?" The man's voice was calm and concerned.

Naomi stared blankly at him for a moment and then began to do a mental assessment of her body. She couldn't feel any pain, so she answered.

"Okay . . . I think."

"Would you like something to drink?"

"Yes . . . thank you." As his face moved out of her vision, she followed him with her eyes turning her head to keep him in view. "Sssswhooo! Ow!" she cried, as a pain shot through her neck.

"What's wrong?"

"It's my neck."

"Just stay still while I get your drink."

Naomi began to check herself in more detail, starting with a cautious wiggle of her toes, then she moved her feet slowly up and down, as she did so she realised that she was covered by a coarse blanket, she clenched and unclenched her hands. With great relief she realised that she could feel her legs and move her arms. She didn't make any attempt to move though until the man had brought her water. He put his arm gently under her neck.

"Does that hurt?" he asked.

When Naomi answered in the negative, he began to lift her towards the water bottle he held in his other hand, then putting it to her lips tipped it just enough for Naomi to sip the water into her mouth. The water was ice cold and the shock of it had the effect of not only quenching Naomi's thirst but clearing her head somewhat. She glanced surreptitiously at him as he concentrated on her lips and the cup. His hair was dark, shoulder length, a tousled, soft, curled mane. He wore a beard of a few days growth, his complexion was brown and ruddy, his features were large but not unattractive, at this point in her perusal his eyes looked up and met hers. They were dark and penetrating, so much so that for a moment Naomi was caught in their gaze. Then, suddenly feeling the embarrassment of the situation, she looked away and lifted her hand to signal she had had enough to drink. The man gently laid her back down and once again disappeared from her view. This time she didn't try to follow him, instead she stared directly at the sky above her which was grey and overcast. She began to wonder how long she had been unconscious then. . .!

"The children! There were children with me, ahh!!" Naomi cried out in pain and grabbed the back of her neck, as she forced herself up to a sitting position, anxiety for the children's welfare overriding any feelings of concern she may have about her own condition. "I need to find them," she looked around anxiously for her rescuer. He was tending a fire close by and looked up at her but stayed bent over the fire as she went on. "I was with four children, two boys and two girls, there were also twenty-six other children and two adults a little way ahead of us. I need to look for them."

"I've checked this area within a three-mile radius and there were no others, only you."

"Well you must be mistaken," Naomi said, putting her hand to her head, trying to think through the dull ache throbbing through it. "Perhaps the emergency services have already got to them . . . yes that must be it." This logic eased Naomi's mind considerably and she relaxed somewhat. Focusing once again on her rescuer she said, "My name's Naomi Kelly," and then waited expectantly for the strangers reply.

"Marcus."

"Do you know what happened?"

"There was an earthquake."

Naomi felt her stomach turn over.

"I need to make contact with the emergency rescue teams. There are people who will be worried about me. I'd be really grateful for your help."

Marcus continued to stoke the fire, and for a moment said nothing. When he did look up, he had the look of someone with very bad news to deliver. Naomi felt suddenly sick and unconsciously clutched her stomach.

"There are no rescue teams."

His matter-of-fact manner had the effect of irritating Naomi.

"But there must be," she declared, in a raised voice. "There are always coordinated rescue efforts in disasters like this. What makes you say that? How could you know that?"

"If there are any rescue teams, they will have their hands full in your towns and cities."

Naomi felt her eyes begin to sting as the gravity of what he was trying to tell her began to sink in, she blinked and managed to stem the tears that tried to force their way down her cheeks. Taking a deep breath, and unwilling to accept what Marcus was implying, and somewhat disconcerted by his use of the word 'your' she asked.

"How do you know the earthquake was so severe? Do you have a radio, or an app on your mobile . . .? Mobile. My mobile!" Naomi quickly located her phone in the inside pocket of her coat. It looked as if it had survived without a scratch, she pressed the on button . . . 'no signal'. She began to wave it about in the air searching for a signal. When that didn't work, she pushed herself up on to her knees and with some difficulty tried to stand. Seeing her struggle Marcus moved over to her and helped her up.

"Thank you," she said, somewhat grudgingly.

Once on her feet it took her a moment to gain her balance. The air felt damp and cool on her face, and as she took her first proper look around, she couldn't tell if it was sunrise or dusk. The sky was blanketed with dark clouds, but even though the light was hazy it was possible to see around quite clearly. She looked at her phone for the time. It was 4.30 in the afternoon, and she could see by the date it was the day after they had set off on the walk. She began to hold the phone in the air again. They were on a grassy verge in a gully, mountains climbing all around them. She made her way falteringly up the grass verge, Marcus following close behind. When they reached the top of the bank Naomi let out an involuntary cry, her knees buckled and the phone dropped from her hand, smashing its way down the rock face. Marcus' arms quickly surrounded her, preventing her from following in its wake.

The picturesque landscape, she and her little group had so admired yesterday, was unrecognisable. Gone were the array of well walked tracks, dust, ash and vast mounds of rubble now covered the once defined scene. Whole mountainsides had crumbled into the surrounding lakes. Fragments of wood splintered and blackened, and household debris floating on the murky waters, the only evidence of the jetties, hotels and homes that had once dotted, the now devoured, lake banks. Trees torn from their roots lay strewn across the landscape, while others stood bent and broken across the rocky plain. In the distance, towers of smoke surged up to meet the sky and merged with the grey clouds that tumbled above.

Marcus sat her down. Naomi stared at the devastated landscape feeling completely overwhelmed. She sat there for some minutes until she heard Marcus' voice break through her grief.

"We need to move on, and find cover for the night, there is a storm on the horizon."

Naomi raised her eyes and looked as far into the distance as she could, and wondered how he could tell a storm was coming from the plethora of black clouds that filled the sky from the smoking debris. Marcus touched her shoulder lightly and helped her to her feet. Automatically, Naomi followed Marcus back to the sheltered camp site. She watched silently as he put out the fire and picked up the blanket that had been covering her, and a long black leather coat which had been her pillow. He put the coat on himself, the blanket in a brown leather bag and placed the bag over his shoulder, adjusting the strap across his chest, and without speaking started to lead the way. Naomi followed, unseeing and unthinking. Her guide made his way deftly across the rocky terrain, often having to stop and wait for her to catch up. They went on like this for some time, until Naomi was brought out of her stupor by a searing pain in her left ankle, she screamed and stopped short. Marcus turned and ran swiftly back to her.

"What's wrong, what happened?"

"It's my ankle, I've twisted it. I wasn't looking where I was going, I'm sorry I..." Naomi burst into uncontrollable tears.

Marcus sat down next to her and waited patiently as she vented her grief.

When she had completely exhausted herself, Naomi let out a few shuddering breaths, and sat, completely spent, with her face in her hands. Then she felt rain begin to splash the back of her neck.

"We need to move on," Marcus said, softly.

"Yes . . . Of course, I'm sorry," Naomi said.

Dazed and confused, Naomi tried to stand up but found her ankle was too painful for her to be able to put weight on it.

"I will carry you," Marcus said.

Before Naomi could make any attempt to protest or apologise at the prospect of his having to carry her, and so further slowing them down, she found herself swept up in his arms, and rather than slowing their progress it had the opposite effect. No longer hindered by Naomi's inability to keep up Marcus moved swiftly and expertly from rock to rock, carrying Naomi as if she were no more than a small child. Naomi secured her arms round his neck and, exhausted, lay her head passively on his shoulder. The motion of Marcus' assured steps rocked Naomi into a stupor from which she was unable to keep her eyes open, and soon, safe in her rescuers' arms, she was no longer aware of the passing of time.

It wasn't until she began to feel her head rock heavily back and forth against Marcus' shoulder that Naomi woke from her semi-conscious state. She lifted her head slightly and looked around her, groggily. Marcus was continuing to make his way swiftly, if not smoothly, over much rougher ground. He coursed his way towards a group of fells, where two in particular stood proudly together, like brothers in arms. As he began to climb up, his breathing became more laboured. Naomi immediately offered to try and make her own way, now that she had rested, but he ignored her and kept his sights on his goal, which turned out to be the craggy base which joined these two fraternal giants.

On reaching his goal Marcus lowered Naomi onto a large boulder. She watched, as he moved a few metres away from her towards the rock face and then vanished behind a wide outcrop. She craned her neck to see where he had gone, but from her position on the boulder it was impossible to see around the outcrop. She pushed herself up to a half standing position to try and get a better look, but it made no difference. Sitting back down she kept her eye on the point of Marcus' disappearance and waited. The lowering atmosphere all around her began to fill her with a sense of foreboding, and she tried putting weight on her ankle, but it was no good it was still too painful to walk on. 'Why doesn't he come back?' she thought. As the minutes ticked by, darker thoughts began to fill her mind like; what if he did come back, and he wasn't alone, what if he meant to hurt her? After all, she had no idea who he was, where he had come from. He was dressed strangely too, for a Fell walker, and out here in the middle of nowhere she was completely at his mercy. Just as she had almost convinced herself that he was some kind of madman, he reappeared. Naomi started! Her apprehension, however, quickly turned to curiosity. He was accompanied by what Naomi thought at first was a small child, but as they made their way towards her, she realised was, in fact, a very small female adult.

"This is Ceraline, she will attend to your ankle."

Naomi was fascinated by Ceraline's appearance, she looked like a little Dresden doll; her skin was snow white with a slight sheen, her eyes, steel blue, oval shaped, and large for her delicate face; her lips were pressed together in a thin red line. She was dressed in an ankle length leather skirt, a fitted leather jacket and boots. Her curly blonde hair, somewhat dishevelled, was pulled back in a ponytail. Naomi took all this in, as Ceraline removed a satchel from around her diminutive body and took from it a small wooden box.

"Please remove your shoe and sock."

Ceraline's voice had an authority which was incongruous with her doll-like features. Naomi obediently removed her shoe and sock and presented it to Ceraline for appraisal. Ceraline examined it with care, then set to work by opening the box and removing from it a handful of green leaves and a smooth black rock. She rubbed the leaves on the rock releasing the sap from them, then she rubbed the moist leaves gently over Naomi's wound, Naomi winced as she touched her. After a few moments, the healer stopped rubbing and took a small round container from the box, removed the lid and scraped some sort of grey paste out of it onto her fingers, and then began to expertly massage it into Naomi's very swollen ankle. Naomi felt heat course through her ankle and the throbbing ease considerably.

"Thank you, that feels much better."

"You're welcome," Ceraline replied, with a curt smile. Then, turning to Marcus, said, "She should be able to walk soon."

"Thank you, Ceraline."

"I only hope you know what you are doing," and with this enigmatic pronouncement, not looking at either of them again, Ceraline packed up her things and nimbly negotiated her way over the rocks, until she disappeared once more around the rock face.

"What did she mean . . . I hope you know what you're doing?"

Marcus stared at Naomi intently for a moment and then said, "She's concerned about my helping you."

"Why?"

"There isn't time to explain now, we need to get under cover, the storm is ready to break."

"Look, I'm grateful for everything you've done for me, but I really would like to . . ." before Naomi could finish, a loud clap of thunder resonated all around them and the rain began to fall in sheets.

Marcus moved quickly towards her. Raising his voice, to be heard over the rain and thunder which filled the air, he called out, "Can you walk?"

Seeing it was pointless trying to argue, under the circumstances, Naomi cautiously put weight on her ankle, and finding the pain was more than bearable she put her now wet sock and shoe back on as quickly as she could. As soon as she had finished Marcus unceremoniously took her hand and hurried her toward the rock face that Ceraline had, a few moments earlier, disappeared around. On the other side of the outcrop there was a narrow crevice. Marcus let go of her hand and took a few steps into it, signalling Naomi to follow him.

"Stay close to the rock face," Marcus called through the swirling wind.

Naomi watched as Marcus put his back to the rock wall and edged his way along. She followed his lead, trying to keep a close eye on her footing, as the rain lashed against her face. They hadn't gone far when Marcus reached towards her.

"Take hold of my hand."

Marcus' hand enveloped Naomi's, they moved a few steps together, the crevice was just wide enough for them to squeeze into. Naomi felt a sudden rush of claustrophobia and turned her head away from the rock wall, that was practically touching her face, towards Marcus. Naomi took a sharp intake of breath, much to her consternation, half of Marcus' body had disappeared into the surface of the rock. Marcus looked back at her reassuringly and gave her hand a slight tug. Reluctantly, but nonetheless completely transfixed by the scene unfolding before her, she continued along through the crevice watching, as if in a dream, Marcus' body completely disappear apart from the hand that held hers. Then, seeing her own hand slip easily through the rock surface, she shuddered and braced herself as the rest of her body appeared to melt into the rock until, much to her surprise, clear skies and bright sunshine filled the sky above her, and they appeared to be standing at the edge of what looked like a small village.

In the near distance there were rolling hills dotted with clusters of trees. In a state of great confusion, Naomi looked back to where she had come from and there, through the narrow crevice, she could see the storm continuing to rage, only now it was as if she were looking at it through a translucent window. She turned a questioning gaze on Marcus.

"Welcome to Oakvale," he said, smiling.

Naomi was too stunned to speak, she just stood, opened mouthed, staring at the extraordinary scene before her. Marcus began to move down, what appeared to be, the main street of the village, Naomi following closely behind him. This was like no other village Naomi had ever seen before. It was set in a valley, that was ordinary enough, what made it unusual were the buildings and the . . . 'people'. Many of the buildings were shaped into the rock faces of the two mountain ranges which formed the valley, the windows and doors of these dwellings were fringed by lintels and architraves decorated with ornate carved masonry. Stone stairways, cut out of the rock face, led down to the street. On the street there were rows of single storey wooden cabins in clusters of three or four, all of which displayed the same kind of carvings as the stone houses above them. The cabins also featured something which Naomi couldn't help smiling at, despite her dumbfoundedness, each of them was adorned with a singular shaped chimney, carved into the form of various types of fish, cats, mice, rabbits and all kinds of birds, all contorted into assorted poses, allowing smoke to billow out of the top of their heads, mouths and beaks respectively, and each of them showing the same expert artisanship as the lintels and architraves. However, even more curious than the buildings themselves, were their inhabitants.

Many of them resembled Ceraline, others were somewhat taller and a lot rounder, with pointed ears and small piercing eyes. They stood conversing in doorways, or engaged in various tasks around the dwellings, washing clothes in wooded tubs, cleaning doors and windows, while others were occupied with masonry or carpentry tasks. Tiny children played boisterously in the street, being alternately shooed or indulged by the adults they disturbed. Gradually, the villagers became aware of their new visitors. They began to stare at them and whisper to one another, children stopped their play and ran to their parents, as if for protection. Marcus returned their stares with a nod of friendly acknowledgement, the villagers returned his nod pleasantly enough, but eyed Naomi suspiciously. Naomi began to feel increasingly uncomfortable, and kept her eyes ahead of her, wishing they would get to their destination quickly. Eventually, they left the main thoroughfare, and the valley began to widen. Here the village became more suburban, populated with slightly larger cabins than those in the main street, surrounded by beautifully kept gardens, and just a few stone dwellings were dotted above them in the hillside. At last, Marcus stopped at the gate of a cabin, the garden of which was, on one side, given over to a lush green lawn enclosed with colourful flower beds, while the other side heaved with the green foliage of root vegetables and herbs. Walking down the neat gravel path to the house Naomi's senses were overwhelmed by the competing scents of flowers and herbs.

Marcus knocked on the door. After a few moments, it was opened by a middle aged woman, who bore similar features to Ceraline, however, she was a little taller with an olive completion, chestnut eyes and dark hair that was tied in a tight bun; she wore a flowered apron, an ankle length skirt and a crisp white blouse, the sleeves of which were rolled up to her elbows. She smiled a welcoming greeting to them both.

"Come in, come in," she cried, bustling them both in through the door.

Naomi was surprised at the woman's relaxed greeting it was as if she had been expecting them. Once inside there was an intoxicating aroma of home-made soup and bread. Naomi hadn't eaten since before she left for the ill-fated walk with Year Six, and up until now food had been the last thing on her mind, but the inviting smell of the soup left her suddenly feeling ravenous.

As if she had read her mind her hostess said, "You must be exhausted, and starving. I've made soup. Your favourite, Marcus, vegetable . . . Oh my dear!" the woman said, inspecting Naomi up and down. "You are soaked through. We must get you out of those clothes before you catch a chill . . . Hmm! You're somewhat taller than I am, but I *think* I have something that you might be able to wear while we dry your clothes, come with me into the bedroom. Marcus make yourself at home, you know where everything is."

Marcus nodded and started to take a bowl down from one of the shelves in the kitchen. Naomi felt her stomach rumble and gave a longing glance at Marcus filling his bowl with soup, as her hostess hurried her into the bedroom and closed the door behind them. Once inside the room her hostess hurried over to an ornate dresser, which stood grandly against one of the walls. She opened the top draw and pulled out a white slip and some underwear, placed them on the bed, then began to rummage through the bottom draw mumbling to herself.

"Mmmm. Right . . . I know it's in here somewhere, no, no, no . . . ah yes! Oh no! No, no ye. . s! Found it!" With somewhat of a flourish, she produced a long white night gown from the drawer and laid it neatly on the bed. "This was my grandmother's, she grew to be five feet tall, one of the tallest of our race *ever*," she said proudly. "Such a beautiful woman, she made this herself, as she did all her clothes. Such a wonderful seamstress, and I learned all I know about baking and gardening from her, and oh what a singing voice she had. People would come from miles around, just to hear her sing at the summer solstice celebrations. She was a wonderful woman . . . I miss her very much . . ."

Naomi waited in silence as her hostess stared lovingly at the nightgown, lost in reverie. Then, suddenly becoming aware of Naomi's presence again, she said, "It will be a little short on you, but it should do." She placed it lovingly on the bed. "Well, I'll leave you while you get changed. When you're done bring your clothes into the other room and I will dry them by the fire. There is a towel hanging behind the door that you can use to dry yourself."

When the door closed Naomi began to change. Taking the towel from the door she dried herself, once dried she untied her wet hair and put it in a turban with the towel. She took the slip off the bed and put it on, it felt like silk, and reached just passed her knees. The nightgown, however, was made of cotton and felt somehow warm and comforting next to her skin, it reached half way down her calves and just below her elbows, fitting loosely about her body. Once dressed she picked up her wet clothes and made to open the door.

Just as she turned the handle, she suddenly remembered that Marcus was on the other side of the door, and she certainly didn't feel comfortable with him seeing her dressed, as she was, in a nightgown. She stood at the door, debating silently with herself as to what she should do, until her stomach began to rumble again, and she knew she couldn't go much longer without something to eat. So, the decision made for her, she began to cautiously open the door, peeking her head round to see if she could see where he was in the room.

"Don't worry! Marcus has gone," her hostess called out, at the sound of the door opening. "He will be back in the morning," she said, as she stood at the kitchen table, ladling soup into a bowl. "Come and eat, you must be starving."

Naomi didn't have to be asked twice she made her way eagerly to the table, passing the wet clothes to the outstretched arms of her hostess, and sitting down began to eat with relish. Everything tasted as good as it smelled.

After placing Naomi's wet clothes on a wooden drying frame at the side of the fire, her hostess took a kettle from the stove, and poured a hot substance into the empty cup next to Naomi's bowl, saying while she did so.

"I've made some camomile tea it has recuperative powers and will help you get a good night's sleep."

Naomi nodded her thanks with a mouth full of soup and bread.

While she was eating, Naomi took the opportunity to survey her surroundings. The room was split into two distinct areas, much like the garden. On one side was the kitchen with a wooden table and several chairs, a stove, cupboards, and a sink. The other part of the room consisted of a cosy seating area with a small sofa and two, comfy looking, mismatched, chairs; a large open fire burned away heartily in the grate. There was a sparkling crystal vase on the mantelpiece, which contrasted strangely with the rest of the plain, but pleasant décor, it was filled with a colourful bouquet of flowers. The vase was flanked on either side by two carvings, one of an owl and the other of a rabbit. A colourful rug lay neatly before the hearth. When she had finished taking in the room Naomi turned her gaze on her hostess, who was busying herself at the stove and sink. Naomi couldn't get over how strange she looked, in fact how strange everyone in the village had looked, and what had she meant when she referred to her grandmother as being the tallest of their 'race'. It felt like she was having some bizarre dream, and perhaps she was. Too tired to think any more, she began to pick up her bowl and cup intending to take it to the sink, but her hostess, seeing what she was about to do, quickly took over the task.

"I'll do that!" She said, firmly. "You go and sit by the fire and dry your hair. There is a brush on the chair nearest the fire."

Naomi took the brush from a wing back chair, and taking its place, listlessly removed the towel from her head and brushed out her wet hair before the comforting flames.

Soon her hostess came to join her.

"I think it's about time we introduced ourselves," she said. "My name is Rochan."

"Naomi."

"That's a beautiful name. What does it mean?"

"Erm . . . I believe it means pleasant. I looked it up on the net once."

"The net?" Rochan looked blankly at Naomi.

"The Internet," Naomi clarified.

Rochan continued to stare at Naomi blankly.

"I'm sorry I do not know what you mean by the Internet," she said. "But never mind, it is a good name, with a good meaning. My name means, bringer of light."

"That's beautiful."

"I do my best to live up to it, by following my grandmother's example and bringing what light I can to those of my neighbours whose lives are sometimes darkened by the vicissitudes of life."

Naomi was touched by this expression of kinship from her new acquaintance and began to feel relaxed, as the conversation; which unlike everything else she had experienced since meeting Marcus; continued in a routine and familiar fashion.

"Have you lived here all your life?" Naomi asked.

"In the village, yes, but not in this house. This was my grandmother's house. I came to live with her after my parents died when I was six years old."

"I'm sorry," Naomi interjected.

"There is no need to be sorry, my grandmother was, as I told you before, a wonderful woman. I've been very fortunate. And you? Where do you come from?"

"At the moment I live in a flat in Manchester," Naomi said, stifling a yawn.

"Oh, your exhausted. Time for bed," Rochan's voice took on an authoritative tone once more. "There will be time enough tomorrow for us to get to know one another. Off you go, and make sure you put the lamp out before you go to sleep."

Too exhausted to argue, Naomi got slowly up and made her way to the bedroom, wishing Rochan goodnight through another yawn. Once in bed she blew out the lamp, as instructed, lay her head down on the plump pillows and slipped into oblivion.

CHAPTER FIVE

A Proper Introduction

Naomi opened her eyes and gazed torpidly at the white ceiling above her. Slowly, she turned her head to one side bringing into vision the tall oak dresser from the night before, the sight of which had the effect of bringing her into full consciousness. So, she thought to herself, it hadn't been a dream, her stomach tightened as she remembered what had happened and at the thought of the fate that had befallen the children and her work colleagues. Swallowing hard, she pursed her lips and blinked back the tears which sprang into her eyes.

After a moments sad reflection, pushing the feelings of sorrow to the back of her mind, she sat up and looked around the room. The sun was shining through the curtained window next to the bed and her dry clothes lay neatly on a chair in the corner. There were noises coming from the other room. Rochan she thought, possibly preparing breakfast . . . Rochan! The thought of the strange little person in the other room filled Naomi's mind and brought with it a cascade of other images; the village, its inhabitants, Marcus, and Ceraline with her 'magical' ointment and finally the devastation she had seen. Trying to make sense of it all was impossible, it seemed so unreal, yet it was real. She sat still in the bed, allowing the tears to flow down her cheeks for a moment, then brushing them away resignedly she got up and dressed.

In the main room Rochan sat by the fire sewing.

"Good morning," she said, looking up on Naomi's entrance, "I hope you slept well? I will get you some breakfast." Rochan made her way to the stove and ladled out a large portion of porridge into a bowl.

"Good morning," Naomi said, sitting down at the table waiting to be served.

Rochan placed the steaming bowl of porridge in front of Naomi, then filled a cup with water placing that next to the bowl. Naomi sat stirring the porridge thoughtfully. A good night's rest had awoken Naomi's curiosity, and she couldn't help staring at her odd little hostess when she thought she wasn't looking. Rochan, however, was fully aware of Naomi's heightened interest in her.

"Is there something you want to ask me?" Rochan asked, looking Naomi full in the face.

Naomi, taken aback at being discovered, was just about to answer a polite no, but staring into Rochan's singular eyes Naomi's sense of propriety, in not wishing to offend her hostess, was overcome by her need for answers, and she found herself saying . . . "Actually . . . yes there is . . . Look I don't mean to offend you . . . it's just . . . that I've never met anyone like you before . . . I mean you keep saying 'your' race, what do you mean by that, what race are you?"

Rochan looked at Naomi, her face wearing a touch of wonder, and said, "Why didn't Marcus tell you? You're in the Land of the Faerie's."

Naomi had laughed before she realised it, but quickly stifled her mirth, seeing, by the look on Rochan's face, that she was completely serious.

"I'm sorry," Naomi said. Then continued, still struggling to control her mirth, "So you're telling me you're a . . . faerie?"

Looking completely benign Rochan replied with a simple . . . "Yes."

Naomi sat stunned, lost between mirth and disbelief, then after a moment of reflection she said, "You know, the weird thing is . . . that after everything that's happened to me in the past couple of days, that actually makes sense."

Rochan looked at her, questioningly.

"Never mind," said Naomi, smiling. "And Marcus. . .is he a . . ." Naomi could hardly bring herself to say it, it sounded so ridiculous, "a faerie?"

"No, he's a halfling. His father was human, and his mother was a wood nymph"

"A wood nymph?"

"Yes. They live in the forests and care for the woodlands."

"How did Marcus' father and mother meet, I mean they can't have frequented the same social events?"

"Well . . ." Rochan said, sitting down opposite Naomi, "that is an interesting and sad story. Freaya, that was Marcus' mothers name, first saw Marcus' father, John was his name, when he was a young boy roaming the forest on his father's land. She was taken by his love for the trees and for the animals that lived amongst them and would secretly watch him as he played his childhood games amongst the branches and roots of the trees, and with the wild beasts that he had a gift for befriending. As she watched John grow into manhood, Freaya was pleased to see that his love for the forest remained firm and that he was not influenced by his father who, unfortunately, did not share his son's love of the forest. He saw the trees only as a commodity and came close to devastating the forest in his greed for the money their fine timber could make him. Eventually, in their distress the trees called out to the wood nymph queen, Latora, for aid. Latora called Freaya to her, as she knew of her fondness for this particular forest. Latora questioned Freaya on the state of the forest, Freaya had no choice but to confirm the complaints of the trees and when she did so, Latora asked her why Freaya herself had not come to her to plead their case. Freaya could not tell the queen of her feelings for John, she could not tell her that she now loved the young man whom she had watched from childhood. Love between humans, and any of our kind, had been forbidden when the link between our two worlds was broken in the long ago by Gaia."

"Who's Gaia?" Naomi interrupted.

"Gaia is the mother guardian, the watcher over all things," Rochan replied, a hint of surprise in her voice that Naomi could somehow not already know this. "Freaya, unable to tell the queen the truth, begged the queen's forgiveness and said she had been playing too much with her sisters and not paying enough attention to the forests in her care. She promised that she would find a way to save the forest. Latora, however, said that it was too late for that and that the forest would not survive another winter. She commanded Freaya to take the life of John's father. Freaya bowed her head and pleaded with the queen if there was not some other way the man could be punished. For though she knew the truth of the trees' complaint against John's father, she also knew that although John disagreed with his father on his management of the forest, and had had many arguments with him on the subject, they loved each other very much, and that their bond was all the closer because John's mother had died in childbirth. The queen, however, would hear no pleas for leniency. She said that one who had caused so much pain to their kind could not be allowed to continue to do so. She said, that while she knew the difficulty of the task she had given Freaya, it had to be done for the good of all, and as Freaya, by her own admission, had been the one lax in her care the task must fall to her.

"Her request for leniency denied, Freaya returned to the forest with a heavy heart, for she knew that no matter how much she loved John and hated to cause him pain, she could not disobey her queen. So, one morning, when John's father and his men were cutting down trees, she caused one of the trees to fall onto him taking his life instantly. John was, of course, grief stricken and spent many days wandering through his beloved forest in deep mourning. Freaya was always close by, unseen, her heart breaking for his loss and her part in it. As the months and years passed, however, John found comfort in repairing the damage the forest had suffered under his father's care. As Freaya watched him plant new trees, cultivate old ones, and cull the forest sparingly, her love for him grew so strong that she longed to speak to him; she had also begun to fear that he would marry and so be lost to her forever.

"One evening, as he took his usual stroll through the forest, she appeared to him through the gloom of the trees. He stopped immediately at the appearance of her ghostly figure. When they came face to face Freaya told him simply that she was 'Freaya of the wood,' then bowed her head unsure of what to do next. They stood silently for a moment then John, without speaking, lifted her head gently, smiled at her, took her hand and they continued the walk through the forest together. Later, John told her that since he was a child he had felt a presence in the forest, as if he were being watched and when he saw her that night he felt as if he had known her all his life. They wanted to marry immediately of course. However, Freaya knew that it would be difficult, if not impossible to get the permission of the queen. She went to her and begged for her permission. At first the queen was unwavering, but when the trees that John had so lovingly cared for, pleaded his case the queen relented and gave her permission. There was a condition to the queen's consent, however, and that was that Freaya could never again see her people, once married, she would belong to the human world. Although disappointed by the queen's decision, Freaya's love for John was such that she was willing to give up everything she had ever known to be with him and, at first, they were very happy.

"After a year Marcus was born, and John adored his newborn son. For Freaya though, the relationship between her son and his father was a reminder of the past, and the secret she held. Her inward sorrow made her melancholy and weary. John worried at his wife's decline in spirits and did all he could to lift her from her depression, supposing it came from her separation from her people. The more John fussed over her though, the sadder she became, until she could bear it no longer. One evening, as they took their nightly stroll in the wood, she poured out her heart to him and begged him to forgive her. John, after his initial shock at the news, said he understood and forgave her, but things were never the same between them. After a few months, John told Freaya that he had been called to fight, in one of those wars that you humans are so keen on having every few years. Freaya knew though that his work on the farm excused him from having to go and believed that his real reason for leaving was because he couldn't bear to be with her. She pleaded with him to stay, if not for her, for their son, but it was to no avail and on a fresh spring morning he kissed her and his son goodbye and that was the last time she saw him. When the letter came announcing his death Freaya was distraught, the only thing that kept her from going mad was her son, but even he couldn't stop her decline, because each time she looked at him she was reminded of his father and what might have been. Gradually, her grip on this life began to wane and she allowed herself to be drawn into the mists of the other world."

"The other world?" Naomi interrupted again.

"Yes, for although nymphs are immortal they can, if they choose, leave this life, die if you like and enter the mists, where they become part of those mists, shapeless, covering the earth each morning and each evening with the living water that ensures the continuance of us all. Before she faded into the mists though, she brought the child to my grandmother. Freaya asked my grandmother to care for Marcus. My grandmother was familiar with Freaya's story and had, albeit in secret, remained her friend. My grandmother took the boy and made no attempt to dissuade Freaya from her course, for she could see, from her countenance, that she was already more in the other world than in this one. On leaving, Freaya kissed the boy and said, 'I have nothing to leave him but my love and this medal given to his father from his people. May he find peace and joy in this world.' Then kissing him gently on the forehead, once more, she left, never to return. My grandmother cared for Marcus until he was sixteen summers, which is for our people the age of choice, then, much to my grandmother's surprise and sorrow, the Wood Queen summoned him to her kingdom, and we did not see him again for many years. When he did return, as a grown man, my grandmother had sadly died. He . . ." Rochan's dialogue was interrupted by a firm knock on the front door. Rochan went to open it. Marcus stooped through the door.

"Good morning, Marcus. Would you like some tea?" Rochan asked, moving towards the stove.

"No thank you, Rochan, I ate breakfast at the inn."

Stopping in mid flow and turning to face him with a look of indignation, Rochan said, "Oh well, if you would rather drink that *muck* Noll calls tea than my home-made camomile, then I'm sure that's your choice, as mistaken as that may be."

Acknowledging Rochan's reprimand with a half-smile Marcus turned to Naomi.

"Did you sleep well."

"Yes. Very well thank you." Naomi said, feeling a little embarrassed by his sudden appearance, knowing that she now knew a little more about him now, than *he* may have wished.

"How is your ankle?" Marcus asked, sitting in the chair lately vacated by Rochan, who was now washing dishes at the sink.

"Oh, its fine . . . in fact I'd forgotten all about it."

"Good." Then glancing back at Rochan, he said, "I presume Rochan has told you where you are."

"Yes."

"And do you believe it?"

Naomi took a moment to answer.

"I don't know," she said at last. "I mean you're . . . *here*, Rochan's here, the village, Ceraline . . . you're all here, right before my eyes . . . but . . . it's a lot to take in . . . I . . ."

"I understand. It must be difficult to believe in a world peopled by races you have only read about in fairy stories." Marcus paused, and took on the expression of a man, once again, struggling to deliver bad news.

"What is it?" Naomi asked. "What's wrong?"

"At the Inn last night . . . I heard rumours . . . rumours concerning some children found on the mountains near to where I found you."

"Oh, but that's brilliant! Do you know where they are? Who found them?"

There was an ominous pause from Marcus, quickly dampening Naomi's initial delight at hearing that the school children had been found.

"The rumour is," he continued, "they were taken by . . . spriggins."

Rochan took a sharp intake of breath.

"What! What are sssprig. . .ins?" Naomi asked, becoming more anxious at Rochan's obvious concern.

"They are mountain folk."

"Little devils is what they are," Rochan declared.

"Will they *hurt* the children?" Naomi cried.

"They are more mischievous than anything," Marcus said. "They probably took the children out of curiosity." Rochan made a sound of derision and Marcus gave her a look of reprimand. "While our two worlds live alongside one another, there has been little or no contact between our worlds for many decades. Most spriggins have never seen a human, so as I say they probably took the children into the mountains out of curiosity."

"Rochan, what do you think? Do *you* think they'll hurt them?"

"No not *hurt* them . . . more . . . frighten them . . ."

"What . . .!"

"Rochan!" Marcus admonished.

"There is no point in lying to the girl, Marcus, you know as well as I do that you need to get those children back."

"Yes! That's what we have to do. But how?" Naomi asked.

"I have already made arrangements for the journey," Marcus said. "We will leave as soon as you are ready."

"I'm ready to go now."

"Very well."

"Thank you for all you have done, Rochan," Marcus said, standing up to leave.

"Yes, thanks very much," Naomi added.

"It is little that I have done, I wish it could have been more," Rochan said, pulling Naomi, who was now also standing, down to her and giving her a firm embrace. "Take care of yourself, child, and follow Marcus' guidance closely." Releasing Naomi, Rochan turned to Marcus, who returned her embrace warmly.

All pleasantries over, and without another word, Marcus went to the door and Naomi followed him, turning back to give Rochan one last smile of thanks. Rochan stood with her hands folded in front of her, a slight frown on her face, she returned Naomi's smile. Naomi closed the door softly behind her.

Once outside, she and Marcus walked side by side further away from the main town, until they came to a large, weather-beaten, two storey building standing alone on the edge of the village. A sign hung adjacent to its heavy double fronted door and bore the inscription:

Oakvale Inn

Welcome All Weary Travellers.

Marcus pushed open the ancient, gnarled door, the hinges of which seemed to groan in protest at his touch. Inside, the Inn it was gloomy and musty with tables and chairs of various shapes and sizes dotted around a large room. One side of the room was dominated by a brick fireplace and the other side by a long oak bar from which, just as Naomi's eyes rested on it, a short round man with pointed ears and a sharp pointy nose popped up from behind. He fixed them with a narrow stare then, as recognition dawned, his eyes opened wide and crinkled at the corners as his whole face broke into a smile.

"Marcus!" he cried, heartily. "Back so soon, well I have your things ready," he said, pulling out from under the counter two well-worn leather back packs stuffed to the brim. So much so that Naomi on seeing them worried that she may not be able to lift hers, let alone carry it for any length of time.

On reaching the counter Marcus undid the straps on the back packs and inspected the contents. Satisfied with his inspection he addressed the barman.

"How much do I owe you?"

"I'm afraid it's three gold coins, some of the things were difficult to get hold of at short notice, especially those . . . bags for sleeping in." As he said this, he gave Naomi a reproachful glance, as if she were somehow responsible for the offending items.

"Thank you, Noll," Marcus said, and taking some coins from his pocket handed them to the little barman. Who, after giving them a quick inspection, placed them in a draw which he pulled out from under the counter.

The transaction completed, Marcus lifted a pack from the counter and gave it to Naomi, she placed it on her back and immediately her legs gave way a little under its weight.

"Is it too heavy?" Marcus asked.

"No! No! I'm fine," she lied. "I just wasn't ready for the weight that's all." Then adjusting the pack she stood as straight as she could and said, "See! . . . Fine."

Marcus didn't seem completely convinced but, giving Noll a parting nod, they left the Inn without another word.

CHAPTER SIX

Too Close for Comfort

The sun was beginning to get higher in the sky as they left the valley. They made their way steadily along a mountain track that gradually sloped upwards, taking them deep into a mountain range. Naomi's fitness was somewhat lacking, and after only a couple of hours she was already beginning to feel the effects of the journey. She began to sweat under the heat of the warm July sun and stopped to take off her coat. Taking the opportunity to rest for a moment, she looked around her. She thought she could make out in the distance, southward, a smoky haze. Not wishing to think about what that meant she turned away quickly. Tying her coat around her waist she hurried after Marcus, who had not noticed her sojourn and was some way ahead. By the time she caught up with him she was breathing heavily, and the sudden burst of speed had turned her legs to lead. Marcus heard her scramble behind him and stopped to look back at her.

"You need to rest," he ordered. "There is water in your pack."

Naomi didn't argue. Sitting down on the nearest rock she began to root through her pack. On discovering a leather pouch with a stopper in it, that made a slopping noise, she held it up to Marcus with a questioning look on her face. He nodded in the affirmative and Naomi twisted the stopper and squeezed the water into her mouth, the water tumbled out causing her to choke.

"Slowly, slowly, just tilt it a little and gently squeeze the bag," Marcus said.

Naomi got her breath back and tried again, this time applying just enough pressure to the bag so that the water trickled into her mouth.

Marcus took off his pack, and taking out his own water pouch began to drink from it. When he had taken his fill, he pushed it back into the pack.

"Are you ready to move on?" he asked.

"Yes." Naomi said, dragging herself up and taking her place in Marcus' wake once more.

They made their way northward, stopping only once to consume a short snack; consisting of an apple and some cheese; which Marcus produced from his pack. It wasn't until the sun was beginning to set that Marcus stopped again.

"We will stop now," he said, looking up at the sky, "and make camp."

With an aching back and leaden legs Naomi gratefully eased herself down onto the nearest boulder. She watched Marcus as he bent down to open his pack and pulled out a brown paper parcel, opened it, and began to eat the contents with his fingers. Naomi felt too exhausted to eat but thought she had better try, so she rummaged through her pack and found a similar parcel. She opened it to discover what looked, and smelled, like pulled pork, seasoned with herbs and spices. She tried a small mouthful. It tasted delicious and awoke her appetite, so much so, that before she realised it, she had finished it all. Swallowing the last morsel, she suddenly thought that this might be the only food they had, and perhaps she was supposed to ration it. She looked up at Marcus who was, thankfully, putting the empty parcel back in his pack.

Naomi was soon sitting, staring vacantly into the flames of the fire Marcus had made, her eyelids becoming heavier and heavier. She was roused from her stupor by Marcus' voice, as he touched her gently on the shoulder.

"I have laid out your sleeping bag for you."

"Thank you," Naomi said, rubbing her eyes. Then stifling a massive yawn she crawled into the bag and fell asleep.

The next morning Naomi awoke, marginally refreshed, and after a breakfast of what tasted like rice cakes was eager to get going. By midday though, her newfound enthusiasm was beginning to wane and she was more than glad when Marcus said they could stop for lunch. Rooting in her bag she found the last of the brown paper parcels, it contained some cold ham and an assortment of root vegetables. She ate it hungrily. She tried not to dwell on the fact that this was the last of the food and that she had no idea when they would eat again.

"When do you think we'll get to where they are holding the children?" she asked.

"It will be at least another day before we reach any of the entrances to the spriggins' caves."

Naomi stared down at the empty paper and began to think that perhaps she should have eaten a little more sparingly after all. Marcus, she thought idly, was probably used to going without food for days, she on the other hand enjoyed her three meals a day, with the occasional snack. Well, more than occasional actually.

"If you are finished? We should move on." Marcus said.

"Of course," Naomi screwed up the brown paper resignedly, and made to follow Marcus again.

They continued on for some hours, stopping only occasionally to quench their thirst. The sun was beginning to lower in the sky when they came over a ridge and began to descend into a valley where there was a lake surrounded by trees. The terrain was rocky, Naomi scrambled her way down watching enviously as Marcus skimmed deftly across the same rocks that she fought to keep her footing on. At last, after some bumps and bruising, they reached the edge of a wood. The air was much cooler here and Naomi was glad of it. She stopped for a moment to enjoy the cool breeze and catch her breath. Marcus, however, continued on into the wood and vanished through the trees. Naomi, on realising she was alone, looked around and becoming slightly panicked and confused, by Marcus' sudden disappearance, hurried up to the line of trees.

Peering into the shadowy gloom, she softly called Marcus' name. There was no answer, she tried again, a little louder, but still there was no answer. Continuing to peer into the gloom, she tried to make out Marcus' tall, dark figure moving through the foliage. Unable to do so she apprehensively stepped into the wood and slowly made her way, continuing to stare keenly all around her in search of Marcus. After some moments, she began to feel as if she were being watched. She quickly looked behind her, her eyes widening in amazement at the sight of the trees, they were moving! Shifting, almost imperceptibly, but definitely moving together, appearing to close ranks, lowering their branches and entangling them together, effectively barring the way back. In a complete state of confusion, Naomi turned and began to run clumsily through the trees, trying not to make contact with the foliage, which was now closing in menacingly all around her. Terrified, she felt something grab her arm, she let out a cry and tried frantically to pull herself free.

"Calm down, calm down, it's me."

Naomi stopped in her frenetic attempt to break loose and fell into Marcus' arms, breathing heavily on his breast. Marcus held her head close to him. Eventually, Naomi managed to get control of herself. She pulled herself away from Marcus' hold, but with her hands still on his chest she looked up into his face.

"It was . . . the trees," she said falteringly, "they were," she stopped short, suddenly feeling ridiculous about what she was about to say; that she thought that the trees were moving, closing in on her, as if they were . . . alive. She glanced furtively over Marcus' shoulder. Everything looked calm and still, there was no evidence of the phantasmagorical scene that had left her a quivering wreck. So, releasing herself from Marcus' hold she said, "It's really . . . close in here isn't it?" Marcus looked down at her keenly. "I just got a bit worried when I couldn't see you."

Marcus continued to frown down at her.

"Stay close to me, we will soon be through to the other side," he said.

Naomi nodded her obedience. They continued on through the trees, Naomi still feeling, all the time, that she was being watched, causing her to follow Marcus' instruction so absolutely that she almost caught the back of his heels a couple of times. At last, they made their way through the maze of trees out to the shore of the lake.

The lake was a welcome sight after the unsettling events in the wood. Naomi took a deep breath. The air was cool and fresh, the sun was just beginning to set, the water glistened with a rainbow of colours. A ribbon of red and orange blazed across the horizon and, as the sky above the flaming display darkened, a more subdued beauty began to take shape. Countless stars were revealed, flickering and sparkling against the black canvas nature had created to best display their beauty. Naomi watched as day turned to night, taking comfort from its constancy.

"We need to make camp."

Naomi tore her eyes from the reassuring scene and turned towards Marcus.

"I will get some wood and start a fire before it gets too dark." he said.

Naomi started slightly## at the mention of going anywhere near the wood.

"There is plenty of dry wood around the shore, I will not need to go far to collect enough to make a fire," Marcus said, reassuringly. "You stay here. I will not be long."

Although relieved that Marcus was not going to enter the wood, Naomi still kept a close eye on him, while he sorted through the scraps of wood that littered the shore.

Marcus was true to his word and before long he had set a fire. Once it was burning well, Marcus walked to the lake, and rather than stopping at the edge, much to Naomi's surprise, he walked straight into it, fully clothed, up to his waist. He then just stood there, very still, staring at the water. Naomi sat on her sleeping bag puzzled and fascinated at the same time. They stayed like that, watcher and watched, for some time, silent and still. Until . . . splash! All in one movement Marcus plunged his hand into the water and pulled out a fish. Naomi let out a gasp, and smiled appreciatively, as Marcus adeptly threw his wriggling captive several meters onto the bank. A few moments later he repeated the process and emerged from the lake. Picking up his catch he returned to the fire, opened his coat, took a knife from his belt and began to expertly prepare the fish for cooking. When he had set the fish over the fire he delved into his pack and brought out a small loaf of home-made bread. Soon Naomi was enjoying one of the most satisfying meals of her life.

"Thank you," she said. When she had taken a last draught of water to finish off her meal. "That was very good."

"You are welcome," Marcus smiled,

"You must eat very healthily . . . I mean living in the wild, and . . ."

Marcus raised an eyebrow at this observation.

"Oh! I don't mean to be rude, I mean . . . living in the countryside . . . you'll be able to have fresh fruit and veg and things . . . I'm sorry if I've . . ." Naomi stopped, suddenly. Marcus was smiling.

"Tchh! You're making fun of me," Naomi said, smiling back at him.

"Not really. I suppose compared to the life you live in the city my life must seem quite . . . *wild.*"

"Well, life in the city can have its own kind of wildness . . . Have you ever lived in a city?"

"No, but I have seen many."

"You sound like you don't think much of them."
"No."

"They've got some good things . . . indoor plumbing for one . . . and there's some beautiful architecture, and the theatre, restaurants . . . well I suppose it's what your used to. I've lived in the city all my life. I had hardly been in the countryside until now."

"And what do you make of it?"

"To be honest. I hated it at first and then it started to grow on me . . . but then there was the earthquake and . . . since then, I've found myself standing in awe of its beauty one minute, then the next, being so overwhelmed by the challenge of its terrain wishing I was anywhere but here.

"That is understandable, and I'm afraid tomorrow there will be more challenges, so you should get some sleep."

Naomi nodded her assent and, pummelling her pack into as comfortable a makeshift pillow as possible, she lay on her side staring out across the lake and up at the moon; which shone down like a giant search light on the still lake; eventually falling asleep with its reflection in her eyes.

CHAPTER SEVEN

In the Dark

Naomi awoke with a start. It was still dark. She took a deep breath, closed her eyes and stretched and yawned. She opened her eyes again, although she wondered if she had or if she was dreaming, because she couldn't see anything. She opened and closed her eyes quickly. No, nothing. There was no longer any moonlight, in fact as she became more conscious, she became aware of the fact that there was no breeze. The air smelled damp, the darkness was oppressive, she felt closed in. She sat up and shivered. She was no longer in her sleeping bag, her eyes scrambled about looking for a chink of light, searching for a sign of Marcus. She was just about to call out his name, when instead she let out a gasp as two eyes flashed open in front of her in the pitch black. Then, to her horror, two more, and two more. Disoriented and frightened, Naomi turned her head frantically. Every which way more and more pairs of disembodied eyes were appearing, floating in the air all around her. When the spectral materialisations seemed to have stopped, breathing heavily, she waited, terrified, for *something* to happen . . . Minutes seemed to pass and still her invisible observers continued to gaze at her, unblinkingly. Naomi's eyes darted, in expectation, from one set of eyes to another. But still nothing happened. The longer this bizarre staring competition went on, the less afraid Naomi felt. Mainly because, as she stared back into the eyes, so attentively fixed upon her, they seemed to be regarding her with intense curiosity rather than murderous design. Encouraged by their lack of movement and their seeming benignity, Naomi swallowed hard and forced herself to call out a tentative . . . "Hello."

Every set of eyes moved back, as if she had pushed them simultaneously. Encouraged further by this passive reaction, she called out again a little more forcefully, "Hello." This time the optical chorus moved forward simultaneously. Naomi let out a startled cry . . . "Whoa!!"

The chorus stopped short but continued their surveillance. After a few more moments of this visual stand-off, Naomi was just plucking up the courage to ask her viewers who they were and what they wanted when all of a sudden, they took their eyes off her and turned their collective gaze elsewhere. Naomi, following their gaze, saw a small chink of light moving slowly towards them through the distant blackness.

All eyes remained fixed on the growing illumination. As it got closer it gradually began to reveal Naomi's surroundings. The exposure of dark craggy walls, and dirt floors with rocks of all shapes and sizes strewn around, soon made Naomi aware that she was underground. The greatest revelation though, was the sight of her observers. She found herself surrounded by a group of very dirty, very tiny, dishevelled children, standing on rocks or ledges all around the cave. Their clothes were ripped and ill-fitting, they were bare-footed, and their hair straggled about their shoulders, from their appearance it was impossible to tell whether they were girls or boys.

"Shoo!"

Naomi's head snapped back towards the light, from where the unexpected exclamation had come.

It had finished its journey, and now hovered in the air so brightly, that it rendered its bearer invisible. She turned back to the children for their reaction and was taken aback to see that they had all disappeared. She searched and squinted to try and make out how they could have disappeared so quickly, as she could see no exit from the cave just solid rock from floor to ceiling. She turned back to the light just in time to see it slowly lower to the floor, diminish in brightness, and reveal a short round man with pointed ears and tiny piercing eyes, staring malevolently in her direction.

"So, they brought you *here*, did they? I told them to bring you straight to me, but their curiosity got the better of them, never seen a human before you see, not this close up anyway"

"Why have you brought me here . . . and who are you?"

Continuing to fix her with a look of malice he said in a voice that matched his look, "Folla me."

With seemingly no other choices, Naomi got up and reluctantly followed her surly guide, who picked up his lamp and lit the way through a maze of narrow tunnels. Shiny metals flecked the water-stained walls and caught in the light of the wavering lamp, causing them to sparkle like fairy lights. The effect so arrested Naomi's attention that she almost tripped and fell over one of the many rocks that littered the floor of the passageway, eliciting a malicious chuckle from her guide. Presently, the passageway began to widen until it opened up into a large cavern, lit with flaming torches. In the centre of the cavern there was an imposing wooden statue of a being, very much like her guide, standing on a stone plinth. In one hand the figure held a spear, the tip of which was metal, in his other hand he held a wooden shield covered in decorative metal work. He stood as if ready for battle, wearing an expression fixed somewhere between anger and determination. Naomi and her guide crossed the cavern floor towards a substantial double wooden door set in the wall of the cave. When they stopped at the door her guide put down the lamp, moved to the edge of the door, and reached out with his hand into a hole in the wall, from which he produced an old and rusted metal key which, despite its obvious age, turned smoothly in the lock of the door. Once unlocked, her guide pushed the heavy frame door open to reveal a small dimly lit cavern and four forlorn figures staring apprehensively at their entrance.

"Miss!" Hannah squealed as she ran towards her teacher, followed immediately by Ruth and Luke. The children almost knocked Naomi over as they rushed to hug her.

"Miss! Miss! . . ." the children began to shout all at once. "We've been so afraid . . . we didn't know what had happened to you . . . it was so dark in here . . . I've hurt my leg . . . where are we . . . how . . .?"

"Whoa, whoa slow down, it's okay, I'm here now. Everything is going to be alright."

The children stopped their cacophony of questions and stared at Naomi. She looked back at them smiling broadly. Then she looked around her to see how many others there might be hidden in the gloom. There was only one other figure, standing a little apart from the others . . . Elliott. And although she was happy to see him, she felt a deep disappointment that there didn't seem to be any others. She quickly checked this melancholy thought. Smiling once again, she looked down at the children.

"It's good to see you all."

"It's good to see you too Miss," the trio chorused.

"Did you say you were hurt, Ruth?"

"Yes, Miss my leg is cut." Ruth lifted her trouser leg. Dried blood covered a substantial gash on her shin.

"Is anyone else hurt?"

"No, Miss, just a few little cuts and bruises, we've been lucky, considering," Luke reassured her.

Naomi turned to her guide.

"Could I please have something to clean and dress this wound with?" she asked, curtly.

"Hhmmf . . . I suppose so," he answered. And with this reluctant reply he left them, locking the door behind him.

"Have you seen any of the others, Miss, did you see what happened to them?" Luke asked.

"It looked like the mountain fell in on itself and took everything with it." Elliott's voice came dully from the back of the cavern.

They all stood in silence for a moment, overwhelmed by the starkness of his revelation. Naomi heard the girls begin to weep quietly beside her, she put her arms around them and pulled them close to her.

"How did you get here?" she asked them. Swallowing back her own tears, not wishing to alarm them any further by what she knew of the loss of the others. The children merely answered her with shakes of their heads and raised shoulders.

"One minute, I was scrambling about on the mountain and the next . . . I was here," Luke said.

"I thought I saw something, Miss, I don't know if I was dreaming or if it was real," Hannah said. "It looked like other children, but really dirty and badly dressed."

Spriggins, Naomi thought, but only said, "Well, anyway, you're safe. Have you been treated well?"

"He hasn't hurt us, Miss, if that's what you mean?" Hannah answered.

"The man I came in with you mean?" Naomi asked.

"Yes, Miss, he's the only person we've seen since we've been here."

As if on cue, their 'host' was heard opening the door and entered carrying a bowl of water and some cloths hung casually over his arm. He placed his burden unceremoniously at Naomi's feet and made to leave.

"Wait a minute," Naomi called. He stopped and gave a surly questioning look in her direction. "Have you had any food or drink?" Naomi asked the children.

"We've had some water and some stale bread," Elliott answered. Looking accusingly at the little man. "If you can call *that* food."

The little man turned his saturnine gaze on Elliott, who returned it with a look of equal contempt.

"These children need something substantial to eat." The guide turned his gaze slowly from Elliot to Naomi and fixed her with the same glowering look of disdain. Unperturbed, Naomi continued to plead her case. "These children have been through a lot, and you've imprisoned them here, for what reason I have no idea, but they're hungry, tired, and frightened . . ."

"I'm not frightened," Elliot interrupted.

Naomi gave Elliot a quick look of annoyance and continued.

"You took no care of their wounds and half-starved them. What sort of people *are* you who would treat *defenceless* children in this way?" This last remark seemed to have some effect on their host, as his look changed to one of indignation.

"You'll be fed," he answered, angrily. Storming out. Shutting and locking the door forcefully behind him.

Naomi let out a slow breath of relief and then set to work cleaning and bandaging Ruth's shin. When she had finished, she looked up into Ruth's anxious face.

"There, that should keep it clean while it finishes healing," she said.

"Miss . . . why *do* you think they've brought us here?" Ruth asked.

"As I said, sweetheart, I don't know, I'm sorry." This complete admission of ignorance on Naomi's part seemed to be the last straw for the girls and they began to sob uncontrollably.

"I want my mum," Ruth cried.

"Me too," Hannah sobbed.

"Girls it'll be okay, calm down now. He'll come back soon with something to eat and drink and then I'll do my best to find out what's going on, and I'll do *everything* I can to get you back to your families as soon as possible." Naomi held the girls close to her and tried to fill them with a reassurance which she herself did not feel.

Thankfully, it wasn't long before their host returned with two women carrying baskets. They entered the cave, set down the baskets and left without saying a word. Naomi removed a soft woollen blanket from the top of one of the baskets and lay it on one of the larger rocks that covered the floor of the cavern, then began to lay the food out on it. There was a variety of cold meats, cheeses, bread and cakes, and despite their obvious concerns, the children couldn't help being attracted to the little feast that was laid out before them. Once the baskets were empty the children looked at Naomi for confirmation that it was okay for them to eat. She nodded her assent, and the children hesitantly began to sample the food, their faces brightening slightly with each mouthful.

"Mizz you should try zum it's really gud," Luke advised, with his mouth full of bread and cheese.

Naomi gave him a half smile and although she didn't feel much like eating, she broke off a piece of bread and taking a slice of cold meat, she made a makeshift sandwich. It *was* good. So good in fact that she decided to sample a piece of fruit cake and a chunk of cheese too, washing it all down with a drink of fresh milk. The consumption of which, despite their circumstances, amused everyone, as their hosts had not brought any glasses, so they had to drink straight from the jug, and they all ended up dribbling milk down their chins onto their clothes. After this short respite from their immediate worries, they all sat, for some time, in silence lost in their own thoughts. Luke was the first to break their quiet state of reflection.

"Do you think the others are okay, Miss?"

Not wishing to alarm the children any further than they already were Naomi said, "Yes they were probably found by rescue teams." She felt terrible lying to them, but there was no way she could tell them about the terrible destruction she had seen, or about Marcus' emphatic, 'There are no rescue teams.'

The little forlorn group fell into another silent pondering, until . . .

"Well, I reckon this whole thing's weird," Elliott announced.

"What do you mean?" Ruth asked, anxiously.

"That bloke, did you have a good look at him, the way he dresses, what's that all about? I mean . . . he's got pointy ears, did nobody else notice that?"

"Pointy ears, I didn't notice that did you?" Ruth addressed her question to Hannah.

"No. But . . . he did have quite long hair, but his nose. I didn't like to say anything, I didn't want to be rude, but it was pretty sharp and pointy just . . . well . . . like Elliott said . . . weird."

"What are you saying . . . do you think that he's, he's not . . . human?" Ruth cried.

"Okay everyone let's calm down a minute. Let's not go imagining things," Naomi admonished them, "they may just be a group of people who have decided to live an alternative lifestyle. It's not unknown for some people to try to get back to nature and shun the modern world." Naomi, of course, knew this not to be the case but thought it best not to confuse Ruth any further under their present circumstances.

"Miss is right there, mate," Luke butted in. "My uncle went out with a girl once who tried to get him to sell his house, move to the countryside with her and join a group who lived off the land. He kicked her into touch smartish though, he wouldn't want to be more than twenty minutes from the nearest pub."

"Erm . . . Thank you, Luke . . ." Naomi said. "Let's try and look on the bright side, none of us are seriously injured, we're safe . . ."

"We're in a dark, filthy cave with no way out, I don't see how that's *safe*," Elliott voiced back, accusingly.

"Elliott . . ."

"But you tell me I'm imagining things," Elliott interrupted. "When you saw *him, and* those women, we all did. There's something weird going on, I'm telling you."

"All right there's something different about them but getting hysterical about it is not going to help, we are just going to have to wait patiently until we can find out more about why they've brought us here."

"That doesn't look very likely, that bloke has hardly said a word to us, and we've been here for I don't know how long, and no one's told us anything and you turn up and you don't know any more than we do."

"Miss I'm scared," Ruth broke in.

"Elliott, if you have nothing positive to say, don't say anything at all."

"But . . ."

"I said that's enou. . ."

"Miss!"

". . . you're just frightening every . . ."

"MISS!!?"

"What!" Naomi turned impatiently in answer to Luke and Hannah's shrill call.

They were staring into a dark corner of the cave, their eyes wide with fear, Naomi followed their gaze. There in the blackness, at the back of the cave, something dark and menacing was gradually emerging from the cave floor. Naomi pushed the children behind her and instinctively put her arms out to protect them. Elliott came forward mimicking her action.

"Elliott, get behind me."

"I'm not frightened."

"For goodn . . ." but before she had time to finish her reprimand, the burgeoning floor gave a low growl. Elliott grasped her hand and together they stood firm, as the mound before them grew ever more daunting.

46

Unable to make any sort of escape, they were forced to watch as the image gradually metamorphosed, before their astonished gaze, into a grey granite man about two meters tall covered in a grey shingle floor length coat adorned with amber buttons. On his head he wore a wide brimmed hat (also grey) with a brightly coloured peacock feather sticking out to one side. Finally, he opened his eyes, which were steel blue and shone in the gloom like two small headlamps. Naomi and the children stood transfixed by this fantastical metamorphose until, metamorphose complete, the 'man' shook his huge granite head, like a dog shaking itself dry, causing Naomi and the children to have to cover their eyes as gravel and earth flew in all directions. Once the onslaught of earth had stopped Naomi heard a defiant Elliott call out:

"Who are you? What do you want?"

The creature's headlamp eyes lit quickly upon him. Naomi immediately forgot her own fear and forcefully pushed a resistant, but somewhat subdued, Elliott behind her and dared the granite figure, with her own steely stare, to come any closer.

"I am Woodlan, I am your guide," the figure answered simply, in a voice that was surprisingly soft compared to its physique.

After a few seconds of confused silence Hannah's voice chimed from behind Naomi.

"To where?"

"The surface . . . I have come to rescue you."

Without another word, he made his way heavily towards the locked door and looked, for a moment, as if he was going to break it down with one blow from his giant fist. However, he instead put his hand in a pocket of his shingle coat and produced a shiny object with which he began to pick the lock. Eventually, they heard the lock begin to turn. Woodlan opened the door just enough for his, not unsubstantial, head to peer into the adjoining cavern. Then, turning back to face Naomi and the children, he signalled with his finger on his grey, dusty lips for them to be quiet and nodded with his head for them to follow him. Naomi turned to the children and approved his signal with her own nod. To their surprise, however, as soon as Woodlan stepped back, to allow the door to open, an army of tiny people, spriggins, and others like their host, ran through the door and covered Woodlan like a swarm of wasps.

They began beating him with sticks, throwing stones at him and kicking and punching him; the latter, much to their own detriment. Amidst the confusion Naomi's former guide, who was obviously leading the charge, and some others, ran towards Naomi and the children and tried to drag them away. Woodlan was throwing spriggins and dwarves, (for that's what they were.) Male and female alike around the cave as if they were rag dolls, but still they kept coming at him. Naomi, Elliott, Luke and Hannah fought as hard as they could with their would-be kidnappers, resisting every attempt to take them and doing all they could to protect, the terror stricken, Ruth from their grasp. Despite their best effort though Naomi and the children found themselves being pulled towards the open door and past the beleaguered Woodlan.

Naomi searched frantically around the open cavern, they had now been dragged into, for a way of escape. The cavern had numerous tunnels emanating from it and bright torches hung from the wet walls. Naomi's eyes fell on the wooden statue . . . and she had an idea.

She was being held by two youths who were both smaller than her by some margin. She suddenly let out a yell of pain, causing her captors to stop for a moment to ascertain the reason for her cry. As they did so, Naomi took the opportunity to scrape her foot down the shin of one of her captors. Screaming with pain he let go of Naomi and bent down to grab his shin. Naomi, with her now free hand, grabbed the hair of her other captor and pulled his head down as hard as she could on his companions. Free of her captors, who were now rolling around on the cavern floor dazed and in pain, she ran towards one of the torches, scrambled up some loose rocks, pulled it off the wall and rushed towards the wooden effigy.

"STOP!" Naomi shouted. "STOP OR YOU'LL BE SORRY!" From her elevated position Naomi's voice was amplified and echoed around the cavern.

Prisoners and captors alike stopped in their various states of confusion to look in Naomi's direction.

"Noooo!" screamed the little guide. Unceremoniously throwing the sobbing Ruth (whom he was holding tightly by the arm) to the ground and running towards Naomi, who stood holding the torch threateningly at the base of the effigy.

"Don't come any closer or I'll set it alight," she said, moving the torch menacingly closer to her target.

The little guide stopped shortly, fixing her with an enraged glare.

"Let the children go, and free . . ." Naomi struggled for a moment to remember their, would be, rescuer's name.

"Woodlan," Hannah shouted, helpfully.

"Yes, thank you . . . Woodlan. If you don't, I promise you I'll set light to this thing."

"THING! . . THING! How *dare* you call the statue of Redcap, the greatest leader our people have ever known, a *thing!*" Their hosts fury at Naomi's slight towards this most venerable of leaders was palpable.

Naomi, trying to sound braver than she felt, repeated her demands.

"Let them go . . . *now!*" There was a quiet determination in Naomi's voice that assured her adversary that she meant what she said, so reluctantly he gave the command.

"Let them go."

The children ran to Naomi, crowding the plinth where she stood like chicks around a mother hen. Naomi continued to stand, holding the torch threateningly at the base of the statue. Their assailants stared menacingly, waiting to pounce. This stand-off lasted a few moments, and Naomi was beginning to wonder what an earth to do nex,t when thankfully the now free Woodlan came charging through from the smaller cavern locking the door swiftly behind him. The door secure, he turned quickly round, and grasping the situation immediately, reached into another of the pockets of his great granite coat, from which he redeemed a rope of massive proportions and began to use it to round up the rest of their assailants. Naomi and the children watched fascinated, as he wound the rope deftly in and around them until he had succeeded in wrapping them into a squirming, squealing bundle.

"Release me you, blockhead, you'll pay for this, how dare you touch me, I'll . . ." the tiny guide screamed.

Woodlan ignored their 'host's protests and turning to Naomi said, in a tone tinged with both surprise and admiration, "Well done, Little Miss. Follow me now, we need to get out of here before a rescue party turns up."

The children looked at Naomi for confirmation of what they should do. She answered their dumb request with a simple. "Let's go."

They followed Woodlan as he led them into one of the tunnels off the cavern, leaving their captors swearing deadly oaths after them.

The little group followed Woodlan down the dimly lit tunnel, staying close together. The tunnel was strewn with small stones which they kept catching their feet on and so made their progress slow. Naomi was worried that they weren't moving fast enough and that they would be caught. She was at the rear and kept looking back, concerned that any minute she would hear their captors following. After some time of stumbling along, the path began to slope upwards. Naomi could hear the children breathing more heavily, she knew they were tiring but not one of them complained, she felt a sudden burst of pride at how well they were coping. They were so young and had been through so much in the last few days and, depressingly, she knew it wasn't over yet. She felt sick as she thought of how she was going to have tell them how desperate their situation really was. At last, she felt a warm breeze brush her cheek and before long they could see daylight and they were climbing out of the passageway to the surface.

Once above ground Naomi and the children stopped to catch their breath.

"There is no time to rest yet, we are still too deep in mountain dwarf and spriggin country," Woodlan warned them.

"Spriggins? What are spriggins?" Hannah asked.

"I have no time for explanations just now, we need to keep moving," Woodlan answered shortly. And before anyone could say another word he strode off over the hills, the little band of followers hurrying to keep up with him.

The children quickly struggled to keep up with the pace set by their guide and soon Naomi was falling behind with an exhausted Ruth.

"Erm . . . Mr . . . Woodlan . . . Mr Woodlan," Naomi shouted.

Woodlan stopped, turned, and with a puzzled look on his face said . . . "My name is Woodlan . . . just Woodlan."

"I'm sorry, M . . .Woodlan. The children really need to rest, they're exhausted."

"I'm not tired, I'm fine," Elliot declared, defiantly.

"Yes, well the rest of us aren't . . . Please M . . .Woodlan, they really do need to rest."

Woodlan stood pensively glancing around the pathetic little group, seeming to weigh up the situation in his mind. Then his glance alighted on the defiant figure of Elliott, and he broke out into an extraordinary smile, extraordinary because his granite teeth were dotted with a variety of tiny gem stones that glittered fascinatingly in the sunshine.

"Aye, well I suppose those who need a rest must have it. You and I lad will keep a look out until the others are ready to move on. Take a position up on that ridge and keep a look out Southward, shout out if you see anyone."

At this command from Woodlan Elliott seemed to stand a little taller and eagerly took up his post. Woodlan patrolled the perimeter while Naomi and the other children sat huddled together, tired out. Some minutes later Elliott gave out an urgent cry.

"Someone's coming!"

Naomi started up and hurried over to Elliott's position, closely followed by Woodlan. In the near distance they could see a dark figure, skilfully, traversing the rocky terrain, making their way swiftly towards them.

"Marcus," Naomi said, softly. Elliott looked at her quizzically. "A friend."

Soon Marcus' lean figure had reached them. On arrival he quickly looked them over and then turned to Woodlan and said, "Thank you."

"Don't thank me, it was, Little Miss there (pointing at Naomi) who gave us our means of escape. She held Redcap hostage," he said, jovially.

"Redcap!" Marcus said in an amused voice.

"Threatened to set fire to him."

"Who's Redcap? And I still don't know what spriggins are," Hannah broke in.

"Spriggins are people who dwell in these hills and Redcap . . . well he is a story for another day," Marcus replied.

Hannah still didn't feel as if her question on spriggins had been answered, but their new companion had such a firm air of authority about him that it acted as a curb on Hannah's natural inquisitiveness, so she didn't pursue it but held off . . . for *another day.*

"Are you ready to move on?" Marcus asked.

Naomi looked at the children for an answer to Marcus' question. Hannah and Luke nodded a tired assent. Ruth, however, looked as if she wanted to ask a question but was afraid to.

"What is it, Ruth?" Naomi asked.

"I'm sorry, Miss but I'm really thirsty, I don't think I can go on much further without a drink."

"I have some water here," Marcus said. Then taking the pack from his back he produced a leather water pouch and passed it to Ruth. Ruth took it a little dubiously.

"You just pull out the top," Naomi said, "put it to your lips, lift the pouch a little and squeeze it . . . *gently.*"

Ruth did this and poured the water awkwardly into her mouth then wiping her chin she turned to Hannah and offered her the pouch. Hannah took it and drank just enough to take the edge of her thirst, making sure she left enough for the others to do the same. Naomi, the last to drink, passed it back to Marcus and, with this modest repast completed, they started south; Marcus taking the lead and Woodlan bringing up the rear.

It was some time before they stopped again and when they did it was between a lake, and a dense forest that was all too familiar to Naomi.

"We will camp here for the night," Marcus said.

The children flopped down where they stood. Marcus and Woodlan gathered wood for a fire. Once that was set Marcus gave Naomi and the children some bread and cheese from his pack.

"Tomorrow we will reach Oakvale and you will be able to get a proper meal and rest," he said.

"Where's Oakvale?" Hannah asked.

"A village that lies on the other side of the forest," Marcus answered.

Naomi, remembering her last encounter with this particular forest, went cold at the thought of having to pass through it again.

"Will we be able to get help there to contact our parents?" Ruth asked.

"We will be able to get help there." Marcus said.

The meaning of Marcus' ambiguous reply was not lost on Naomi, and she gave an inward sigh.

There was only one sleeping bag. Marcus opened it out and laid it on the ground.

"You will have to share this for tonight, I'm afraid I have no pillows, and my coat will have to suffice as a blanket."

The children, almost asleep sitting up, crawled onto the sleeping bag and lay down. Marcus covered them as best he could with his coat. Seeing that it didn't quite do the job Naomi took off her coat and finished covering the, already sleeping, children.

"So we're going back to Oakvale?" Naomi said.

"Yes. The children need food and rest and Oakvale is the nearest village," Marcus answered.

"I know you said that there were no rescue teams, but I need to try and get these children back to their parents, I'm not going to able to do that on my own . . . will you help me?"

"I will help you."

"Thank you," Naomi said, stifling a yawn.

"You need some sleep," Marcus said. "I have no bedding to offer you, but you might use the pack at least to rest your head on.

Naomi nodded her appreciation and lay down near the fire, resting her head heavily on the makeshift pillow.

CHAPTER EIGHT
The Wraith of Tramar

Naomi awoke the next day, shivering and stiff. The sun was low in the sky and the birds were singing a dawn chorus. The children lay sleeping, having hardly moved from their positions of the night before. The fire was still burning low, Naomi sat up and placed another log on the glowing embers rubbing her hands in front of the flames, which licked appreciatively at the new fuel. Looking around her she could see no sign of Marcus or Woodlan. The forest looked dark and ominous, Naomi turned her back on it and looked across the lake; it was covered with a thick mist. She sat for a while scanning the grey cloud, until suddenly she saw a dark figure coming towards her out of the mist. It was Marcus, he was carrying two large fish. Breakfast, she thought and greeted his arrival on the shore with a smile.

"Well at least we won't starve," she said.

Marcus bid her good morning, then began to prepare the fish for cooking.

"Where's Woodlan?" Naomi asked."

"In the mountains, he will be back soon."

It wasn't long before the aroma of cooking fish filled the air.

"I can smell food," Luke said, sitting up.

"What?" Hannah asked, sleepily.

"Did someone say food?" Elliott said.

"I'll have a large fries please," Ruth ordered, still asleep.

"Fries! There are fries?" Hannah cried, waking up fully now.

"No! No!" Naomi corrected. "Only fish."

"I don't care what it is," Luke said. "I'm so hungry I could eat my shoe if you put some ketchup on it."

"No you couldn't," Hannah admonished, "and where would we get ketchup out here?"

"Oh shut up Hannah," Elliott chided.

R. E. BUSBY

"What's going on? I'm absolutely freezing. Where am I?" Ruth exclaimed.

"We're still in the Lake District with Miss," Hannah answered.

"Oh!" Ruth looked crushed.

"Come and get warm by the fire all of you. The fish is nearly ready," Naomi called, as cheerily as she could manage, under the circumstances.

Before long they were all greedily eating their fish breakfast on leaf plates.

Woodlan returned, just as they were washing their hands in the ice-cold water of the Lake, and marched straight up to Marcus, who was putting out the fire.

"There is no sign of anyone following us," he said.

"Good."

"Hello, Mr Woodlan . . . sorry . . .Woodlan," Hannah called from the lake.

"Good morning, young'uns."

"It's time we were leaving," Marcus called out.

Naomi and the children shook their hands in the air and dried them on their clothes as they made their way over to Marcus and Woodlan.

It may have been early in the morning, with a bright sun breaking through the mist, boding well for another warm day, but the forest was dark and close, and as they entered its confines Naomi's stomach tightened. The children made their way slowly at first, until their eyes became accustomed to the gloom, and they were able to make their way somewhat more easily. Naomi did her best to fight off her feelings of apprehension at once more being closed in on all sides by, what she couldn't help feeling were, hostile trees. She nonetheless found herself jumping every time she was touched by a falling leaf, or an unseen bird disturbed the branches above her. Even Ruth was coping with the conditions better than she was. At last, the trees began to thin out and Naomi knew they were coming to the end of the forest. She was just beginning to relax when suddenly she heard one of the children cry out.

"Ow!"

Naomi turned quickly at the sound of the cry of pain and saw Hannah attempting to disengage herself from the branch of a tree.

"It's okay, I've just caught my hair in something," she said.

Ruth moved towards her to help, and to everyone's astonishment appeared to be deliberately slapped back by another branch hanging from the tree. Elliott rushed forward and he too was likewise summarily dismissed. Naomi ran forward calling for Marcus as she ran, only to see him run swiftly past her, but before he could make it anywhere near the struggling Hannah he was, all at once, lifted up in the air by the branches from another tree and held immobile in the air. Naomi and the children, following his flight, were astonished to see that Luke too was hanging likewise above them. Hannah, meanwhile, was becoming more and more distressed, as a mass of black twigs and branches bent over and around her, until they had practically engulfed her. Naomi looked around her wildly for some way of freeing Hannah, and as she did so was stopped in her frenzy by the bizarre sight of a pair of eyes blinking out from the trunk of a tree.

"It's Woodlan, Miss . . . I recognise his eyes," Ruth cried.

Naomi studied the eyes carefully for a moment, and then not only did she see that they were indeed Woodlan's eyes, but she could also make out his outline, held tight as if he were tied with rope within the gnarled giant trunk.

"Miss!" Elliott's frantic cry pulled her attention away from the fantastical picture.

Elliott was staring in horror at an opaque, dark figure, floating malevolently in front of Hannah's 'gaoler.' Naomi moved towards the tree once again, but her way was blocked by the figure and she watched helplessly as Hannah disappeared into the bowels of the tree, but just before she was completely swallowed up Naomi thought she heard her call to her. It was a faint desperate cry that filled Naomi's whole being, turning her feelings of distress to ones of anger. Lips parted and eyes steeled, she looked up at the menacing ethereal figure and felt a darkness of her own stir inside her. She took a step towards it. The figure grew in size and darkened in colour, but Naomi sensed the smallest feeling of uncertainty from it, a feeling which she somehow seized upon, holding it in her mind.

Keeping her gaze fixed on the dark figure, she began to intensify its own impressions of doubt, as she did so she felt, rather than saw, the figure diminish slightly in size. Naomi, now sensing confusion from the figure, continued to intensify her concentration towards it.

"Let the girl go," she said, in a voice that did not sound like her own.

The figure increased in size once more and stayed fast to its post.

"Let . . . her . . . go." This time, Naomi didn't the words out loud, she thought them. The figure challenged her, but the strange connection between them allowed Naomi to fix the command in the mind of her enemy, she could feel herself beginning to control it.

Realising the danger, the figure tried to fight her power over it, but Naomi continued to fill its being with the single thought, 'let the girl go.' Gradually the figure began to grow smaller and smaller, it shrank until it was no larger than a feather, then Naomi blew it away up into the treetops, where it disappeared out of sight.

Still entranced, Naomi moved resolutely towards the tree that held Hannah and placed her hands on it. Slowly, every branch, twig and root began to untangle until the tree began to surrender its quarry, and Naomi was able to take the hand of a very pale and distressed looking Hannah, lifting her up, and out onto the forest floor. The power she felt filled her with an overwhelming euphoria and she lifted her hands high in the air and with her mind commanded the release of Marcus and Luke, who were placed gently down next to the shaken Hannah. Then, she turned to the release of Woodlan, who emerged unharmed from his wooden prison. Her task complete she lowered her arms and fell into a swoon.

*   *   *

Naomi awoke to a sea of concerned faces looking down at her.

"She's awake . . . Are you all right, Miss . . . Give her some air let her breathe," the children cried in unison.

"Hannah! Where's Hannah?" Naomi asked, sitting up abruptly.

"She's fine, Miss . . . thanks to you," Ruth answered.

Then, they all moved aside to reveal an extremely shaken Hannah leaning against Woodlan, who had his huge arm wrapped softly but securely around her. She managed a faint smile at Naomi who breathed a sigh of relief at the sight of her.

"You were *awesome*, Miss," Luke cried out.

"So awesome," Ruth agreed.

Marcus looked puzzled and clearly didn't understand awesome, so Naomi enlightened him.

"It means they think what I did was good."

"Good!" Elliott protested. "It was way beyond good it was . . . well . . . it was . . . *awesome*."

"How did you do it, Miss?" Luke asked, eagerly.

"To be honest I'm not sure," and not really wishing to discuss it right there and then she said, "and I have a bit of a headache and . . . I'd really love to get out of this forest."

"Me too," said, a jaded, Hannah.

So, with Woodlan carrying Hannah, and Marcus supporting a shaken Naomi, they left the confines of the forest as quickly as they could.

Stepping out into the open they all took a moment to catch their breath.

"We need to keep moving," Marcus said eventually, "if we want to reach Oakvale by nightfall."

No one argued, they all wanted to get as far away from the forest as possible. So, with Woodlan continuing to carry Hannah, they soldiered on.

The sun was just beginning to set as they entered the village and passed the Inn. The children were almost dead on their feet. A welcoming light shone from the kitchen window of Rochan's cottage; Marcus knocked on the door.

"Who's there?" they heard a voice call out, apprehensively.

"Marcus."

A moment later, they heard the door unbolt and a concerned Rochan stood in the doorway. On seeing the weary travellers, she quickly ushered them in.
"Oh my dears. You poor children, you look worn out. Here sit by the fire I will get you something to eat and drink."

The children, surprised by their hostess's appearance, but too tired to question it, flopped down into the chairs which surrounded the glowing fire; Woodlan placing Hannah gently in the chair Naomi had vacated just a few days before.

Rochan bustled about getting out crockery and cutlery and emptying her cupboards of whatever cold victuals she could find.

"Let me help you, Rochan," Naomi said.

"No! No, child. Sit down at the table and rest. My goodness, I can only imagine what you have been through."

Naomi, Marcus and Woodlan sat around the table, which was soon filled with a veritable feast. The children at the smell and sight of the food and milk perked up a little. Rochan filled plates and cups for them and waited on them all. Insisting that the children stay by the fire and eat.

"You must be exhausted," she said.

Once they had all eaten their fill, all except Woodlan, (who it appeared needed neither food nor drink) Ruth sat rubbing her leg. Rochan, on learning of Ruth's injury, insisted on examining it. She carefully removed the, loose and grubby, dressing and set about cleaning it and applying some sap; from what looked like the same leaves Ceraline had used on Naomi's ankle; to it, finally redressing it in a fresh bandage. This accomplished, she ushered the children off to bed, putting the girls in her room and the boys in the room Naomi had used.

Once the children were settled Rochan joined Naomi, Marcus and Woodlan, who were now sitting thoughtfully around the fire.

"Would anyone like anything else to eat or drink?" Rochan asked.

Marcus and Naomi both shook their heads, and they all sat for a few minutes in a heavy silence, until Marcus got up.

"Woodlan and I will lodge at the inn for the night and return in the morning," he said.

"Not too early," Rochan admonished. "I don't want those children disturbed, let them wake when they are ready, you've worn them out."

"What was that thing in the forest?" Naomi broke in, unexpectedly.

Marcus turned back slowly from the door.

"A wraith," he said.

"The Wraith of Tramar to be exact," Woodlan added.

A flicker of disquiet crossed Marcus' face at Woodlan's elucidation.

"Tramar?" Naomi asked.

"Tramar is the name of the forest," Woodlan continued.

Naomi's brow furrowed.

"Why do you call it, The Wraith of Tramar, exactly?" she said, with a slight edge to her voice,

"Because this particular Wraith has haunted the forest of Tramar for centuries. There is a . . ."

"Am I understanding this right . . ." Naomi said, interrupting Woodlan and rounding on Marcus. "You *knew* about that thing, and you *still* took the children in there?"

"Wraiths come to the dying to lead them to the other world. They are rarely seen by the living," Marcus said, calmly.

"Well that one was," Naomi said, furious at Marcus' seeming lack of concern for the danger he had put the children in. "What were you thinking? Hannah could have been killed! How could you put the children in such danger?"

"We had to go through the forest. There was no way around it."

"Well you could have least given me some warning."

"It didn't look to me like you needed any warning, she proved to be no match for you." Woodlan said. "It seems what Marcus has told me about you is right, the power of the old ones runs through your veins,"

"The power of the . . . what is he talking about?" Naomi said.

Marcus gave Woodlan a look of admonishment which Woodlan returned with a look of complete innocence.

"Well . . .?" Naomi insisted.

"It is late. I think it would be better if we continued this conversation in the morning," Marcus said.

"No! You tell me, and you tell me *now* what this is all about, because I don't believe you when you say you didn't think that thing in the forest would show itself. There's something going on here . . . something you're obviously hiding from me." Marcus stood, resolute. "Rochan!?" Naomi pleaded.

"Why don't we all just sit back down?" Rochan said.

Marcus remained resolute for a moment and then took a seat back at the fire.

"I lied . . ." he began. "When I said I hadn't seen any others except you on the mountain . . . I found bodies scattered all over the mountainside, adults . . . and children . . . all dead." Naomi started at this stark allusion to the fate of her pupils and colleagues, tears stinging her eyes. "Then I found you, lying in the gully . . . with only a slight cut to your head . . . and you weren't just lying there as if you had fallen, you were laid on your back your arms across your chest . . . it was as if you had been put there out of harm's way."

"You're suggesting that someone came along and saved me?" Naomi interrupted. "But who and . . . why . . . why me and not any of the others?"

"Not someone . . . something." Rochan said, thoughtfully.

"What do you mean some . . . *thing*?" Naomi asked.

"I'm beginning to understand now why Marcus brought you here and revealed our world to you," Rochan said.

"Would someone like to tell *me,* so I could understand?"

"Of course, child," Rochan said, taking Naomi's hands comfortingly in her own. "When the links between our two worlds began to weaken so did humankind's links with the very earth which sustained them . . . In times past, we are taught, there were some humans whom Gaia blessed with the gift to . . . *communicate* with the natural world. The other races, though part of that world were, and are still, limited to their own sphere of nature, but some humans had the ability to bridge those spheres and bring the Essential Harmony; that is the communication between different elements and forces;

a harmony that often provided protection for those who call earth their home, from her more harmful forces. As the earth became less and less important to humankind as a place of husbandry, and became more a place to exploit, the gifts of Gaia were no longer nurtured and so those gifts were lost.

"The powers of old were passed down from generation to generation, and while any knowledge of that power may have been lost over the decades, the abilities that are contained within that power continue to flow through the bloodline, whether the holders are aware of it or not. If your ancestors belonged to that small group of humans chosen to maintain the Essential Harmony, then their abilities will flow through your blood and if your blood touched the earth, it would have to recognise your right of protection in respect of the ancient laws, which were founded when Gaia was made mother of all."

"Is that why you took us through the forest," Naomi said, pulling her hands from Rochan's hold and turning to Marcus, "as some sort of test, to see if I really possessed this power?"

"No, what I told you is true, Wraiths rarely show themselves to the living." Marcus said.

"But you suspected something might happen . . . you must have, because we had already felt the Wraiths presence the first time we travelled through the forest . . . hadn't we?"

"Whether I suspected or not, as I have told you it makes no difference, we had to go through the forest, there was no other way."

"But even if I did possess this . . . *power*, what difference does it make? I still don't understand why you brought me here, why not just take me back to my own people?"

"There was a time when both our worlds lived in harmony, even at times married," At this latter remark a cloud crossed Marcus' face and Naomi remembered the story of his parents. "Then humankind invented machines which they used to choke the air, their minds became polluted with greed, they no longer saw the world around them as a place to be nurtured and cared for, but a means to wealth and power. Those humans who tried to hold onto the links binding the two worlds found themselves overcome by want and need, forced into the growing cities just to survive. At last, all but a very few embraced the material world, and our world became a fable recounted only in stories to amuse children. For centuries we have lived so, the gap between our two worlds ever widening. Gaia, the mother of all things, eventually hid our world to protect us from the relentless onslaught of humankind. She has kept this balance between our two worlds for many years, but now the earth is calling out for justice against humankind and Gaia has heard its call and answered it; the earthquakes and extreme weather conditions are an indication of that. I brought you here for two reasons. The first is, I don't believe that our world is immune to the effects of Gaia's justice and the other is . . . I have ranged the borders of our two world for many decades and learned that there are still men and women willing to fight for the rights of the earth which sustains them, my own father was such a man, and it is for him and others like him, as well as the welfare of the faerie races that I have brought you here."

"What is it that you think I can do?"

"Ancient legends tell us that, in times past, humans who possessed the power of the old ones were able to commune with Gaia, ask for her help and guidance. I believe that a personal plea from one who holds this power now, may save both our peoples from the worst of Gaia's justice."

"You want *me* to make a plea to . . . Gaia . . . this mother of *all* living things . . .?"

"Yes."

"I'm a primary school teacher . . . you need a . . . politician or a scientist."

"It is not science or politics that will save your people now, only the ancient efficacy," Rochan said.

"Even if I do have this . . . ancient power. I would have no idea how to use it."

"You would do anything within your power to save the children under your care," Rochan said, taking Naomi's hands within hers once more. "Even, if necessary, I think . . . give your life to save theirs."

Rochan's words touched Naomi to the core. 'Give her life for them.' She had never thought about it in those terms, she felt responsible for them yes, but die for them . . . then she remembered her dead colleagues and pupils, and was almost overwhelmed by feelings of grief and pain for their loss, and with tears stinging her eyes once more she knew, in that moment, that she *would* do *anything* she could to save her little band of misfits from the same fate.

"Yes." she said, faintly and then with more conviction. "Yes! I would."

"It is that desire that will lead you to find the powers of old that lie latent within you. You will find a way." Rochan said.

"I think it is time Woodlan and I left," Marcus said. "We will return in the morning."

"Aye. I think you have given the lass enough to think about for now," Woodlan added.

Rochan saw them out, then returned to the fire.

R. E. BUSBY

"You and I can sleep here by the fire tonight, she said. "We can put the chairs together and with a few cushions and blankets we will be snug enough."

"What happens now?" Naomi said, hardly heeding what Rochan was saying. And without waiting for an answer added, "What about the children?"

"There will be enough time to discuss all that tomorrow," Rochan answered. Then, continuing matter-of-factly, she said, "Now, can you help me move these chairs?"

CHAPTER NINE
The Nexus

Naomi stood at the cottage window watching the children, under Rochan's tutelage, learn all about the various medicinal properties of the flowers and herbs which she grew in abundance in her garden.

The children had awoken early and refreshed. Rochan had delighted in preparing breakfast for them and in watching them devour it heartily. Naomi on the other hand had had little appetite. She had spent most of the night, going over again and again everything she had experienced in the last few days, trying to make sense of it, but coming to no conclusions except that the more she thought about it the more confused she became until at last, overcome by fatigue, she had fallen into a restless sleep. The children, fully rested, were full of questions about when they would be leaving and how long it would take to get home. Questions which Naomi had no answer for. She had merely told them that they would have to wait until she spoke to Marcus. Rochan, in order to save Naomi from any more questioning, had kept the children busy tidying up the breakfast things and then taken them out into the garden.

Naomi's gaze wandered from this restful domestic scene to the road where she saw Marcus and Woodlan approaching the cottage. Hannah spotted them at almost the same time and called out a greeting to them; the other children turned their attention from Rochan to the visitors, eyeing them with mixture of awe and apprehension.

"Good morning, young'uns, did you sleep well?" Woodlan asked, good naturedly.

"Yes, thank you." Hannah said, speaking for the whole group, and looking as if she would have liked to say more, but was given no opportunity to do so as Woodlan merely nodded his approval and quickly followed Marcus, who was already opening the cottage door.

Naomi greeted them with a perfunctory, "Good morning."

"Did you sleep well," Marcus asked.

"No."

"Well, that's understandable, lass, you have a lot on your mind," Woodlan said.

"That's an understatement," she said.

"Perhaps we should sit down, I'm sure you have a lot of questions," Marcus said.

"A few," Naomi said, with a slight raise of her eyebrows. "You said last night," Naomi began, when they were all seated round the table, "that in order to help my people and save the children I would have to make a plea to Gaia. How am I supposed to do that, exactly?"

"First you will have to join The Nexus," Marcus said.

"The Nexus?"

"It is a council of all races," Woodlan answered. "It has not been held for many years."

"I have called for a meeting for this morning," Marcus said. "I do not know how many will come. However, I am hopeful that the recent rumblings and the news I have spread of one who holds the gifts of old may be enough to bring them together, or at least enough of them to hold the council. The last shaking was felt well within our borders, that should cause some to question our position of safety, and others will come because they simply do not want to be left out."

"And what will joining this Nexus entail?" Naomi asked.

"As Woodlan has said, it is a council of *all* races, humans included. You will take the place of your people on the council. The journey to Gaia will be a difficult one, many of our people believe that humankind is merely reaping what they have sowed and will do all they can to stop us from reaching Gaia. The council must be persuaded that it is in their best interests to sanction our journey, because without their support our journey may prove impossible."

"So, you want *me* to somehow persuade them to give their approval for our journey?"

"Yes."

"No pressure then."

"I'm sorry?"

"Nothing, it doesn't matter . . . you said the meeting is midday today."

"Yes."

"That doesn't give me much time to prepare. I mean . . . what do I need to know . . . what sort of protocol is there . . . is there anything I definitely should or shouldn't do, or say?"

"Just follow my lead, and do not speak until you are spoken to."

"Right," Naomi answered, feeling less than reassured by Marcus' curt advice.

"You'll be fine, lass," Woodlan said, cheerily. "We will be with you the whole time."

Naomi gave Woodlan a smile of thanks.

"What about the children?" she asked.

"They will stay here, for now, with Rochan," Marcus answered.

"Then what? How are we going to get them back to their parents?"

Marcus gave Naomi a look she was beginning to become familiar with, a look that signalled bad news. She braced herself for the worst.

"Since you have been here your people have suffered under the burden of many more storms and quakes. They are struggling to survive their ruinous effects. There is no time to take the children home . . . even if they still have a home left to go back to . . . I am sorry."

It was damning news and Naomi blinked back tears as she contemplated the catastrophic consequences it implied and felt sick at the thought of telling the children that they wouldn't be going home . . . that she couldn't keep her promise.

"I am afraid there is no more time for discussion. We need to leave now if we are to make the meeting place on time," Marcus concluded.

As they pushed back their chairs and made to leave, the door of the cottage flew open and the children, followed by a beaming Rochan, tumbled in.

"I'd like to cut the vegetables," Ruth was saying. "I'm never allowed to do that at home."

"I'll peel them," Luke added enthusiastically. "That's always my job at home."

"Oh, Rochan! Can I help cook them and choose the herbs?" Hannah pleaded. "It will be just like being on one of those cooking programs I watch with my mum."

Elliott was quiet, but there was a smile playing on his lips, evidence of how much he was silently joining in the others enjoyment.

Naomi was pleased to see the children so happy, but all their talk of home made her glad that she was going out, and the dreaded conversation was postponed.

"Oh, Miss!" Hannah cried. "We're all going to make a vegetable casserole for lunch. We picked the vegetables and herbs ourselves, and Rochan taught us so much about what goes best with what and what all the different herbs were for and . . ."

"I'm going to cut the vegetable, Miss," Ruth interrupted.

"What's your favourite vegetable, Miss?" Luke asked, but not stopping for an answer continued. "Mine is potatoes because you can make chips with them . . . I love chips."

"That's lovely, children," Naomi said. "I'm glad you're enjoying yourselves. I have to go out for a little while. You're all going to stay here with Rochan, so I need you all be really good."

"Will you be back for lunch, Miss?" Hannah said, anxious that her teacher have the opportunity to taste her cooking.

Naomi glanced questioningly at Marcus.

"As long as you do not eat too early," he said. Then added, good-humouredly, "But if we are a little late do not forget to save us some."

"Oh we won't," Hannah assured him.

"Where are you going?" Elliott asked.

"Erm . . ." Naomi stuttered, taken off-guard by Elliott's directness.

"There is just some business I need Miss to help me with," Marcus said. "And we are late already."

Marcus swept from the cottage, before Elliott could ask the next question that was already forming on his lips. Woodlan followed him out giving the children a grin and nod goodbye.

"I'll be back as soon as I can, be good!" Naomi admonished once again.

"We will all be fine, do not worry. My helpers and I will have a hearty meal ready for you when you return," Rochan said.

Naomi gave them one last smile as she closed the door.

*   *   *

Once passed the Inn they followed a path which led to a dense forest. Naomi stopped short, reluctant to cross its perimeter.

"Don't worry, Miss. Stay close to me. All will be well," Woodlan assured her.

Inside the forest Naomi stayed so close to Woodlan she had to be careful not to catch her feet on his solid bulk, while further trying not to trip over the many tree roots which covered the forest floor.

Thankfully, much to her relief, it was not long before they came to a large clearing surrounded by twelve silver birch trees. The trees stood tall and stately, the sunlight shining through their leaves and branches creating a glistening circle. Within the centre of the circle there was a large, round wooden table, itself surrounded by seven, singular looking, wooden chairs. Some of the chairs were covered with deeply ornate carvings while others were more prosaic, seeming merely to serve their purpose. Between one of the more practical chairs and one of the more ornate ones there was a gap, as if one of the chairs were missing.

Naomi only had a few moments to take in her new surroundings before she was left shocked and confused, as a familiar little man, with an extremely round face, pointed ears and exceptionally small eyes, that surveyed his surroundings with a look of suspicion and malevolence, burst through the trees and acknowledging Naomi and Marcus with the same look of suspicion and malignity, seated himself defiantly in one of the more prosaic chairs. It was the dwarf who had held her and the children captive!

Naomi made to speak, but Marcus touched her arm firmly as a sign for her to keep silent. There was a short awkward silence before the next visitor arrived, the appearance of which, left Naomi wide eyed and open mouthed.

A satyr emerged through the trees and proudly made his way towards the table, stopping short to acknowledge Naomi and Marcus with a low bow, then took his place, regally, in one of the chairs carved with many leaves and branches. Naomi hardly had time to come to terms with being bowed to by a satyr, before a centaur entered the clearing, followed immediately by a creature that looked like a wolf, although it was the size of a small horse. The wolf-like creature climbed into a chair carved with many different types of animals and sat head erect acknowledging no one. The centaur stood in the gap in the circle of chairs, he too made no acknowledgement of those around him. The centaur had no sooner taken his place, when the air was filled with the most intoxicating aroma.

Everyone in the clearing closed their eyes and took a deep, involuntary, breath. Naomi felt the scent infuse her body with a deep sense of calmness. She slowly opened her eyes and started slightly as there were now, seated on either side of the centaur, two of the most beautiful women she had ever seen. One was black as ebony, with soft brown eyes, her sleek burnished hair fell in copious black curls across her shoulders down to her waist; she was dressed in luxurious robes of rich red and green hues, and a smile played across her full copper lips. The other, by stark contrast, was pale and ethereal yet no less beautiful. Her alabaster hair, which ended at her feet, formed a natural cape around her, lightly covering the rest of her pale vesture, which hung from her slight frame like cobwebs. Her eyes were emerald green and, from under their pale lashes, eyed all around her with a hint of suspicion. Both of the woman sat in a chair which complimented their form, carved with foliage and river icons respectively. There were now only two chairs left unfilled at the table. One was engraved with images of mountains and lakes; the other was conspicuous by its plainness; it was high backed, made of oak and devoid of any decoration.

Suddenly, out of the hanging silence, the dusky beauty spoke.

"Will she not take her place with us?"

Naomi blanched as the extraordinary company directed their collective gaze towards her. She turned uncertainly to Marcus who, in answer to her mute question, raised his arm and directed her towards the plain oak chair. Overcome with a sense of confused obedience she made her way to the seat between the satyr and the other, still empty, chair.

Sitting down she found the oak seat, surprisingly, comfortable. However, unlike the others, whose chairs seemed made to measure, this one had obviously been made for someone much larger in stature, so Naomi felt, and looked, like a child sitting in an adult chair. This somewhat ridiculous position was not lost on the others and they all looked at her with varying degrees of amusement. All except the pale beauty, who's demeanour remained impassive. Naomi, blinked and shuffled embarrassedly and trying to draw attention from herself, looked up at Marcus expecting him to take the final chair.

To her surprise, though, he moved away from her towards the dusky beauty. As he reached her chair the dusky beauty turned her head and with a slight lowering of her eyes acknowledge his presence. Marcus bowed a low bow then took up sentinel by her chair. As Naomi watched on, she wondered if this was the queen who had ordered the death of Marcus' father; it was an unsettling thought.

With Marcus by her side the dusky beauty placed one of her hands on the table and closed her eyes, the other creatures immediately followed suit. Naomi sat staring around the table. Unsure of what to do, she once again looked to Marcus for advice who indicated that she too should place her hand on the table. Marcus then placed his hand on the shoulder of the dusky beauty and closed his eyes. Naomi looked down at the table and saw the imprint of a large hand, looking around the table, and seeing that the others were resting on similar indentations, she placed her hand, gingerly, onto the oversized imprint. . .

"She should not be here . . ." "They must be represented . . ." "They are nothing to us . . ." "Why are we here . . .?" "What is there to discuss . . .?" "It affects us all . . ." "You are a fool . . ." "No one is safe . . ."

A cacophony of voices filled Naomi's head it was so overwhelming that she pulled her hand out of the imprint almost as soon as she had laid it down, her involuntary movement causing all the others to do the same. The centaur, wolf and the dwarf fixed her with reproachful stares, while the others looked at her questioningly, all except for the sable beauty, who gave her a smile of reassurance.

"She is unfamiliar with the link," Marcus said.

"She should not be here," the dwarf protested, vehemently.
"She has a right to represent her people," Marcus replied.

"Her people," spat out the dwarf, "abandoned the link centuries ago. They forfeited their rights then."

"Marcus is right, in the present crisis all should be represented," the sable beauty said, in a voice as rich and smooth as her complexion.

"It is her kind which have brought the crisis upon us," the dwarf cried. "If we involve ourselves with them our chances of survival will be diminished. We must cut all links with them."

"All links, Bathon?" The dwarf did not answer Marcus' pointed question he merely moved, uncomfortably, back in his chair and spoke no more. Naomi assumed Marcus was referring to his own human connections. "It is true," he continued, "the humans have played a major part in the present instability, the effects of which we are all feeling, however, they are also an essential part of the balance, we cannot restore it without them."

As Marcus finished speaking a low howl penetrated the air. All eyes were now on the wolf. The sable beauty answered his cry.

"Amorok, of course, we must restore the link." Then looking around her she addressed the others. "This time it may be better if we take some time to introduce ourselves to our . . . guest. We will each take our turn to speak, I will begin, if no one objects." (No one did.) Then looking directly at Naomi she signalled with her hand that she should follow her lead and place her hand once more on the table. Naomi did so. This time there was silence, at first, then . . .

"I am Latora, Queen of the Woods, welcome to the council of elders. We have met in places such as this since Gaia was given charge of the world. It is many years since a human has sat among us and, while my people have chosen throughout those years to distance themselves more and more from them, there are still many among us who remember the times of old. Times when we lived in peace and the chosen humans kept the Essential Harmony. A harmony which maintained a balance of kinship and joy amongst us all. If Marcus has indeed brought us one who could restore the ways of old, my people are keen to hear and help. I, therefore, welcome you to the council."

Latora fell silent and another voice filled Naomi's head.

"Guthran," the centaur introduced himself baldly. "I speak for all my kind when I say we will follow the will of the council. However, we urge the council to err on the side of caution when dealing with the humans, they have proved themselves deeply self-serving in the past. Nonetheless, we recognise the need for harmony and bid the human a . . . cautious welcome to the council."

"Amorok," the wolf growled, and continued slowly and deliberately. "My kind have experienced nothing but pain, suffering and death from the humans. I see no reason to help them."

"See, Amorok agrees with me. Why his kind would be extinct if Gaia had not hidden them from the murdering humans. They . . ."

"Bathon! You will have your time to speak, *please* allow others theirs." Latora's voice was soft but firm and silenced Bathon immediately.

Amorok continued, "What Bathon says is true. My kind once roamed this land with pride. We had no quarrel with humankind, but they were not willing to share the land, and so accused us of ruining their crops, stealing their livestock and even eating their children. It will take much to convince my kind to help the humans."

Amorok's deep, round tones were replaced by the soft, light tones of the satyr.

"Lixell," he said by way of introduction. "So you would become like your enemy and treat them as they treated you, without mercy. That is not a solution, Amorok, it is revenge, and revenge leads only to further death and destruction. I for one think it would be most *interesting* to renew ties with the humans and bid you a *warm* welcome on behalf of all my kind." Naomi felt such a direct playfulness from the satyr, as his smooth voice filled her head, that the blood rushed to her cheeks, leaving her with an involuntary sense of confusion. Indeed, Naomi was finding the link deeply invasive and was fighting a strong desire to sever herself from its effects.

"Bathon, of the mountain dwarves, and I speak for *all my* people when I say we must strive to protect our own borders. The humans must be left to their fate the old links have long been severed, and for good reason. At this very table there is an empty chair, the elves know better than to waste their time with futile attempts to ally ourselves with the humans, an alliance that will bring only death and destruction. You need only to look around you to see the devastation they wreak upon each other and all that surrounds them, greed and hate fills their hearts. Restoration of the Essential Harmony? Bah! I warn you now that if we involve ourselves with the humans any hope for *harmony* will be lost." The vehemence of Bathon's angry tirade left Naomi feeling shaken, as the power of the link caused her to feel his fury as if it were her own.

No one spoke for a moment, then the light, penetrating, considered tones of a women broke the heavy silence.

"I am Cachada Queen of the River Folk . . . my people have long felt the scourge of humankind as they have polluted our rivers and lakes, plundered the great seas, murdered the giants of our oceans and left a trail of loss and pain that runs through our world like an open sore . . . Talk of harmony with the humans has for us a hollow ring to it . . . Nevertheless, I will hear with an open heart her words and the words of the council."

Naomi felt a deep sense of shame rush through her body when Cachada had finished speaking. The link was becoming increasingly oppressive, she began to feel overwhelmed by the cacophony of emotions directed towards her; shame, anger, embarrassment, pity, curiosity . . . just as she was about to pull her hand from the table, unable to stand the confusion any longer, Latora's voice pulled her back.

"The child is not used to the link we must curb our feelings. We are placing all the wrongs of her kind on her shoulders it is unjust of us. Let us allow her to speak for her people."

Naomi now felt their collective consciousness directed solely towards her. She took a moment to try and collect her thoughts.

"I'm Naomi," she began. ". . . I . . .erm . . . well actually . . . Marcus believes . . . that I have some inherited power that can be used to bring back this . . . Essential Harmony . . . that could in fact be used to help . . . in the present situation."

"You see! The girl herself does not believe that she holds the power," Bathon cried.

Naomi felt the inadequacy of her words and was silenced by the truth of Bathon's reproof.

"But Marcus does!" Latora exclaimed. "And he must have a strong reason for this belief."

"I do!" Marcus proclaimed. "When Gaia shook the earth, I found her, not amongst the bodies of her companions, but lying safe, far from them, a single scratch upon her cheek." Naomi started at this sudden reminder of the lost children and her colleagues, tears stinging her eyes. Marcus paused for a moment as they all, involuntarily, felt her grief . . . "She could not have gotten there herself. I believe a drop of her blood touched the earth beneath her and, following the ancient laws, forced the elements to protect her from the havoc they wreaked . . . I believe she possesses the gifts of the ancients. That is the only explanation for her surviving the manifestation of Gaia's retribution, for even Gaia is subject to the laws of the ancients."

"This is not evidence, just a vain hope . . . in a weeping child."

Naomi felt a sudden rush of anger towards Bathon at this blatant show of contempt for her grief for all those who had lost their lives. As the feeling within her reached its height Bathon involuntarily stiffened in his chair, as if he had just received an electric shock. A sense of surprise rippled through the link and once again Naomi felt the collective consciousness directed towards her.

"That is not all," Marcus continued. "She subdued the Wraith of Tramar, forcing it to return one of the children in her care, and to release all those who were with her that it held captive."

This created another ripple of surprise through the Link, but Bathon was not to be won over.

"I tell you the real evidence lies in Gaia's chastisement of the humans," Bathon had quickly recovered himself, however, Naomi thought she detected a little less confidence in his voice as he tried to win the council over to his side. "It is the demonstration of *Gaia's* power we should concern ourselves with."

"I came to this meeting with little hope," Guthran said. "And when I saw the girl, I too felt she was merely a child, and that Marcus had called us on a fool's errand, but she has shown humility, and a deep concern for others that cannot be ignored. Also, it took strength to withstand the power of the link. Where you see weakness, Bathon, I see hope."

"No one has felt the total disregard that many humans show for nature than those of us who guard the waters," Cachada said, "but Guthran is right, there is an aura about the girl, we have *all* felt it present in the link. Perhaps if you were not so blinded by your anger and *fear*, Bathon, you too would be able to admit to the possibilities the girl may hold."

Cachada's further rebuke infuriated Bathon.

"Angry? Of course I am angry, angry that the council would think of taking such a foolish step as to invite the very cause of our problems into the council. We must forget the humans and go to Gaia ourselves and plead with her. I believe she will hear us. Did she not separate our worlds in order to protect us from the humans' destructive nature? Why would she desert us now?"

"Much of what you say is true, Bathon," Marcus answered. "But it is also true, that despite the separation between our two worlds we have all felt the effects of the earth trembles, and the raging tempests that are growing in intensity. You ask why Gaia would desert us now, perhaps it is because she feels that we have deserted her. Gaia did not create the division between our two worlds so we could hide and watch idly as humankind wreaked devastation and destruction all around us. Thinking we could wait out the tempest and when it is all over come out from our hiding places and inherit a world renewed, a world we had no part in making. We must go to Gaia, and yes plead with her, but we cannot go without a human advocate to plead for forgiveness for *all* of us." They all felt the truth of Marcus' words and even Bathon was silenced.

"Marcus is right," Latora said. "Since the Essential Harmony was lost, we have all increasingly isolated ourselves from one another. This, *my* people feel, is ultimately detrimental to us all. Only by one who possesses the old power can we have any chance of appeasing Gaia and calming the storms that are already impacting across our lands and waters. It will, however, be a difficult task for anyone to reach Gaia. There are many forests and waters, as well as others of our kind, that wish Gaia to succeed in destroying the humans, they will do all they can to stop you from reaching her"

"I am willing to take that chance," Marcus replied.

"That may be ... but ... are *you* willing?" Cachada asked.

Naomi, who had been listening intently to the others, started at Cachada's question which once again drew all attention to herself. She couldn't think. Overwhelmed by all the different emotions flowing through the Link she pulled her hand from the table and said, vocally.

"I need a moment to think ... I ... excuse me."

Leaving the table she stumbled into the forest past, a concerned, Woodlan. Forgetting, in her distress, her newfound fear of woodland, she stopped only when she thought she could no longer be seen by the others, then sank down onto the forest floor, closed her eyes, and tried to think.

Her head swam with all the voices from the Link. Did she really have some sort of undiscovered power that she could use to help save humankind, or was she just a 'weeping child'? Was she the answer to some ancient law? She shook her head at this, still, unbelievable idea and put it to one side. What *did* she know? She had experienced something truly terrible, and she had survived it; she had wrestled with some unknown entity and overcome it; she also knew that she had stepped into a fairytale land that was real and somehow held the answer to all the devastating events that were happening in her world. Events, that she was being asked to play a key part in preventing from causing any further destruction, a part she felt completely inadequate for. "Oh God!" She heard herself cry out and found herself praying; something she hadn't done since she was a child.

"Please help me ... I don't know what to do, so much seems to depend on me ... *me* ... of all people. It's too much, I'm just seriously not up to this."

After a few moments, she was startled out of her contemplation by a strange sound. Kukk ... kukk ... kukk ... She looked around and discovered a squirrel crying out towards her from a knothole in the side of a beech tree. Presently, four smaller squirrel heads squeezed out round their mother, curious to see what the fuss was about. The mother gave Naomi several more warning calls and then scurried her young back into the hollow and quickly disappeared after them.

Naomi raised her eyebrows to the sky.

"I think I understand," she said, with a half-smile. "The children!"

While she couldn't take on the thought of the responsibility for the whole world, the keenness she felt in her responsibility for those four lives back at Rochan's cottage meant she could and would, do all she had to save those children from the same fate as their classmates. If that meant she had to go along with this *belief* of Marcus', then so be it. If he was right about her latent abilities, then all well and good, if they helped her to ultimately save the children, and if . . . No! She wouldn't think beyond that, one step at a time. She had to get a hold of herself, focus on the children. Filled with this new resolve she went back though the forest and placed her hand back on the table.

There was silence as they all waited for her to speak.

"In answer to Cachada's question I say . . . Yes! I *am* willing to go."

"You understand there will be many dangers," Latora said, "and the journey may cost you your life?"

Latora's stark warning shook Naomi somewhat; that was the second time in two days she had been reminded that the coming journey could cost her her life; but she held her nerve and responded with a simple.

"Yes."

"When will you begin your journey?" Latora asked.

"Tomorrow at sunrise," Marcus answered. "We will go north overground to the Kingdom of Fionn,"

"You will find no welcome in the land of Fionn, he feels as we do towards the humans," Bathon broke in.

"We shall see," Marcus said.

"Hmmf! You are a fool, Marcus and . . ."

"What is it you wish of the council, Marcus?" Latora added, cutting short another tirade from Bathon.

"I ask that the council use all its power to aid us in our journey, and that they will use the influence they have over those they represent here to help them see that unless old links are renewed, both our worlds are in danger of destruction."

There was a *general* silent assent to Marcus' request felt throughout the link, only Bathon remained defiant. Without another word they each left their places at the table and disappeared into the forest.

When they were alone Naomi turned to Marcus.

"This journey we're undertaking," she said. "I don't relish taking four children with us, you and the members of the council made it very clear that it could get extremely dangerous. Is there no way we could get them to safety, even possibly back to their homes, before we start the journey?"

"No. There is no time," Marcus answered, flatly.

"Will the children be able to stay with Rochan then?" Naomi persisted.

"No. That is not possible."

"Why? She adores them, and they've obviously taken to her."

"Rochan could not keep them safe."

"Safe! Safe from what?"

"Bathon for one, he knows how much the children mean to you, it is possible that he might try to recapture them."

"I didn't like the look of that wolf either," Woodlan warned.

"I'm afraid they will have to come with us . . . for now," Marcus said, finally

*   *   *

When they reached Rochan's cottage, Naomi began to feel in earnest the weight of the task ahead of her. There was no more avoiding telling the children that they weren't going home. She still had no idea how she was going to tell them. How she could make them understand, what she didn't really understand herself. Marcus opened the cottage door and Naomi steeled herself for the inevitable tears and questions. The first person she saw was Ruth, relaxed and smiling, laying the table for lunch. The others were huddled round the stove, happily following instructions from Rochan. Seeing them so happy made the thought of her task heavier than ever.

"Oh! You're back, Miss and just in time," Ruth said, cheerily.

"They're back, Rochan," Luke cried. "Can we eat now?"

"Of course we can . . . you all take your seats, and Hannah and I will serve."

Hannah smiled, obviously relishing the idea of serving a meal which she helped so much in the preparation of. Ruth took it upon herself to seat everyone else. Soon they were all enjoying Hannah's casserole, as Ruth kept calling it, much to Hannah's delight. All, of course, except Woodlan. Who sat smiling by the fire watching them.

When they had all finished, Naomi thought it was time to break the news of their impending journey to the children.

"It will be time to get ready to go soon," she said, taking her opportunity during a lull in the conversation. All the children eyed her expectantly, she swallowed hard. "I know you're all expecting to start off for home straight away but . . ." this qualification of their expected journey caused a slight furrow to appear on the brows of the children. Naomi did her best to ignore their looks of concern and continued, "Marcus and Woodlan have somewhere to go before they can take us home, so we need to be patient."

"Are we going with them, Miss?" Hannah asked.

"Yes . . . we are," Naomi answered.

"Are we leaving now?" Ruth asked, anxiously.

"Yes," Marcus answered.

"Where are we going?" Elliott asked.

Naomi and Marcus looked at one another.

"We're going," Naomi began, then stopped and let out a sigh, what could she tell them? She didn't want to lie to them, but she didn't want to frighten them either. She thought for a moment, and then said, "You know that there was an earthquake?"

"Yeees," Elliott said.

"Well Marcus and Woodlan need to go somewhere to make sure that there isn't another one."

"And we're going to help them?" Elliott said, excitedly.

"Not exactly . . . we just need to take part of their journey with them. It's a journey they can't delay by taking us home."

"Then when will we get to go home?" Ruth asked.

"Oh, Ruth! This is far more important than us getting home. You don't want there to be another earthquake, do you?" Luke admonished.

"Well, no . . . but . . . it's just I miss my mum," tears began to steal down Ruth's cheeks.

Hannah rushed to put her arms around her friend.

"I miss my parents too, Ruth," Hannah said. "But we have to be brave. We haven't said much about the earthquake . . . because it's too upsetting, but I think we all know that since then some strange things have happened. I mean the mountain dwarves and spriggins, and it's obvious that Rochan isn't exactly . . . human . . . and Woodlan certainly isn't . . . no offence."

"None taken," Woodlan said.

"There is something going on here," she continued, "that we don't fully understand, but I feel it's important, don't you?"

"Yes," Ruth said, reluctantly.

"Me too," the boys chorused.

"Everything is going to be okay, Ruth, if we all stick together and listen to Miss, and do what she tells us."

At the conclusion of Hannah's discourse, Naomi, overcome by Hannah's display of wisdom beyond her years, joined the girls in their embrace.

"Hannah's right," Naomi said, smiling at the boys. "Everything will be okay if we stick together."

"Oh! Come here you two," cried Rochan, pulling the two boys, who looked surprised but pleased, into a hug around her tiny frame.

CHAPTER TEN
The Hamadryad

Within an hour they were packed and ready to go. Rochan, with help from Naomi and the children, had made up food parcels. While Marcus and Woodlan had left the cottage returning a short time later with several back packs, which Naomi guessed must have come from, the ever resourceful, Noll. Some of the packs were already filled with bedding, and the others they filled with the food parcels. Marcus gave the children the packs containing the bedding to carry, while he and Naomi carried the ones containing the food. Woodlan took charge of the heaviest pack, which was filled with the items they would need for cooking. Rochan bid them a teary goodbye and they set off.

The first day of their journey was uneventful and, as it was all on the flat, not so arduous as their escape from the mountain dwarves. The children chatted easily with one another and asked endless questions of their guides about the countryside they passed through. They loved staying up late eating food they helped cook, around a campfire they helped build, and listening to Woodlan who told them all about the stars they were sleeping under. Unfortunately, the calm was not to last and during the night of the second day as they slept, camped by the edge of a dense forest, they were awoken by a fierce storm.

The children awoke confused and startled. Marcus and Woodlan were calling to them, through the howling wind, to pick up as much of their bedding and supplies as possible. Naomi was already scrambling about trying to grab what she could. The children followed suit for a few minutes then, as a flash of lightening seared across the sky directly above them, Marcus and Woodlan herded them into the nearby forest.

Once far enough into the forest, to be protected from the worst of the storm, they stopped. Naomi and the children huddled together, shivering from cold and apprehension, and listened anxiously as the storm grew in intensity with every passing moment. The roaring of the wind was deafening, and so strong Naomi wondered if their forest sanctuary would be able to withstand its power as the branches above them danced wildly under its force. Lightening streaked violently across the sky and the thunder, which followed its incandescent blaze, mingled its roar with the blasting wind, amplifying further the ear-splitting sound that filled the forest and shook the terrified children to the core. The children covered their ears and winced at every new flash and clap. The rain whipped all around them driven, by the relentless wind, through the leaves and branches and round the giant trunks, soaking them to the very skin. Marcus and Woodlan stood on either side of the little group, wearing expressions of deep concern, trying to protect them as much as they could with their bodies.

Just when Naomi was beginning to think that the storm was never going to ease, the thunder and lightning began to roll off into the distance and the roar of the wind gradually began to quieten, until all that could be heard was the sound of the rain splashing heavily through the, now eerily, still branches. Eventually, the rain too eased and the sun began to rise, shedding a welcome light through the branches of their oppressive shelter.

"The worst is over now," Marcus said, softly, and led them back out to their campsite.

At the sight of the campsite the children let out a collective sigh. There was nothing left of it. No sign of the fire they had made or of any of their belongings. It was as if they had never been there. In fact, apart from the sodden grassy areas, the place seemed no different from the night before when they had decided to camp there.

Naomi looked after the storm clouds as they continued Westward and felt a deep disquiet as she imagined the damage they had no doubt done, and were about to do, elsewhere.

"We must start a fire," Marcus said, "so we can eat and dry off. I will have to go into the forest to try and find dry wood. Elliott and Luke, you will come with me."

The boys followed eagerly in Marcus' footsteps.

While they were gone Woodlan, Naomi and the girls went through what they had managed to save from the night before. Mostly it was bedding but thankfully Woodlan had managed to grab a bag of food, so at least there would be something to cook for breakfast.

It wasn't long before Marcus and the boys returned and Woodlan was cooking bacon and fried bread, over a blazing fire, in the only pan that had survived the storm. The children sat close to the fire, enjoying the aroma and waiting patiently. They hadn't managed to save any of the cutlery, so when the food was ready, they ate it with their fingers straight from the pan. It wasn't ideal but no one seemed to care they were all so hungry. They stayed at the campsite most of the morning, drying themselves and their bedding and allowing time for the children to get some of the rest they had missed the night before. When they did eventually continue their journey, their progress was slow. The path was more rugged than it had been, and the children were tired and sluggish from their nights adventure, even Elliott was struggling to keep up a show of defiance.

They travelled for hours, stopping now and again for a few minutes in order for the children to rest and drink, but both were in short supply and Naomi worried how long the children could go on like this. She knew that they must be hungry, and their pace was slowing with each endless mile, but still they dragged themselves on.

At length, the way became less rocky and began to level out into a sandstone track lined with trees. After a short distance, the trees began to thin out and the path widened out into a patch of open ground on which stood a neat little farmhouse. White smoke billowed from its chimney and its walls were draped in shades of pink and purple honeysuckle. On one side of the garden there was a lone willow tree and on the other side was a little girl working in a vegetable patch. As they got closer to the house the little girl became aware of them and looking up, she broke into a beaming smile and ran towards them, throwing herself into Woodlan's arms. Woodlan swung her around heartily, which alarmed Naomi somewhat as the child was such a delicate looking thing. Woodlan's great, granite-like, hands enveloped her tiny waist, Naomi wondered how she could breath, but the little girl merely smiled and giggled, unharmed by her giant playmate. After three or four turns Woodlan placed her gently down. On landing, continuing to smile broadly, she turned to Marcus.

"It is good to see you again, and you have brought friends," she said, bestowing a welcoming smile on Naomi and the children. They all smiled back, all except Elliott who merely gave her a quiet look of appraisal.

Now she was standing still she looked even more delicate. She was slim to the point of being bony. Long blond hair straggled around her shoulders, and her clothes; which consisted of a long sleeved, dirty, brown dress and pumps of a similar shade; were extremely worn. Her eyes, of nut brown, made a stark contrast with her flaxen hair and when she looked at Naomi, Naomi felt as if she wasn't looking *at* her but *inside* her. Despite her somewhat disconcerting air Naomi felt drawn to her, there was a calmness about her that seemed to touch everyone and everything around her.

"We need somewhere to stay until morning and I'm afraid we got caught in the storm and are in need of new supplies," Marcus said.

"Of course, of course. You all look tired out and I'm sure you are all very hungry. There is soup and fresh bread, enough for all, come, follow me."

Inside the house, the girl called for them all to make themselves comfortable and signalled them to sit around a large, rectangular, oak dining table. The table was surrounded by seven chairs and dominated the, somewhat, sparsely decorated room. As they followed her direction, she lit the fire under a large pan and took out an impressive looking loaf of bread from the oven. The whole room filled with the wonderful, homely, smell of fresh bread. Placing the bread in the middle of the table she smiled, shyly, at the wows it elicited from the children. The loaf was fashioned into the shape of a bunch of roses, standing proudly in an intricately plaited, bread vase.

"I like roses," she said, continuing to float around the room making dinner and chatting cheerily.

"I am so glad you have all come today I do not get many guests . . . except Woodlan." She gave Woodlan another beaming smile. Woodlan sat himself down in a large, well cushioned, chair near a plain empty fireplace looking as if he had done so many times before. Marcus stood beside him with his back to the fireplace. "The air was so clear, and the sky was so bright this morning, after last night's storm, that I knew that something wonderful was blowing my way, and here you all are. I hope you will enjoy the soup; it is onion and leek. The bread was made this morning."

And so, she continued to fly around the room, putting out bowls, pouring out soup, and cutting bread, until before they knew it the table was set, and they each had a bowl of steaming hot soup, a large portion of the artisan bread and a mug of milk in front of them. Woodlan stayed by the fire contentedly.

"I think it is time for introductions now," the young girl said, when the meal was almost done. "I am Laifolia. Marcus?"

"Of course," this is Naomi, Hannah, Ruth, Luke and Elliott." They each nodded at the mention of their name.

"I am very pleased to meet you all."

Relaxed, by the meal and the introductions, the children began to question their, singular, benefactress.

"Do you live here all alone?" Hannah began.

"No, we are seven," Laifolia answered, simply.

"There are seven in your family you mean?"

"Yes."

"Where are they?" Elliott asked.

"Everywhere."

"They live near-by then?" Hannah continued.

"Yes! In the forest, in the hills, here in the garden, by the river . . . everywhere," Laifolia answered, airily.

"I didn't notice any other houses close by," Elliott said, in a suspicious tone.

"There are no other houses. This is our home."

Elliott's brow furrowed at this, less than clear, answer.

"How long have you lived here?" Ruth asked.

"Everyday."

This surprisingly enigmatic reply, combined with the rest of Laifolia's, somewhat, curious answers to the children's questions, brought an embarrassed smile to the children's lips and they passed each other surreptitious glances round the table, but asked no more questions.

After the meal was over and they had all had second helpings; all except Laifolia herself who in fact only seemed to be eating to keep them company; Laifolia showed the children to their rooms for the night. Each of the rooms had two beds, a dresser with a vase full of fresh flowers on top of it, and a small wooden table covered with a porcelain bowl and a hand towel. Hannah and Ruth shared one room, Luke and Elliott another. The children said very little, their exhaustion was obvious. They wearily wished Naomi and Laifolia goodnight and crawled into their designated beds, falling asleep almost immediately.

Once the children were settled Laifolia began to clear the dinner things. She refused all offers of help from Naomi, placing everything into a large basket which, when she was finished, Woodlan picked up for her.

"There is a river that runs at the back of the house, we will wash up there," she said.

"I really wish you would let me help you," Naomi pleaded.

"I have Woodlan to help. Please you stay here, and rest," she said, and left the cottage.

Naomi took up a seat near the fire, where Marcus stood leaning against the mantelpiece lost in thought. Naomi looked up at him about to ask about their plans for tomorrow, but something in his expression stopped her. Instead, she found herself examining his dark, brooding features, and thinking how little she knew about this man in whom she was putting so much trust. Marcus suddenly turned his head and met her gaze, Naomi felt herself flush.

"You . . . you look worried," she said, awkwardly.

Marcus gave her one of his unreadable looks.

"We must begin our journey as soon as possible tomorrow," he said. "We have lost a lot of time because of the storm. You should try and get some sleep. I will see you in the morning. Goodnight." And with this charge he left the cottage.

Naomi, however, didn't feel like sleeping and stayed sitting, staring into the empty fireplace, lost in pensive reflection. She had not been sitting long, when she thought she heard the sound of someone singing. It was coming from outside the back of the house. Naomi went to the back door and opened it, the singing seemed to rush in on her and she felt herself shiver with delight. She peered out into the darkness looking for the source of the music. Then, at the end of the garden through the fence, in the moonlight, she saw two figures, one large and solid, the other slight and ethereal, sitting by a river looking up at the stars. Laifolia's voice filled the night air with its crystal clarity as she sang . . .

> *Seven there were, who cared and tended,*
> *The forest ancient and strong.*
> *Drifting through its shady hollows*
> *scattering colour and life.*
> *Lovingly, they roamed its endless expanse,*
> *Dancing amongst its shimmering groves.*
> *Scattering seeds that flowered and grew,*
> *Reaping a harvest sublime.*
>
> *Seven there were, who cared and tended,*
> *The forest ancient and strong.*
> *Sisters all as one in form,*
> *Oak, Ash, Beech, Hazel, Elm and Cherry.*
>
> *Until on the horizon dark forms did appear.*
> *In their hands, metal, glinting a threatening glare.*
> *Swiftly they fell, helpless to save,*
> *Oak, Ash, Beech, Hazel and all.*
> *Seven there were who cared and tended,*
> *The forest ancient and strong.*
> *And now that forest lies broken and torn,*
> *And many a flower is no more.*
>
> *Lost is their beauty, a thing of the past.*
> *Tall trees now hewn and felled,*
> *Waiting their turn to be craven and sculpted,*
> *Into shadowy images of themselves.*
>
> *Gone are the seven who cared and tended,*
> *Grieving for all that is lost.*
> *Their tears with the mists mingle together,*
> *Covering the few that are left.*
>
> *One remains, saved for the morrow,*
> *Preserving the memories of old.*
> *Still stands the Willow,*
> *Last of the Seven, who cared and tended . . .*
> *The forest ancient and strong.*

Standing, mesmerised by the scene, Naomi felt someone gently take her hand, it was Ruth. Neither of them spoke. They both stood spellbound until the last strain of Laifolia's song floated away on the night air.

"What do you think it means, Miss?"

"I'm not sure."

"She is singing of her sisters, the Hamadryad." Marcus appeared out of the darkness.

"Hama . . . Hama . . .?" Ruth stuttered.

"They are tree nymphs who care for the forest," he said.

"Where are they now?" Ruth asked.

"The Hamadryad are bound to a particular tree, when the tree dies, they die."

At this sad revelation Ruth looked toward Laifolia.

"So, all of her family are dead," she said, with a catch in her voice. "Doesn't she have a mother or a father."

"No."

"So, she's all alone."

"No. She has Woodlan, myself . . . and as she said, her sisters . . . their . . . spirits, if you like, are all around her in the m. . ."

"Mists," Naomi interrupted.

"Yes," Marcus said, giving Naomi a questioning look.

"That's so sad." Tears began to shine in Ruth's eyes.

"I think it's time we got you back to bed," Naomi said, wishing to change the subject.

Naomi led Ruth back to the room she shared with the sleeping Hannah.

The main room was still empty when she returned to it from settling Ruth. The door to the garden was open. She looked out and saw Marcus sitting on a fallen tree trunk, that lay between the river and the fence, staring out into the starry night. She went outside and stood next to him. He made no acknowledgement of her presence. She looked back down to the river; she could no longer see the shapes of Woodlan and Laifolia.

"How did Laifolia's sisters die?" Naomi asked.

"A mighty forest used to cover the land here," he said, continuing to look out into the night. "Laifolia's sisters and many of their kind before them had cared for it for centuries. Then humankind began to inhabit the land around the forest, at first the men came with axes and felled just a few trees, to build their homes and feed their fires; there was still the connection between our two worlds then and they came to know the Hamadryad and respected them. They made sure that the trees of the Hamadryad were not touched. They passed this knowledge down to their children, so the forest and the people lived in harmony for many years. Little by little though, more and more people began to encroach on the forest's boundaries; people who knew nothing of the Hamadryad and dismissed those who tried to teach them, accusing them of making up stories so they could keep the land for themselves. It was during this time that the first of Laifolia's sisters was cut down. Those who knew and loved the Hamadryad did all they could to protect the rest, but as humankind discovered the wealth the forest could bring to them, they brought machines that could hew down trees in a much shorter time than the axe. They hacked through the forest from every direction. Laifolia's sisters were caught in the frenzy, unable to do anything to stop it. When only one was left she called out to Gaia for help to save Laifolia. Gaia heard her cries and sent Woodlan. By the time he got here only Laifolia remained, a mere sapling, not worth the effort to cut down. Woodlan built this house and fenced in the garden to keep Laifolia safe."

"So Laifolia is . . . bound to the Willow tree in the garden?"

"Yes. She is the last of her kind in these parts and continues to care for the woodland that is left."

"Woodlan . . . what is he? I mean he's not a faerie . . . *is he*?"

"No. Woodlan is an Earth Guide."

Naomi wanted to ask what an Earth Guide was but, as she stifled a yawn with the back of her hand, Marcus said, emphatically, "You should go back in the house and get some sleep."

"Where is Laifolia?" Naomi asked.

"She will not sleep in the house tonight. She is roaming the forest with Woodlan. We will see her in the morning before we leave."

Naomi made her way back to the house, picked up the lamp from the table and settled down in one of the remaining bedrooms for the night.

CHAPTER ELEVEN
Bloody Cranesbill

When Naomi awoke the next day, the sun was burning through the gossamer curtains which adorned the cottage window. Naomi dressed quickly, worried that she might have slept late, and hurried into the main room.

"Miss! Did you sleep well?" Ruth was helping Laifolia set out the breakfast things and Naomi gave an inward sigh of relief that she had not overslept.

"Yes, thank you, and you?"

"Really well, Miss."

"The others, are they up yet?"

"Hannah is in the garden with Woodlan, and the boys are down by the river with Marcus."

"Oh right. Is there anything I can do to help?"

"Breakfast is almost ready so you could call the others in," said Laifolia, as she laid a plate, piled high with fresh buttered toast, in the middle of the table.

"Okay. No problem."

Naomi went out into the garden. Hannah and Woodlan were sitting, deep in conversation, on the same trunk Marcus had occupied the night before. As she came up behind them, she heard Hannah saying . . .

"How does that work? Do you become the object? How do you break down the molecules in your body? What does it feel like?"

"I do not know how it 'works' as you say, I have never thought about it, it is just what I am what I have always been. As to how it feels, can you tell me how it feels to always walk through the air on two legs"

Hannah's brow furrowed at this question, and she thought deeply for a moment.

"It depends on the weather," she said, finally.

Woodlan gave her a puzzled look.

"What I mean is. If I'm walking and it's sunny it feels warm, if it's raining it feels wet, if it's snowing it feels cold. That's the only way I can explain it really." With this pragmatic reply she fixed an expectant gaze on Woodlan.

Woodlan remained puzzled for a moment.

"It is the same for me," he continued. "If the earth is wet I feel wet, if it is dry I feel dry, if it is warm I feel warm."

"Really!" Hannah said, eagerly. "That's so in . . ." Hannah stopped as she caught a glimpse of Naomi out of the corner of her eye. "Oh! Hello, Miss. Woodlan has been telling me all about himself its really interesting. He's an Earth Guide you know."

"That is very interesting. Laifolia and Ruth have asked me to come and tell you that breakfast is ready."

"Ooo! Good. I'm starving. Are you coming, Woodlan?" Before Woodlan had a chance to answer Hannah was asking him another question. "Do you eat? Oh! Of course you don't, or perhaps you eat earth and rocks, do they have a taste? I suppose there is no way of you being able to explain what they tasted like, even if they did have a taste and then they would probably taste differently to you than to me . . . Do you sleep?"

Naomi couldn't help smiling as she watched Hannah and Woodlan make their way back to the house; Hannah questioning, the perplexed, Woodlan as if he were no more than a foreign exchange student. She continued on down to the river, where the boys were standing on the bank intently watching Marcus. Marcus was standing, motionless, knee deep in the water. Naomi remembered the night she had similarly watched him and knew what he was doing. She made her way towards their position on the riverbank, reaching them just as Marcus snatched a fish from the still water.

"Whoa!" the boys called out in simultaneous admiration.

"That was awesome!" cried Luke.

"Could you teach us how to do it?" Elliott asked.

"Perhaps?" Marcus said, putting his wriggling captive back into the water. "But right now I think breakfast may be ready." Marcus added, looking over the boys' heads at Naomi.

The boys turned around and on seeing their teacher broke into an effulgent discourse on all the cool things Marcus had been showing them.

"Did you see him catch that fish, Miss?" Elliott cried.

"That's not all he can do," Luke continued. "He showed us how to set a trap for a rabbit and how to start a fire without matches and . . ."

"He knows loads of bird songs, Miss," Elliott interrupted. "It was as if he was talking to them."

The boys sang Marcus' praises all the way back to the house, continually interrupting each other in excited rapture.

At the breakfast table the children shared stories of all they had learned about their newfound friends, stopping only to fill their mouths with toast and soft boiled eggs and to turn to Naomi for suitable comments of appreciation and confirmation. Naomi obliged, in best teacher fashion, with some appropriate adjectives. 'Brilliant, sounds excellent, wow, stupendous, fascinating, well done.' It was wonderful to see them so happy after all that had happened to them.

Breakfast was over all too soon, however, and before long they were making ready to leave.

"Laifolia has made up some bags of food for us," Ruth said, smiling appreciatively at Laifolia as she placed two leather bags on the table. "And some bedding packs," she added, with even greater admiration in her voice.

Marcus gave each of the children a bedding pack, reserving the leather bags for himself and Naomi. Woodlan was already laden with a pack full of cooking utensils. When they were ready to go Laifolia gave each of them a hug. She seemed to hold onto Ruth for just a little longer than the rest and, seeing Ruth was about to burst into tears, gently touched her cheek gazing intently into her face. In that moment, Naomi thought, it was as if some of Laifolia's calm, gentle strength imprinted itself onto Ruth. Ruth swallowed down her tears and forced a smile.

With many exchanges of thanks, they made their way out of the cottage and back onto the road, Laifolia waving them goodbye from the cottage gate.

This was their second, bitter-sweet, goodbye in almost as many days. Naomi wondered uneasily how many more such goodbyes there would be before their journey ended.

*   *   *

For two days, after leaving the comfort of Laifolia's cottage, they walked and walked, only stopping to eat and sleep. The children, who had started the next part of their journey in high spirits, by the third day said little; reserving all their strength for the punishing pace that Marcus silently demanded of them. Only Elliott seemed to thrive on keeping up with Marcus.

Woodlan, meantime, did his best to keep them cheerful and take their minds of their seemingly endless trek. He pointed out to them the many wildflowers and mosses that lined the path. At first the children had delighted in his discourse, but their initial enthusiasm was now waning. Even Hannah was so tired that she no longer questioned Woodlan's information, but merely nodded or gave a cursory 'that's lovely,' so as not to hurt his feelings.

Mid-afternoon on the fourth day they reached a wide gully.

"We will stop here to rest," Marcus said, suddenly.

Grateful for this unexpected respite the children plonked themselves down where they stood.

Marcus climbed up a nearby ridge and looked all around. Then, in an urgent voice, called Woodlan to join him. Naomi wanted to go to see what was wrong but stayed with the children; not wishing to alarm them. However, she kept one eye on the children and one eye on Marcus and Woodlan, who stood on the ridge, deep in conversation. At one point, Woodlan shook his head and Marcus put his hand on his shoulder as if he was trying to convince him of something. Eventually, Woodlan's head drooped slightly, and he gave Marcus a reluctant nod.

Elliott too must have been watching this dumb show because when they returned, he immediately demanded, "What's wrong?"

"The storms have somewhat changed the route we are to take," Marcus answered. "We will have need of a boat or two, so Woodlan and I must leave you for a while." The children started at this piece of unexpected news and even Naomi had to work hard at keeping her face passive. "There is no need to be fearful," Marcus said, in answer to their looks of alarm. "We will set a fire, and we will be back before nightfall."

The children accepted Marcus' assurances silently and, under Woodlan's direction, began to collect wood for the fire and sort out the bedding. While the children were thus engaged Marcus took the opportunity to speak to Naomi alone.

"Once the fire is lit make sure that the children stay close to it, and that it does not burn *too* brightly." Marcus' veiled caution of the dangers that could be close by was clear to Naomi.

"I understand," she said.

Once Woodlan and Marcus had gone, Naomi kept the children amused by playing games. Which, despite their initial reluctance; because of their tiredness, and the fact that they thought they were *too old* for 'games; they were all soon laughing and joking and playing. After several games of, I went to the market, Chinese whispers, twenty questions and finally charades, they all ate their evening meal in good humour.

As the sun began to set and the temperature began to drop, they all huddled round the fire. It wasn't long before the children's heads began to droop. Naomi was just about to settle them down for the night when they were all shook out of their languor by, what sounded like, rocks falling nearby.

The children raised their heads in unison, like a mob of meerkats, towards the sound. A few seconds later, they all tensed at the sight of a tall, hooded figure emerging from the blackness and striding straight towards them.

Almost without thinking Naomi grabbed one of the larger pieces of kindling that lay near the fire and placed it quickly in the flames.

"Who are you? What do you want?" she demanded, pointing her flaming weapon at the oncoming, hooded stranger.

The hooded figure stopped in mid stride but did not speak.

"You heard her, who are you?" Elliott pressed, standing next to Naomi holding his own makeshift flaming sword.

"Don't come any closer?" warned Luke. Who was now standing on the other side of Naomi with Hannah and Ruth, each of them holding a large stone in their hands aimed, threateningly, at the stranger.

The stranger stopped short in their advance, and lifting their hands to their hood, lowered it, revealing a man so strikingly handsome that his appearance caused Naomi to stare at him, open mouthed, caught in a moment of confused admiration. His eyes were forest green; his hair, of strawberry blond, brushed the collar of a black leather jerkin just visible underneath his grey flowing cape, and a seductive smile played on his full lips. He began, once again, to move towards them which started Naomi out of her immobility and she shook the glowing stick at him, gesturing him to stay back. The stranger stopped once again. His face had a look of suppressed amusement. Then, after a moment of contemplation, his face broke out into a broad smile.

"I am Lugh of the Northern Kingdoms friend to Marcus Mac Freaya," he said, jovially. This rather unusual introduction left them all stumped for an answer, recognising their confusion he continued. "I have come to join the quest of Marcus and Nimonee." Obviously feeling that he had said all that was needed to justify his being there he stood resolutely awaiting their reply.

Before Naomi could say anything, Hannah piped up.

"I think he means you, Miss . . . Nimonee . . . Naomi?"

"Oh of course . . . Naomi. My name is Naomi," she corrected.

"What does he mean, Miss . . . the *quest* of Marcus and Naomi."

"We'll discuss it later, Hannah, we're a little busy right now."

"Yes, Miss . . . Sorry, Miss."

"What proof do we have that you are who you say you are?" Naomi asked.

"Why Marcus will vouch for me . . . where is he?" His handsome head surveyed the camp looking for the answer to his question.

"He's gone to get . . ."

". . . some wood for the fire." Naomi cut in, before Ruth could give away their vulnerability. "He's nearby . . . with a friend."

"Another friend! Who might that be?" Lugh demanded, good humouredly.

"Woodlan," Elliott declared. "And he's a . . . a *giant* so you better go before they get back."

"I remember Woodlan as tall but . . . a *giant* . . . well we shall see. For you see young warrior he too is an old friend of mine and I look forward to seeing him again."

By now the kindling, that had been slowly burning away in Naomi and Elliott's hands, had reached a point where they could no longer hold onto it and feeling the flame begin to warm their fingers, they both dropped them at their feet in quick succession with a cry of pain. Then, endeavouring to rearm themselves as quickly as possible they both bent down to grab another piece of kindling only to find they had both picked up the same piece, each let go of it in preference to the other, then seeing it fall to the ground they both grabbed for it once again, banging their heads together in the attempt. The other children watched on in confusion, while Lugh, looking around him and seeing a rather large tree branch picked it up.

"Will this do?" he said.

Naomi looked up, rubbing her head where she had bumped it with Elliott. Lugh was standing over her with the sizeable branch in his hand and a, now open, look of amusement on his face. Naomi couldn't help feeling the ridiculousness of the situation and moved her hand to her mouth looking down at the ground in an effort to hide a smile of her own. Elliott, however, took this offer of help as a sign of aggression and ran at Lugh and began to kick and punch him. The other children were about to follow suit, well Hannah and Elliott anyway, but were stopped in their tracks as Lugh picked up Elliott by his collar and held him flailing in the air.

"You're feisty for one so small. I will give you that."

"*Small* . . ." Elliott cried, furiously. "I'll show *you* who's small," and he began to thrash about even more ferociously."

"Put him down . . . *please*."

Ignoring Naomi's pleading Lugh continued to hold Elliott up, laughing at his flailing captive. The other children made a run at Lugh.

"No! Stay where you are," Naomi shouted. Then turning on Lugh she said, "Put him down . . . ***Now***."

All at once Lugh bent forward and grabbed his stomach, dropping Elliott in the process, it was as if he had buckled under the force of Naomi's verbal command. The children stared at Naomi with looks a mixture of admiration and surprise. Lugh was still holding his stomach with a shocked expression on his face. Naomi had no idea what had just happened she was just as surprised as the children, until the incident in the link with Bathon flashed through her mind, with this thought she continued to stare at Lugh, challengingly.

Lugh, having recovered himself, smiled slowly.

"Well," he began, "now we have all got to know each other a little better, perhaps you will allow me to share the warmth of your fire."

Holding his gaze for a moment, Naomi nodded a slow assent.

Lugh moved assuredly to the fire bending over it and warming his hands, the children and Naomi stood a little apart, still slightly apprehensive of their uninvited guest. Undaunted by their continued distrust of him Lugh continued in his easy fashion.

"Come sit by the fire, the night air is cool, surely I have proved to you I mean you no harm."

"I don't think holding me in the air shows that you mean us no harm!" Elliott cried.

"I was merely defending myself."

"Defending yourself . . . defending yourself . . . *you're* the one who came into *our* camp uninvited. Who do you think you are?"

"I have told you who I am. I have not had the pleasure of learning your name however."

Elliott stared furiously at the complacent Lugh.

"All right that's enough," Naomi said. Then signalled to the children to move back to the fire.

They all followed her instruction, all except Elliott who stubbornly stayed where he was. Naomi didn't try to coax him. She knew that his pride was hurt, and he was embarrassed by his altercation with Lugh, so she took a blanket and laid it over his shoulders and returned to the fire.

She had hardly sat down when Elliott exclaimed, "Now we'll see if he's telling the truth."

They all looked up expectantly and saw two figures coming towards them from the crest of the mountain. By their outlines, against the moonlit sky, it was clear to see that they were that of Woodlan and Marcus. The children ran towards their approaching figures, bombarding them with varying accounts of Lugh's unexpected arrival as they went.

Marcus and Woodlan reached the fire, surrounded by the excited children, with bemused expressions on their faces then, on seeing Lugh, they both smiled.

"My friends," Lugh cried, "it is good to see you once more."

Within seconds they were hugging each other and exchanging greetings.

"What brings you so far from your kingdom in the north?" Woodlan asked Lugh.

"My people are not so far north that the doings of the council do not reach our ears. I have come with the blessing of King Donald, to aid you in your quest to reach Gaia before the coming darkness; that *we* of the north have long portent; covers us all."

"Your help is most welcome," Marcus said.

"I must admit though, I had not expected to find littluns involved in this."

"It is a long story, my friend, and one I will explain to you later, but now we need to get these 'littluns' settled for the night. They will need all the rest they can get for the coming days."

The children, fascinated by this mode of conversation, and curious to hear more, made some protests at this call for their dismissal. Woodlan convinced them, however, to settle down by admonishing them in a gentle but firm manner that he 'didn't want to be held up by tired bairns.' The children took some umbrage at this puerile description of themselves but gave in with no further protests; partly because they really were exhausted and partly because they were beginning to grow fond of Woodlan, and didn't wish to wilfully oppose him and so incur his possible disappointment.

Once they were sure that the children were sleeping soundly, Marcus recounted their story, so far, to Lugh. Culminating in he and Woodlan going in search for a boat to cross the lake.

"Lake! I thought it was a good fifteen to twenty miles to the nearest lake from here."

"Not anymore," Marcus said, pointedly.

Lugh furrowed his brow and Marcus continued his explanation.

"Just over that ridge, at what used to be the foot of the mountain, there is now a lake."

Lugh gave him a look of incredulity.

"You mean it has covered the whole . . ."

"Yes . . ." Marcus said, cutting Lugh short with a cautionary look, which Naomi picked up immediately.

"What is it? What aren't you telling me?"

"Do you think it is wise to take the littluns over such a . . ." Lugh paused, obviously unsure as to what to say.

"Such a . . . *what*?" Naomi demanded, checking the volume of her voice so as not to disturb the children.

Marcus looked at her and was silent. She recognised the look on his face it was one she was, unfortunately, getting quite used to, it was the look he had when the news he had to tell her was particularly bad. She met his gaze and steeled herself for what was to come.

"At the foot of the mountain there used to be a village . . . a human village . . . now there is a lake."

Naomi stood, for a moment, in shocked silence.

"I see," she said, at last.

"Is there no way round it?" Lugh asked.

"It would take many days to find a way round and we don't know what other difficulties we might find hidden along the way. Crossing it is our best option. Woodlan and I managed to find two boats along the new shoreline, we can use them to cross tomorrow. Your arrival is most fortuitous my friend. You can steer one of the boats. Woodlan will of course make his own way across."

As Marcus was speaking Naomi began to take in the true difficulty of the journey they were about to make. She realised that there were bound to be some signs left of the flooded village, and some of those signs may be deeply disturbing. She was going to have to make sure that the children didn't look too closely into the lake.

"How long will it take us to cross it?" she asked.

"Some time," Marcus answered. "It was a large village."

Naomi let out a long sigh.

"I will row one boat with you and Ruth and Hannah," Marcus continued. "Lugh will row the other with the boys."

"I think it might be better if Lugh takes the girls and myself, and you take the boys." Naomi said, recalling the recent altercation between Lugh and Elliott,

Lugh gave a half smile, "I think Naomi is right," he said.

Marcus looked a little puzzled by their request but agreed.

"Very well, we will start at sunrise."

Naomi nodded her understanding and suddenly, feeling utterly spent, she excused herself, and made her bed up close to Ruth and Hannah. As tired as she was, she lay for a long time staring up at the, star-strewn, sky contemplating the task ahead of her. When she did manage to fall asleep her dreams were filled with images of shipwrecks and unsuccessful attempts, by her, to save the children from drowning.

She awoke with a start, having just witnessed Ruth sink to a watery grave while she swam frantically towards her unable to make any headway. Taking a deep breath and shuddering slightly she looked around her. It was just getting light; the girls still lay sleeping beside her. Sitting up she saw Luke and Elliott cooking breakfast in hushed voices, under the direction of Woodlan; Marcus and Lugh were sitting on large boulders, a little way from the fire, passively viewing this domestic scene. Naomi stood up and, stretching and yawning, made her way over to the fire.

Luke greeted her enthusiastically.

"Look what Lugh brought, Miss," he said, presenting her with the sight of bacon and eggs. "Would you like some?"

Naomi smiled, "Absolutely!"

It wasn't long before the girls woke up, and after they had all breakfasted, they made their way up the ridge and then down towards the lake.

"Oh! Isn't it beautiful, Miss!" Ruth exclaimed.

The lake was surrounded by purple heather covered hills dotted with an array of colourful wildflowers. It sparkled, in the fresh morning light, below them and gave no sign of the sorrow that lay beneath its placid demeanour. Naomi was surprised by its beauty, it seemed wrong somehow, that it bore no mark of grief for the loss its creation had caused.

"Don't you think it's beautiful, Miss?" Ruth persisted, gently.

"Yes . . . it's very lovely," she answered.

Once they reached the shore of the lake, Naomi had at last come up with an idea to keep the children's eyes off the water and on the shore opposite.

"Children . . ." she began haltingly. "I have something . . . difficult to tell you." The children turned to Naomi and watched her keenly, causing her to swallow hard before she spoke again. "Err . . . Marcus has told me that this lake wasn't here a few days ago, in fact it was open countryside. The earthquake, and the storm, caused the lake to form and . . . unfortunately, there were probably . . . animals which got caught up in the storm and killed and sadly their remains may be floating beneath the water . . ."

"Oh! That's awful!" the girls interjected.

"Indeed, it is," Naomi continued, pleased with the girls' reactions. "So, it's best if you keep your eyes on the opposite shore . . . rather than on the water . . . just in case."

The girls looked appropriately concerned. The boys, however, much to Naomi's consternation, looked intrigued.

Marcus was not blind to the boys look of increased interest either.

"Yes, and you boys are with me," he said. "And I need you to keep your eyes on the shore while I'm rowing, so I keep straight. Do you understand?"

"Yes, Marcus," the boys chorused back, obediently.

"Good," he said, exchanging a look of shared comprehension with Naomi.

The boys climbed into one of the rowing boats, Naomi and the girls into the other. Lugh and Marcus pushed the boats into the water and jumped in. Woodlan remained on the shore.

"Aren't you coming with us, Woodlan?" Hannah cried in a concerned voice.

"Aye! But the boats will not hold my weight, I will make my own way across and wait for you on the other side. Be sure to look out for me." Naomi knew this last request was another attempt to keep the children's eyes from the water and was grateful for it.

Woodlan waved to them then, standing perfectly still and closing his keen blue eyes, crumbled into the shore of the lake and disappeared. The children watched on, awestruck, as Marcus and Lugh began to row towards the opposite shore.

Naomi watched the children keenly as they crossed the lake. Her stomach tight with anxiety for what they might discover should they examine the water beneath them too closely.

At first, they all kept their heads up, facing towards the opposite shore. It wasn't long though before Elliott's head turned, surreptitiously, towards the water. Marcus called out to the boys to ask if his heading was straight, calling Elliott's gaze back to the shore. Naomi breathed a sigh of relief. Her relief was short lived, however. As, after a few minutes, she once again saw Elliott covertly surveying the water; and no matter how many times Marcus called out instructions to keep the boys' attention towards the shoreline Elliott's attention was always drawn back to the water. Naomi watched on, helplessly.

They had travelled almost a third of their way across the lake when Naomi was alarmed to see Elliott examining a log, floating a little way off from his boat, then suddenly snapping his head back to the shore. Alerted to the danger, she kept her eyes on the girls as the log floated towards their boat, ready to call their attention back to the shoreline should their eyes stray towards the passing branch Fortunately, the girls had noticed some colourful wildflowers growing out the rock face on the other side of the lake and were deep in discussion as to what they could be and how beautiful they looked, and so the branch passed by them unnoticed. Naomi, however, felt compelled to see what had disturbed Elliott and looking tentatively into the water, steeled herself for whatever it might be.

At first, all she could make out was the branch with something, silver-like, glinting through its leaves and a dark shadow underneath it. Gently, the tree branch floated a little nearer and was turned slightly by the flow of the water. Then she saw it! She shuddered as the ghastly picture revealed itself. Held down by the branch was the body of a woman, floating face down, her long, dark hair entangled with the branch. In her hand she was clutching the broken handle of a child's buggy; and it was this that was glinting just above the water. Tied to the handle, by a blue ribbon, was a small teddy bear, its glass eyes shining benignly through the murky water. She dragged her eyes away from the awful sight and looked back up to the girls, who were still in discussion about wildflowers. She caught Lugh's eye and knew immediately that he too had seen the gruesome sight. Lowering her head she blinked away the tears that stung her eyes.

Gaining control of herself she pinned her eyes on the boat ahead, and their destination. Elliott's gaze no longer wandered from the shoreline.

Relief rushed through Naomi when their boats bumped onto the shore. Once out of the boat, the girls rushed towards Woodlan, who stood waiting for them, pulling him towards the wildflowers, keen to get a closer look and ask him about them. Marcus and Lugh, with a little help from Elliott and Luke, pulled the boats further from the shore and took out the packs.

"Miss! Miss! Come and see these flowers they're so lovely," Hannah called out. "Woodlan says they're called Bloody Cranesbill, pardon my language, and you can use them as a medicine for cuts and things. Isn't it wonderful, Miss, that they're both beautiful *and* useful?"

"Yes . . . it is," Naomi said, forcing a smile.

Naomi and the girls stood for a moment admiring the flowers. They certainly were lovely Naomi thought, with their purplish pink colour and faint red leaves. Bending down, she carefully picked a small bunch and walked to the edge of the lake where she threw them, gently, onto the water. The girls followed Naomi to the water's edge.

"Are you all right, Miss?" Ruth asked. Without speaking, Naomi put her arm around Ruth and pulled her close to her. "It's so sad about the animals isn't it, Miss?"

"Yes," Naomi said. "It is . . . very sad." These last words were directed over Ruth's head to Elliott, who now stood by them. She looked at him pointedly and he gave her a sideways glance, their eyes met for a moment and there was an unspoken understanding between them, that what they had seen they would not burden the other children with.

There was little time to grieve or ponder over the watery grave though as Marcus quickly bid them pick up their packs and follow him.

CHAPTER TWELVE
Spriggins

Lugh was a welcome addition to their little troupe, bringing a much-needed interjection of renewed energy with his light-hearted manner and his story telling, which he took great pleasure in. Many of his stories told of ancient battles between mountain dwarves and elves; many of which Marcus would raise a wry eyebrow at, and a faint smile would cross his lips, but he would say nothing to contradict his friend's recitals.

On the second night of his arrival, as they sat lounging around the campfire, Lugh began a to tell them of a particularly heated battle between the elves and dwarves. The children sat enthralled. Even Elliott who, still smarting from the fracas of their first meeting, kept his distance from Lugh; preferring to walk close to Marcus and treating Lugh's stories with looks of disdain; had his eyes fixed closely on Lugh, listening intently to his every word.

"Why is it that the elves and the dwarves are such enemies?" Hannah asked, when Lugh had finished.

"There has always been animosity between the two, but there is a particular story told of how their dislike of one another moved from, finding expression in angry words, to heated battles fought to the death." Here Lugh paused and stoked the fire, a glimmer of a smile on his lips.

The children stared at him in silent anticipation, Lugh merely continued his stoking of the fire.

"Lugh . . . would you tell us the story?" Luke asked.

"I would have thought you would have had enough stories for one night."

"Oh no!" Hannah, Ruth and Luke declared; Elliott remained silent, pretending indifference. "We'd love to hear another story."

"Well, if you are sure."

"We're sure!"

"Very well then . . . In the time when men were fewer on the earth and faerie folk ruled the mountain lands, there was in the far north a small plot of land protected by a giant fjord. To humans it was uninhabitable but to elves and dwarves, who love to sculpt and dig their homes from rocks and ice, it was highly prized, and both elves and dwarves desired to build a kingdom there. They argued over the land, and who should possess it, for many months. When they could come to no agreement, they signed a treaty promising that neither would inhabit the land, but both would protect it from any who might also discover the land and try to build on it. The truce lasted seven years, until a band of spriggins . . ."

"Spriggins!" Hannah exclaimed. "We were captured by spriggins, and I'm still not quite sure what they are."

"Spriggins are faerie creatures who love mischief. They grow no larger than a small child, and no matter how old they get they still love causing mischief. These particular spriggins were of the worst kind, in that they went about far and wide seeking ways and places to cause chaos and confusion.

"As they passed through the country, they heard of the treaty between the elves and the dwarves and saw a prime opportunity to cause havoc; and cause it they did. They went to the land in dispute and set about creating signs of building. They dug a tunnel in the side of the fjord and took tools, which they had already stolen from the dwarves, and hid them, not *too* carefully, throughout the tunnel. Then, on another part of the fjord, they began to sculpt faint outlines into the ice and rock, as elves do when they build their cities.

"Spriggins, by the way, are also adept craftsmen and women but waste their talents on playing tricks like this one. Anyway, once they had finished preparing the scene, they split into two groups. One made their way to the land inhabited by the elves the others to the land of the dwarves. They told of how they were just passing through, visiting the north lands, and had run out of supplies. The elves and dwarves were happy to replenish their stores, for the spriggins always carry many precious stones with them, which they mine in the deep dark caverns they call home.

"As they gathered their newly bought goods they began to spread rumours about the disputed land. Telling of how they had passed through a lovely valley, and how fortunate they thought those who were building there were to be able to live in such a beautiful place. As you can imagine the elves and dwarves were furious at this news and dispatched messengers to see if the spriggins' reports were true.

"When the messengers returned, and affirmed the spriggins' reports, the elves and dwarves sent delegates to their opposing kingdoms demanding answers. Of course, each denied any wrongdoing and when presented with the evidence each accused the other of putting it there. Infuriated, by what they each saw as the others deception, war was declared and a fierce battle commenced, arrows and axes, lances and chains, felled elf and dwarf alike.

For three days the battle raged until the valley was strewn with the bloodied bodies of the dead. Headless torsos and severed limbs were scattered like broken dolls across the ground. There was no victor in the end. When each side could no longer lift a weapon to fight with, they limped away; much to the spriggins' delight, who watched the whole thing atop of the fjord, clapping with glee at the success of their prank."

"That's horrible!" Ruth cried, clinging tightly to Hannah's arm. So tightly that, much to Hannah's consternation, she had almost cut off the circulation.

"That's spriggins for you," Lugh concluded, matter-of-factly.

"Didn't they ever find out that it was the spriggins?" Hannah asked, while gently, but firmly, removing the clinging Ruth from her arm.

"There were rumours, but such was, and is, the hate between the two that they each blamed the other for spreading them."

"Lugh . . ." Hannah began but was quickly interrupted by Naomi.

"No more questions tonight, Hannah, it's time for bed."

"Oh . . . okay, Miss." Hannah said, disappointedly.

The children settled quickly, as they always did, exhausted by their day's exertions.

Naomi returned to the fire.

"They are fine young'uns, strong and uncomplaining," Lugh said.

"Yes, but I'm afraid as good as they are and hard as they are trying, this journey is getting too much for them. They don't say anything, but I can see that it is getting harder and harder for them to rouse themselves in the morning and their pace is slowing more each day," Naomi said.

"Except young Elliott, he seems to be taking the whole journey in his stride," Woodlan said.

"Perhaps," Naomi said, thoughtfully.

"Tomorrow we will reach the castle of Fionn. If we can win his promise to care for the children, they will be safe there," Marcus said.

"The wife of Fionn is childless and is known for her love of children, she may be the key to winning the promise of Fionn," Lugh added.

"First, we must gain entrance to the castle and if the rumours are true Fionn has closed his gates to all and will let non travel through his lands since the troubles began, and Bathon was right he has no love for the humans, gaining an audience with him will not be easy," Woodlan cautioned.

"The queen may also be our key to gaining our audience," Lugh said.

"Why is that?" Naomi asked.

"Queen Olwen was found crying, as a babe, on the shore of Lake Firgineis, which lies on the edge of Fionn's land and where the land of the elves begins. A group of elves, going to the lake to swim, took pity on her and brought her to the elf queen who, recognising greatness in her, took her into her own household and taught her the ways of discernment." Naomi here gave him a look of incomprehension. "How to read signs and minds. They say she was so gifted, that she even learned the elf queen's ability of sensing a persons true worth. That is, not only what or who they are, but who they may become, and what they may accomplish. I believe the queen's curiosity will be stirred by hearing that there may be one who has demonstrated a gift for the power, that can challenge even that of her own *and* the elves."

"We must hope you are right, Lugh or our journey to Gaia will end at the castle gates," Marcus said.

Naomi was filled with dread once more, as she pondered on how much of their succeeding in gaining access to Fionn's kingdom rested on her presence. Not wanting to hear any more, she rose quickly from her place at the fire and wishing them an abrupt 'goodnight' made her way over to the sleeping girls.

*   *   *

After another fitful night, Naomi awoke before dawn and lay staring at the sky wishing she were in her own bed and that this was all a dream. Suddenly, she heard wood being thrown onto the fire, she turned her head, it was Woodlan. Carefully, so as not to disturb the sleeping children, she got up to join him. Lugh was sleeping near the boys and Marcus was nowhere to be seen.

"Where's Marcus?" Naomi asked, in hushed tones.

"He has gone ahead a little to check the path for danger. He will be back soon."

"Danger! What kind of danger?"

"It will be alright, try not to worry, Little Miss!"

"That's not possible, what with the children and . . ." Naomi stopped short and stared into the glowing fire.

". . . And what, Little Miss?"

Naomi hesitated for a moment.

"It's all so confusing . . . and frightening . . ." she said, the words tumbling out, in her need to unburden her thoughts and fears to someone, "this power *thing*. I go over and over in my head, all that Marcus has told me, about it being an ancient power that Gaia gave to selected humans, that it's supposed to be used for keeping this *Essential Harmony* and, most confusing and frightening of all, that I . . . *somehow* . . . am one of those few. I know so little about it, and there seems so little time to learn anything else, yet so much depends on my possessing it, *and* being able to use it."

"I could tell you what I know of it, if that would help?"

"Right now, any information would be useful," Naomi said, eager to hear what Woodlan had to say.

"It is, as Marcus says, the old power, although it is perhaps better to say the oldest power. The first power to exist on the earth when the earth was first formed, and Gaia was made her Guardian, and humankind were the first to be formed, made in the image of the Great Ones. . ."

"The Great Ones?"

"The Creators: those who brought the elements together from the void and formed the earth and made Gaia guardian. After Gaia, came the lesser guardians, the faerie folk, Latora and Cachada and the like; created from the souls of the elements and plant life; then those of the woods, flowers, mountains, seas, all working together to form a link between the humans and the planet. Finally, the Advocates were chosen, these were humans given the power to keep the balance between Gaia and all the others created. Eventually, humankind became proud, fixed on a path of selfish discovery. So much so, that the balance, or Essential Harmony, was slowly eroded as they rejected Gaia's guardianship. Those who possessed the power of the Advocates were killed by men of ignorance, or they lost the power because of their own lack of vision. At last, the knowledge of old was overwhelmed by new philosophies; which recognised none of the old links; until we ended up where we are today."

"This power . . . when I felt it in the forest of Tramar, it was overwhelming and . . . frightening. I was in control . . . but not in control. It was as if the evil in that . . . *thing* . . . was in me."

"In time you will learn to control it."

"But how?"

"By using it. Evil is everywhere, it cannot be avoided, it must be faced and won over, and sometimes to win something over we must know it, know how it works, feel what it feels, so we can understand its motive and defeat it . . . with a greater one."

After a moments reflection Naomi asked, "Have you seen Gaia?"

"Me! No."

"It's just that Marcus said that, when Laifolia's sister called out for help, Gaia sent you."

"That's true enough. She called me by name, I'll never forget it. I recognised her voice, even though I had never heard it before, not out loud anyway."

"What do you mean?

"Well, while I've never seen Gaia and I hadn't heard her voice before that day, or since I might add. Her presence is always with me. Gaia is *my* guide, the reason I am what I am."

Naomi wanted to question Woodlan further, but just then Marcus arrived back in camp.

"The way ahead is clear, as far as I can tell. It is not far to Fionn's Kingdom from here, we should make it safely."

"Should I wake the children now?" Naomi asked.

"No. As I say, it is not far to Fionn's Kingdom, they can sleep a little longer."

"Well if that's the case, I think I'll see if I can get a couple of more hours of sleep myself."

Naomi left Marcus and Woodlan by the fire and returned to the spot where the girls continued to sleep soundly. Lying down, she found she couldn't think any more and fell into deep sleep almost immediately.

She awoke with a start to the sound of someone shouting and the laughter of children.

Turning towards the sound, her bleary eyes were met by the sight of Lugh shouting and hopping up and down, frantically trying to brush something, obviously unpleasant, from his person.

"What is it! Is it a rat!? I hate rats!"

The children, meanwhile, were standing by watching Lugh's display of distress in fits of laughter. Woodlan was sitting by the fire with a broad grin on his face.

"What's going on, what's wrong!" Marcus called, running in on the scene.

"It seems Lugh's found a rat in his bedding," Woodlan said, with a distinct hint of amusement in his voice.

"What! A rat in these parts?" Marcus said.

"I felt it on me, it was crawling up my leg," Lugh insisted. "There it is." Lugh pointed towards an indistinct brown mass a couple of metres from where he had been sleeping.

Marcus made his way towards it and bent down to examine the offending creature, then picked it up.

"Is it dead?" Lugh cried.

"Oh yes, it is quite dead."

At Marcus declaration there was another burst of laughter from the children. Lugh looked at them and furrowed his brow.

Marcus by now had turned round and was standing, with a half-smile on his face, holding up what looked like a long plait of hair. He walked towards the group of giggling children.

"I think this belongs to one of you." he said, struggling to keep a straight face.

The truth began to dawn on Lugh.

"Wha . . .! Is that . . . wha . . . did they . . .?" Lugh stood open mouthed staring at the children, who were now heads down trying to hide their continued mirth.

At this point Naomi felt she should do something to take the situation in hand.

"Children what did you do . . .?" but, before Naomi could finish her reprimand, there was a roar of laughter from Lugh.

"It was only a joke, Miss we didn't mean any harm," Hannah giggled.

"Well, what is it?" Naomi asked.

Marcus handed the offending item to her. Naomi stared at it for a moment then, suddenly realising what it was, looked up at Hannah and cried, "Oh Hannah! Your beautiful hair."

"Well, it won't catch on anything now Miss," Hannah said.

In a flash Naomi understood.

"No . . . of course . . . who cut it . . . and what with?"

"Woodlan cut it for me, Miss, with his knife."

Woodlan gave Naomi a benign smile. Naomi forced a smile back.

"I'm glad you're not mad, Miss," Ruth said, "because . . ." and turning round she finished, "I had him cut mine too."

Naomi let out a resigned sigh.

"Whose idea was it to put it in Lugh's bedding?" she asked.

"I was the one who told the littluns that Lugh was afraid of rats, so I suppose you could say it was my doing," Woodlan said.

Despite Woodlan's admission, Naomi was sure she saw a gleam of satisfaction in Elliott's eyes, and couldn't help smiling to herself as she thought, 'revenge is sweet.'

"Well, that's enough frivolity for one day," Marcus gently admonished. "We need to get moving."

"Frivolity? What does frivolity mean, Miss?" Hannah asked.

And Naomi was glad to see that in losing her hair Hannah had lost none of her inquisitiveness.

"Erm . . . messing about."

"Oh . . . Okay," Hannah smiled.

CHAPTER THIRTEEN
Fionn's Castle

After a couple of hours of hiking they reached the base of two rolling mountain ranges joined by a gigantic, forked crevice, here Marcus stopped the troupe. The children flopped down where they stood.

"How long will it be before we reach Fionn's castle?" Hannah asked.

"We are here," Lugh announced.

Naomi and the children looked all around them for a sign of the castle.

"Where is it?" Elliott asked.

"Hidden, to protect it from detection by humans," Lugh said.

"In order to see it you need to put this paste on your eyes and then wash it off with water that falls from these mountains." Woodlan said, while taking a small, wooden box from one of the many pockets scattered around his coat. He then led Naomi and the children to a waterfall, cascading down the mountainside, and offered each of them the box. The children took their turn scooping up some of the paste onto their fingertips. Naomi helped each of them to wash it off then repeated the process herself.

"I don't feel any different." Elliott said, drying his eyes with his sleeves and looking around him.

"Wait! You will *see,*" Woodlan promised, leading them back to where Marcus and Lugh were waiting.

Looking beyond Marcus and Lugh, to their astonishment, the returning troupe saw that the mighty mountain crevice had been replaced by a grand, granite castle. Its expansive walls, which stood proud from the mountainside, were adorned with fairytale turrets which seemed to touch the sky, and a massive oak gate sat at the centre of its impressive exterior.

Marcus began to climb up to the great castle gate. He had almost reached the gate when a voice, calling from the battlements, stopped him in his tracks.

"Who approaches the Faerie realm of Fionn, King of the Northeast Kingdom?"

"It is Marcus Mac Freya come to beg an audience with the mighty King Fionn."

"You are not alone, Marcus Mac Freya, if my eyes do not deceive me, you have *humans* with you." The questioner spat out the word humans as if he could not bear it in his mouth. "*Humans*! Are not welcome here."

"One of the humans I bring holds the power of old. She has battled and beaten the Wraith of Tramar Forest."

Suddenly, a head appeared above the parapet, it was that of an old man; he eyed them suspiciously.

"Stay where you are, Marcus Mac Freya, approach no closer. I will tell the king you seek an audience," he said. Then disappeared from view.

On his disappearance two men armed with bows and arrows appeared and, with steely glares, stood ready to fire.

As Naomi stood with the others waiting for the old man's return, caught under the glower of the unflinching bowmen, she couldn't help noticing that the structure of the castle showed signs of wear and tear. There were stones missing from one of the turrets, that framed the great gate. There was also a significant fissure from the base of the wall up to one of the many narrow windows, which dotted the castle walls. She wondered how many centuries the castle had stood here, hidden from the ramblers and rock climbers who passed by enjoying the magnificent views, while those inside watched them with, at best disdain and at worst outright hatred.

At last, they heard the gate being unbarred from the inside and the great doors began to open. The children, who had been too scared to move until now, moved forward slightly, forgetting the guards above them in their curiosity to see who would emerge from the castle. They were disappointed to see the old man step through the gap in the gate. He stood tall and proud and fixed them all with a watery-eyed glare.

"Marcus Mac Freya, and the human who is said to possess the power of old may enter . . . no others," he commanded.

Marcus turned to Naomi, and she reluctantly made her way up to where he stood and they entered the castle.

Once inside, the doors were immediately shut and barred behind them and two guards, with vicious looking spears, stood sentinel at either side.

The old man led them across a large courtyard, up some steps then through an open doorway into a great hall, the walls of which were laden with silk fabrics and coats of arms. In the centre of all this grandeur was a low platform where two resplendent figures sat on ornately carved wooden thrones. One, a woman tall and willowy with handsome features and gentle grey eyes; the other, a man slightly taller than the woman and whose muscular frame was evident even through the heavy robes he wore. His face was broad and pale, his features looked as if they had been chiselled out of marble, and a look of suspicion shone from his pale blue eyes, a suspicion that was soon to be confirmed in his voice. Naomi and Marcus stopped when they reached them and Naomi, awkwardly following Marcus' lead, bowed as the old man announced them.

"My Lord and Lady, Marcus Mac Freya and . . ." the old man looked questioningly at Naomi.

"Naomi . . ." Naomi announced, timidly.

"Naomi . . ." The old man repeated, with a tinge of contempt in his voice, as if her name were somehow not good enough for such lofty company.

King Fionn nodded regally. "Claymore tells me, Marcus Mac Freya, you have brought one who possesses the powers of old." Then turning to Naomi he said, in a tone that matched the ever-growing suspicion in his countenance, "Is this . . . her?"

"Yes, my Lord."

At Marcus' confirmation, King Fionn turned to his wife, who immediately left her throne, stepped down from the platform and stood in front of Naomi, looking down at her; for she was a good twenty to twenty-five centimetres taller than her; fixing Naomi with thoughtful, searching eyes. Naomi quailed slightly under their invasive gaze. After a few moments, the queen put her hands out in front of her in invitation, Naomi, mesmerised, placed her hands obediently on the queens, who enclosed them with a firm yet gentle grip, never breaking eye contact. Naomi, remembering Lugh's story of the queen's past with elves knew; as she felt her whole body acquiesce to the queens unspoken command and yield to her cerebral examination; that all Lugh had heard was true.

Eventually, Queen Olwen released Naomi hands. Naomi swayed and was about to fall to the floor, but Marcus caught her and held her firmly in his arms. The queen turned to her husband and slowly nodded her head then took her seat once more at his side.

"I will hear your plea, Marcus Mac Freya." King Fionn's voice remained etched with suspicion and contempt.

"King Fionn, lord of all . . ." Marcus began, with, the still shaken, Naomi in his arms. "I ask permission to cross your lands with, Lugh . . .Woodlan . . . and Naomi, conqueror of the Wraith of Tramar."

"To what purpose would you journey across my lands?"

"To gain an audience with Gaia."

"And what would be the *purpose* of this audience?"

"To plead for mercy from the signs of Gaia's growing wrath."

The king sat thoughtfully for a moment.

"I cannot grant you passage across my lands," he said. — A fleeting look of disappointment crossed over Queen Olwen's face — "I know your purpose, news of it has reached every corner of our world, you wish to take this girl to plead for the humans. Even if she does possess the powers of old, why should I help the humans who have done nothing but desecrate the land?"

"I will tell you what I told the Council of Elders; we cannot escape the coming destruction. If it is not tempered there is no way of knowing how much it will affect us all. The very walls of this castle show signs that they have felt the effects of the earth tremors," Marcus said.

"What you say is true, the castle *has* been touched by the tumults wreaked on the humans, however, helping the humans may only ensure that we are caught up in their destruction. I will not risk the safety of this castle, or those who dwell in it, or on my lands, for the sake of the . . . *humans*."

The disgust on his face and in his voice when he uttered the word human caused Naomi to recover somewhat, as a feeling of indignation fired through her. Straightening up, and firmly releasing herself from Marcu's hold, she faced the king and began to speak, strengthened by a growing sense of injustice.

"Excuse me . . ." the king gave her a long look of condescension, the queen on the other hand raised her head slightly and her face wore an eager expression. "It's obvious you don't think much of humans in general, and perhaps you have good cause . . ."

"Perhaps. . .?" The king sneered back at her.

Undaunted, Naomi continued.

"It's true that humankind has done a pretty bad job of living in harmony with the nature that sustains them, but for you to help wipe us out . . . indiscriminately, is just as wrong as anything you accuse us of. I have four children with me, children who have no part in the destruction caused by their elders, and given a chance could learn a new way of living with the earth, rather than using her. If the old links between our two worlds could be renewed, then we could work together, rebuilding a world where we could all live in harmony with nature."

"Those are pretty words, but they sound hollow in the mouth of one who belongs to a race which has spent centuries finding new ways to exploit nature. Harmony is not what they want, only domination of the world and all its resources will satisfy humankind."

"You're right, that's true of many, but I also think recent events will have made them more likely to listen, and there are voices among us who have called for change, and have tried to make changes to the way we use the earth and its resources . . ."

"Token changes" Fionn interrupted, his voice rising, "that have come too late. You expect me to endanger the lives of my people, on the hope that a few voices of dissent among your people may overcome the tidal wave of destruction caused by humankind's greed, which has covered the earth?"

"I'm pleading with you for those four children out there," Naomi persisted. "And the millions of others like them who could, given the chance, make a difference, help to bring about a more peaceful age. You have condemned us all without really knowing *any* of us. Spend time with the children who are with us and you'll see that they aren't senseless destroyers, but a generation ready for change.

"If the links between our two worlds are renewed, and they can learn to communicate with the earth in the way that the races I have encountered on this journey do, a literal, tangible communication; that I never thought possible; I believe that a sense of their real identity will be reawakened in them. The part of their identity that will bring them to a fundamental realisation of their literal connection with the world they live on, and that to destroy the world is to destroy themselves," Naomi stopped, surprised at the strength of her own conviction. It was as if all the thoughts that had been running around in her head; ever since she had encountered this new world and been made aware of the flaws in her own; now found a voice in her plea to King Fionn.

King Fionn did not answer but sat back in his throne, somewhat disgruntled by Naomi's speech.

"My Lord," Queen Olwen spoke up. "I feel it could do no harm to see these children."

King Fionn sat for a moment.

"Very well," he said. "Have them brought to the Great Hall."

"Perhaps husband, would be better to meet with the children . . . in a less formal setting."

Naomi felt a gush of gratitude towards the queen for her thoughtfulness. She knew the children *would* be overawed by the grandeur of the hall, and these two majestic personages, and so may not present themselves at their best.

"I leave it in your hands, my lady."

With this command, the king stood up abruptly, and strode from the hall, without another glance in Marcus' or Naomi's direction. Queen Olwen nodding her assent as he left.

"Claymore" the queen ordered. "Have our guests brought into the castle and have food brought and set out for them, so they many refresh themselves." Her command given, the queen gracefully descended from her throne, gave Marcus and Naomi a smile of goodbye, and followed in the wake of her husband.

"This way," Claymore said. Leading Naomi and Marcus; with a continuing look of suspicion and thinly veiled contempt on his face; to a small ante-chamber off the main hall, where he left them without saying another word.

"Claymore has always been a man of few words," Marcus said, with a smile.

"You know him then?"

"Yes . . . I spent part of my youth here. The Woodland Queen brought me here. Claymore was serf to the old King Owen, Fionn's father. Fionn was much the same age as I was, and the Woodland Queen requested King Owen that I might be a companion to the young prince, and so learn the skills of hunting and fishing, and the ways of the warrior. King Owen agreed, his mother, like mine, had been a wood nymph and he had known my mother before she married my father. He was a good man, like a father to me. Fionn and I became great friends, but when the Woodland Queen came to take me back to the forest, to fulfil my role as a Guardian, Fionn thought I should not follow the council of a woman, that I should stay with him and become the leader of his palace guard. It was a great honour, but I refused. I tried to explain to him that my first allegiance must be to my people. He said that guardianship of the borders was the job of a servant and accused me of being led by a woman's fancy and, if that was the case, he would have nothing more to do with me. His father tried to make him see sense, but it was no good. I never saw him again until this day.

Just as Marcus finished his story the door of the antechamber opened and several servants entered laden with food and drinks, and set them out on a large, round table that sat in one corner of the chamber. When they had finished, and were just about to leave, they were stopped in their tracks by Woodlan, whose impressive figure now filled the doorway. The servants moved aside in deference to the new arrival, and Woodlan strode into the room followed by the children, whose eyes widened at the sight of the feast that burdened the table. Finally, Lugh entered, smiling broadly.

They were soon all sitting, eating and talking easily. The children were filled with questions about the castle and its inhabitants. Marcus took the opportunity to educate the children in the etiquette they should use when meeting the king and queen, how they should address them as My Lord and My Lady and make sure to bow. The children listened very carefully, with looks of awe on their faces.

Lugh told them a story of how King Fionn had inherited the castle from his father Owen, but how his cousins in the low countries had contested his right to the throne, saying that Owen had stolen the kingdom from their father Lucas, by poisoning the mind of the old king Gryffud; their grandfather; against him. He was just in the middle of describing the great battle that took place, and how Fionn slew his cousins and won the day, when the door opened, and a young serving girl entered. Bowing low, she asked them if they wished for anything more to drink or eat.

"Some castle brew would no go amiss!" Lugh exclaimed.

The young girl gave a short nod and left the room, returning soon with a young man who was carrying a small keg which he set down on the table. The young girl began to distribute mugs to the adults, Naomi declined the offer. The young man filled each of the men's mugs from the keg, the men drank down the frothy brew, appreciatively.

"Is there anything more I may get you?"

The young girl addressed herself to Lugh, with a look of open admiration. Lugh looked round the table to see if anyone wanted anything, but seeing that no one did, he dismissed her with a playful smile, which the girl returned shyly.

Lugh continued his story, while filling his mug once more from the keg. The children hung on to his every word as his description of the battle became more elaborate with each refilling. Eventually, the story and the meal were over, and the table was cleared. The group moved over to the fireplace, where there was a large couch and several comfortable chairs which they somnolently sank into.

After a few moments of satisfied silence, Hannah began to look curiously at Lugh.

"Lugh ... may I ask you a question?" she asked.

"Aye, of course, ask away."

Well ... what are you? I mean we know that Woodlan is an Earth Guide and Marcus is part Wood Nymph ... I just wondered who your people were?"

Naomi wondered where Hannah had learned that Marcus was part Wood Nymph, she had certainly never told her, and she had not seen her have any lengthy conversations with Marcus. Then she remembered Rochan, whom she thought Hannah would no doubt have questioned fully regarding her new friends, and smiled.

"We are human like yourself," Lugh said. "But we have not lived as part of the human world since Gaia separated the two worlds. My people are expert artisans and . . . storytellers."

"Artisans?" Hannah said.

"And who's Gaia?" Elliott added.

"Well Gaia is the mother of all living and artisans are craftsmen, builders, artists that sort of thing. The first ones singled us out and blessed us with superior ability in all the art forms. We are concerned with the aesthetics . . ." Seeing here another look of incomprehension in Hannah's face, Lugh corrected himself, "the *beauty* of the earth, its structure and form. After the separation, Gaia kept my people within the faerie world, to allow us to more freely roam the earth, protecting and repairing, where we could, the damage done by our fellow men and women. Unfortunately, as the years have passed, we have found it more and more difficult to make any difference. Humankind are constantly finding more and more efficient ways to consume their environment, and while we have long worried about the consequences of such behaviour, we could see no way to stop it. When we heard of Marcus' quest, and that he had found one who held the power of old, I was chosen to represent my people and do all I could to further their quest."

Hannah sat, open-mouthed, a million questions on her lips

Just at that moment, and much to Naomi's relief, the door of the chamber opened, and Claymore entered.

"Her Majesty . . . Queen Olwen." Claymore's announcement startled them all out of their repose and they all jumped up, the children following the adults lead, bowing low, as the queen glided into the room. She acknowledged their obeisance with a smile and a slight nod of her head, walked stately towards them, then took a seat near the fire and said, with a wave of her hand.

"Please, be seated."

Once they were all seated, the queen's demeanour softened as she glanced over the children, who sat staring at her deeply overawed by her stately presence. The Queen turned her smile directly on Ruth.

"Child, come here and take my hands," she said.

Slowly, Ruth arose and, tentatively, placed her hands on the queen's outstretched palms. The queen enclosed them with her long, delicate fingers; as she had Naomi's earlier.

"What is your name, child?"

"Ruth . . . My Lady."

Gently inspecting Ruth's face, the queen was silent for a moment.

"There is much . . . apprehension in you, young one," she began. "Do not be afraid of it, let its voice of warning be a guide to you as you travel your journey in this world, rather than a chain that holds you in one place. Accept the fear inside you, and you will release yourself from its restraints." With this profound advice she let go of Ruth's hands and gently motioned her back to her chair.

Next, she motioned to Hannah. Who stood up smartly, eagerly placing her hands into the queens.

"Your name, child."

"Hannah, Miss... Oh... I mean... My Lady."

Smiling, at Hannah's mistake the queen said, "You have an agile mind, it needs some training, but there is great potential in you to learn and understand the things that matter. For that is the most important thing Hannah, learning is never enough, only true understanding brings wisdom." Hannah's eyes widened at the queen's counsel, but she said nothing and, released from the queen's hold, sat down thoughtfully.

Next, she motioned to Elliott, who followed the lead of the others with a slight reluctance. On taking hold of Elliott's hands, the queen closed her eyes, and a troubled look crossed her face. After a few moments, she slowly opened her eyes.

"You have the heart of a warrior," she said. "Strong, steadfast and loyal, it will serve you and those you travel with well." Elliott's eyes widened at the queen's words, and he returned to his chair wearing a look of proud satisfaction.

Naomi's face, on the other hand, wore a frown of concern.

Finally, Luke, with a face full of anticipation, eagerly placed his hands in the queens. Almost immediately on their touching the queen smiled back at him, broadly.

"There is an understanding within you that belies your years," she said. "You say little but think much. I sense in *you* ... greatness. We will talk again child," and with this startling revelation, she let go of his hands. "Naomi has spoken the truth. The ways of the old ones still exist in the hearts of the young humans. You may cross our lands. Is there anything more you wish of us, Marcus Mac Freya?" The queen asked this question in a tone which suggested that she already knew the answer to it.

"There *is* one more thing, My Lady ... I ask if, My Lord and Lady would care for the children, until our quest is completed?"

"Indeed, it would give me ... I mean *us* ... great pleasure to offer the children a safe haven here until you return."

"What ...! Miss ...! What do you mean?" the children called out collectively. All, except Luke.

"I'm sorry, children, but you will have to stay here until we return," Naomi said.

"Return from where . . .?" Hannah cried. "I thought you said that we only had to go part of the way with them. Why are you going on with them?"

"That's the 'quest', Hannah," Naomi answered. "You remember what we talked about the earthquakes?" she continued, addressing all of the children. The children nodded a slow assent. "Well, Marcus thinks that I can help stop these things from happening, the way I stopped the creature in the forest from hurting Hannah."

"Is it because you have this . . . *power* Lugh was talking about . . . the power of old?" Hannah asked.

"Yes," Naomi said.

"But I don't want to stay here!" Elliott cried.

Naomi raised her hand to silence, the indignant, Elliott.

"The journey's becoming too dangerous," she said. "You have to stay here. You'll be safe here."

"But what about you?" Elliott called out, unable to hold his peace any longer.

"I appreciate your concern, Elliott, but I have an obligation to your parents to do all I can to keep you safe."

The sudden mention of their parents caught the children by surprise and subdued them immediately, because if truth be told, the children had been so caught up in their adventure that they themselves hadn't given their parents much thought. Ruth and Hannah were now close to tears and Luke wore a mixed expression of sadness and guilt. Elliott, however, felt quite differently.

"Well you don't need to worry about my parents, they don't care whether I'm alive or dead!"

"Elliott! I'm sure . . ."

"Don't try and tell me they *really* love me," Elliott tore through Naomi's attempted protestation. "You know nothing about it. I haven't seen either of them in months, and what's more, I don't care if I never see them again. I want to come with you, you heard what the queen said. *I* have the heart of a warrior. *I* could be of use to you."

"I'm sure the queen meant that when you're grown up . . ." Naomi made a mute appeal to the queen for support, but she merely looked passively on and said nothing.

"You see!" Elliott continued, taking the queen's silence as support for his own argument. "She thinks I should come with you."

"Well I'm your teacher," Naomi declared, somewhat surprised, and a little annoyed, by the queens lack of support, "and I'm responsible for you and it is up to me whether you stay or go and I say you, *stay*."

"What about what you said, about it *all* being okay if we all stick together?"

"If you remember Hannah *also* said that you need to listen to me and do as I ask."

"I!"

"NO more arguments! Nothing you say is going to convince me to let you go."

Elliott sat staring at his teacher, seething.

"There is no more to be said," Naomi declared, matching his gaze.

Reluctantly, Elliott remained silent.

"I'm sure you have had a trying journey," the queen said, "and could all benefit from some rest. Claymore."

"Yes, My Lady."

"See that our guests are shown to their rooms."

"Of course, My Lady."

"I will see you all again at dinner." With this final announcement the queen swept out of the room.

Leaving Marcus, Woodlan and Lugh in the antechamber, Naomi and the children were escorted up the imposing stairway, that dominated the entrance hall and shown to their rooms.

Naomi's room was furnished with a four-poster bed, covered in sumptuous bedding, and surrounded with heavy embroidered curtains. Laid out on the bed were some clothes; which included a beautiful purple, silk brocaded dress; and a pair of white pumps laid neatly on the floor. Naomi presumed these were for her to wear to dinner.

Other imposing items of wooden furniture littered the room but best of all, there in front of the fire, which blazed away in the room; because despite it being mid-July the thick walls and the small opaque windows meant the room was gloomy and cool; was a hot steaming bath. Naomi had never been so grateful for anything in her life, and turning the key in the bedroom door she undressed and climbed in. Taking a deep breath, she closed her eyes allowing the water, for a short time anyway, to wash away all her cares.

CHAPTER FOURTEEN
The Magician

Eventually, the water began to cool so Naomi roused herself, washed and then; wrapping herself in the soft, floor length towel that was laid out, so conveniently, on a chair in front of the fire; sat curled up in the chair, her wet hair draped around her shoulders.

She sat there for some time, staring into the flames, lost in thought, until she was pulled out of her reverie by a gentle knocking on the bedroom door. She stood up, slightly alarmed, wondering how much time had passed. Worrying that she may have missed dinner and upset her hosts. Wrapping the towel tightly around he she cautiously unlocked the door and opened it just wide enough to be able to peek her head around it. Standing outside the door was a young serving girl.

"I have come to help you dress for dinner, Miss," the girl said, bobbing politely.

"Oh, thank you," Naomi said. Then pulling the towel even more tightly around her added, "but that won't be necessary. I can manage."

"Very well, Miss, I will see if the little Misses require any assistance."

"Right."

Naomi closed the door, and feeling a little chilled, carefully laid a new log on, the now dying embers, of the fire. Remembering the clothes laid out on the bed, she began to dress. Everything fitted surprisingly well right down the white pumps, which her feet slipped easily into. Fully dressed, she bent down to adjust her hem, straggles of damp hair fell against her face, taking a piece in her hand she realised it must be a mess. There was a dressing table in the room, adorned with an ornate framed mirror. Sitting down at the mirror, she took a silver-backed brush from the table, brushed her hair and using some pins, that were lying in a silver tray, managed to shape it into a reasonable attempt at a French twist. She had just put the last pin in place when there was another light knock on her door. Standing up, and straightening her dress, she went to open it.

"Oh, Miss! You look beautiful."

Ruth and Hannah stood in the brightly lit passageway looking, for all the world, like two little princesses. The ragged ends of their newly cut hair had been straightened and curled, and each wore a headband with a bow. Hannah's was blue, to match her blue and gold gown, and complimented her blond hair and pale complexion perfectly; Ruth was adorned in red and silver, which was equally as complimentary to her darker colouring.

"You don't look too bad yourselves," Naomi smiled. "Girls, you look lovely."

Just then, a door at the end of the passageway opened and Luke appeared, looking resplendent in a blue knee length tunic, with matching trousers and soft leather shoes. He was followed by, a deeply uncomfortable looking, Elliott, who was similarly attired in green.

"Wow!" The girls chorused.

"You look extremely smart, boys," Naomi added.

Luke smiled broadly at the girls and Naomi's compliments, but Elliott squirmed and pulled at the neck of his tunic.

"I feel stupid," he said.

"Well perhaps we should make our way down to dinner," Naomi said, quickly.

The inside of the Great Hall looked magnificent. A table laden with gold and silver plates, cups and cutlery was now in the place where the dais had been. Two high back chairs, ornately carved with gold inlay, looked out grandly across the table onto the hall; several smaller chairs, low backed and rounded were placed either side of them. At one end, there was one final chair, twice the size of any of the others, roughly hewn out of oak; Naomi presumed that one was reserved for Woodlan.

The hall was filled with an array of flowers arranged magnificently in vases, which were so beautifully painted and crafted, that they almost outshone their florid contents. Colourful bunting was strewn across the ceiling; the rich fabrics, which had adorned the wall earlier in the day, had been replaced by intricately woven tapestries. The whole place was filled with the hustle and bustle of servants rushing here and there, putting the finishing touches to the decorations on and around the table, bringing in plates of food, and carefully carrying large pitchers, filled to the brim, with liquids of various smells and colours. Lugh, Marcus and Woodlan stood near the table drinking and talking. Naomi and the children stood in the doorway unsure as to what to do. Lugh, on spotting them, rushed towards them.

"My! My! Three of the most beautiful maidens I have ever seen."

Dressed in an emerald green outfit, and looking more handsome than ever, Lugh's dashing smile and easy compliments, brought a smile to Naomi's face, and the girls grinned and giggled bashfully.

"Marcus . . . have you ever seen such beauty? The queen is said to be the most beautiful woman in the land, but she will have competition this evening. Do you no think so Marcus?"

Marcus smiled at Lugh's good humour.

"Indeed," he said, resting his gaze for a moment on Naomi, causing her to blush involuntarily.

"Let's not forget these two handsome lads," Woodlan said, ruffling Elliott's hair. Who, on seeing Lugh and Marcus also dressed for the occasion, had become less self-conscious and managed a half smile at Woodlan's good natured jibe.

"You look very smart too, Woodlan," Hannah said.

Woodlan looked as if he had dusted and polished himself thoroughly. His granite body and amber buttons now had a brilliant, shiny hue to them.

"Why thank you for noticing, young miss."

As this conversation was going on, the same serving girl who had brought Lugh his keg of ale earlier, brought in a plate of cold chicken and placed it on the table. On seeing Naomi and the children she asked them if they would like something to drink, they all replied in the affirmative. The young girl retired to the kitchen, soon returning with a tray of glasses filled with a smooth purple liquid. The children and Naomi each took a glass, inspecting it for a few moments before putting it to their lips.

"This is delicious," Luke exclaimed.

"What's in it?" Hannah asked.

"It is made from a variety of fruits grown in the castle orchard," Lugh said. "The recipe is, however, a secret known only to the castle cooks, they pass it on one to another and are sworn to secrecy. I remember my first taste of it as a boy. I enjoyed it so much; I commanded my father's cook to make it for me but no matter how hard he tried he could never get it quite right."

"Please . . . please . . . It is time to take your seats." Claymore bustled in, interrupting their conversation. "You!" he said, abruptly pointing at Luke, "The queen has requested that you sit next to her. Then you," pointing at Ruth. "You," Elliott. "And you," Hannah. "My, Lord Lugh you will sit next to King Fionn then the Miss, Marcus Mac Freya and Master Woodlan."

Once Claymore had ordered them to their seats, he hurried to a door leading off the Great Hall closing it behind him. A few moments later it reopened, and he announced the king and queen. At the entrance of the king and queen they all stood. The queen looked stunning. She gave Luke a satisfied smile as she took her seat next to him, and then she and King Fionn greeted all their guests with deferential nods of acknowledgement. There was a moment of majestic silence, then King Fionn opened his arms as a signal for them to start eating. The children began by filling their plates sparingly. Until, seeing that Lugh did not stand on such ceremony, but filled his plate to the brim, the children: tempted beyond measure by the banquet before them: quickly followed his lead.

Lugh talked as freely as he ate and kept everyone entertained with his conversation.

Even the king came out of himself when Lugh shared stories of the times they had spent together in their youth, learning the skill of the sword and the bow. Adding his own stories of how they had led their elf neighbours a merry dance on many occasions; stealing into their camps by night and causing havoc.

"Do you remember, your father was furious, said we would start a war if we did not stop our antics!" Lugh declared, exuberantly.

"Indeed, indeed . . . and we almost did when we stole the Elf King's sword, *right* from under his nose!" the king laughed.

"Aye . . . Dramon came flying to the border with an army ready for battle."

"My father said he knew nothing of it, but Dramon did not believe him . . ."

". . . All hell was about to break loose . . ."

". . .They readied bows and brandished swords, made to attack. . ."

". . .Then your father calls out . . . Dramon is that not your sword in the scabbard of Ascon your First Guard. . ."

". . . And of course it was . . ."

". . . For you see . . ." Lugh said, addressing the rest of the guests, "we had not stolen it, we had exchanged Dramon's sword for Ascon's sword. . ."

". . .The look on Dramon and Ascon's faces . . ."

". . . "We could hardly keep from laughing out loud right there and then."

Lugh and the king laughed loud and heartily.

"My Lord," Queen Olwen said, when their mirth subsided, and just before Lugh could begin another reminiscence. "I think we have all eaten our fill, perhaps now would be the time to introduce our entertainment."

"Of course, my love, as you wish."

King Fionn clapped his hands, and servants appeared, buzzing around, clearing the table, leaving only the goblets the guests were drinking from.

Then they brought in three large bowls of fruit, laying one in the middle of the table and one at either end. When this was done, and the servants had disappeared, the king clapped his hands once more. The great doors of the hall swung open, allowing a tall, dark figure to sweep through them and glide airily towards them. On reaching the table, the figure bowed low the king and queen.

The august visitor wore a short, neatly cut, curly beard, his head was completely bald, and his eyes were as black as night. He wore a floor length cape of burgundy silk, embroidered with geometric symbols. Without a word, he fixed them all with a penetrating stare from his ebony eyes. Then, deliberately unfastening his cape he cast it around his shoulders into the air, where it opened wide and floated down until it hovered wondrously next to him. The children and Naomi all let out a gasp, stars and planets glistened and winked on the black lining, but it wasn't in two dimensions, it was as if he had opened up a window on the night sky. Thoughtfully, and much to the awe of his onlookers, he picked a star from this wondrous piece of the heavens. The tiny, shimmering light hovered just above the palm of his hand for a moment, then lifting it up to his lips, he blew it gently towards, an astonished, Ruth. Here it hovered for a few seconds more, then broke into a tiny fireworks display, the trail of each flash transforming into green stalks and leaves, culminating in tiny sparks which exploded into a variety of coloured roses, each of which bound together to form a bouquet, which ultimately dissolved into a glittering mass, leaving a single, white rose, shimmering and floating in the air.

"Take it, my child, it is for you," Queen Olwen said.

Ruth, cautiously, took the rose from in front of her, smiling contentedly as she smelled its exquisite scent. Her smile seemed to wake the children from their silent awe, and they broke into appreciative applause.

The Magician remained unmoved by the children's ovation, and picking another star repeated the previous process, only this time, Hannah was the recipient of the heavenly body. Hannah's eyes were wide with anticipation as she watched the star begin to pulsate with different colours then, much to her delight, and surprise, the colours split apart and transformed into tiny butterflies. The butterflies fluttered delicately around her, until they joined together to form a cape, which floated gently down onto her shoulders. Another round of applause filled the room.

The boys sat, eagerly waiting to see which of them would be next to receive a star but, much to their disappointment, the magician took no more stars from his magical cloak. Instead, with a sweep of his hand, he caused it to once more cover his imposing frame and turned his attention towards a large tapestry hanging from one of the walls. The scene woven into the tapestry depicted jugglers, acrobats and dancers in various performance poses. Raising his hands expansively towards the tapestry he shouted out a command.

"Incantia corpus . . . habeas revelous."

The audience held their breath . . .

The dormant dancers, jugglers and acrobats, instantly flew from the tapestry, swirling and tumbling across the floor. A ballerina, spinning en pointe, spiralled up to the ceiling then floated, elegantly back down, mingling seamlessly with her fellow dancers who were all whirling and leaping across the floor. Jugglers, expertly passed and threw innumerable balls, clubs, rings and plates at one another and into the air. Acrobats performed spectacular feats of tumbling and balancing, bending and contorting themselves into, seemingly impossible, positions.

The audience watched the performance enthralled, all except King Fionn, who looked on indifferently, as if he had seen it all before.

Amidst all the revelry, the Magician raised his hand towards Elliot, the scene of carnival behind him slowed, and all eyes turned towards the Magician and Elliott. Elliott was staring at the conjurer, entranced.

Gradually, Elliott's chair began to shake, Elliott grabbed on to the seat, there was a loud bang, at which they all jumped, and Elliott and his chair burst into flames. Ruth and Hannah squealed with fright, and Naomi gasped, jumping up from her chair, looking to the queen for answers.

Queen Olwen merely smiled and raised her eyes upward. Naomi, following the queen's signal, looked up catching her breath in shock and astonishment. The acrobats had created a six-tier tower, on the apex of which, Elliott was balanced, smiling from ear to ear. Naomi let out a cry of consternation, as the acrobats casually flipped, the grinning, Elliott, who somersaulted high into the air landing, much to Naomi's surprise and relief, safely back on the shoulders of the top two gymnasts.

The show, however, was not finished there. They then proceeded to sway Elliott about the room, causing the girls to let out screams of alarm and delight as he swept across the table, almost touching their heads. Circling back upwards, and before anyone could catch their breath, Elliott was once more being thrown into the air. This time he tumbled down the tower, taking the place of the flying acrobats as they jumped nimbly down to the floor between each of Elliott's assisted somersaults. Naomi flinched at each tumble. Until finally, the acrobats landed him expertly onto the floor. The audience broke into a rapturous round of applause for this gravity defying feat. Naomi fell back into her chair, exhausted. Elliott bowed and waved a hand of recognition towards his 'team-mates.' Then, with a self-conscious laugh, ran back to his seat; while the players from the tapestry, span and tumbled back to their backdrop abode, followed by their fellow artists.

When the applause subsided, the magician turned his attention to Luke, signalling him, by a wave of his hand, to come out to him. Luke readily obeyed the Magician's invitation and was quickly standing next to him, his eyes aglow with expectation. The Magician put his hand into his cloak and dramatically produced a green and blue mottled sphere about the size of a tennis ball. Then, opening his hand, the sphere began to float in the air directly in front of Luke. Luke stood staring at it, open-mouthed.

"Try to make it move."

Luke was momentarily startled by the deep baritone resonance of the Magician's voice, but quickly recovered himself.

"Me?" he questioned.

"Merely believe." The Magician's tone left no room for dispute.

Luke stared intently at the sphere.

"Up." he said, hesitantly. Nothing happened. He tried again. "Up."

"Try to *imagine* the sphere moving," the Magician said. "Rather than commanding it with words . . . *will it.*"

Luke tried again and, wearing an embarrassed smile, scrunched up his eyes at the sphere. Just at this moment the magician gently, but firmly, touched Luke's right arm. Luke's face changed almost immediately from one of embarrassed awkwardness, to one of complete concentration. Everyone felt the change of mood, and waited with bated breath to see what would happen. Within seconds the sphere began to move upwards. Luke, astonished by his accomplishment, turned to Naomi.

"Miss look . . . it's moving."

The moment Luke turned from the sphere it began to fall, everyone gasped, and Luke, alerted to the danger, quickly turned back to the sphere and with an upward glance drew it back up into the air. Encouraged by his success, Luke began to, tentatively, move the sphere in different directions; using his hands to speed up and slow down the movement of the sphere. By pulling his hands apart, he discovered that he could make the sphere grow in size he smiled, enraptured by this new discovery. As the sphere grew larger and larger, hills and seas, meadow, plants and flowers began to appear on its surface, the audience stared on in astonishment, it was as if they were watching the genesis of a planet. Just as it looked as if the growing planet would absorb them into its burgeoning terrain, they heard the Magician's voice call out.

"*DIMINUTUS.*"

The next moment, they were all sitting as if they had just woken from a dream. Luke continued to stare, fascinated, at the now once again ball like object he held in his hand.

"That was . . . *mega awesome,*" he said, looking up at them all, and breaking into a broad grin.

Everyone, once more broke into rapturous applause. Luke seated himself back next to the queen, who smiled down on him, thoughtfully.

"That was the most *brilliant* illusion *ever,*" Hannah cried.

The Magician, who was bowing in acknowledgement of the rapturous appreciation, suddenly stopped mid bow, and raising himself to his full height looked down on Hannah with a countenance so cold, it was palpable.

"I am no . . . *illusionist,* a purveyor of party tricks . . . *I am a Magician* . . . a man of science." And with this emphatic declaration, he covered himself with his cloak, turned into a piece of black granite, and exploded into a thousand glittering pieces, which disappeared as they touched the stone floor of the Hall.

"I'm sorry . . . I didn't mean to upset him," Hannah said.

"Do not worry, child," The queen said. "Quinn is always upset at something. I think he quite enjoys feeling under appreciated."

"I remember the first time I saw him," Lugh said, "when I was a lad. King Owen had kindly organised a birthday party for me here at the castle. Quinn blew a star in front of me, the way he did tonight. All of a sudden it began to sprout hair, and two beady eyes appeared right in front of my face." Here Lugh paused for dramatic effect, his hands, fingers wide, close to his face, his eyes staring at the invisible manifestation. "Then tiny sharp little teeth began to shine through the fur . . . RAT!!! I shouted." All the children jumped. "And clouted it . . . WHACK! With the butt of the new knife my father had given me for my birthday . . . but much to my surprise and shock, what lay in front of me was no a rat . . . it was a rabbit, one of those big furry ones.

"Ohhhh that's horrible!" The girls chorused.

"Aye! It was indeed. You can imagine how frightened I was, thinking a rat was going to eat my face, and then seeing the poor wee rabbit lying there . . . dead as a doornail . . . right in front of me."

"How awful for you, on your birthday too. How old were you?" Hannah asked, in a deeply concerned voice.

"Twenty."

"TWENTY!" Naomi exclaimed, unable to keep *her* own shock and surprise out of her voice.

"Aye. Exactly . . . Quinn was furious, but then what did he expect? I was just a lad."

Naomi sat, opened mouthed and speechless. Hannah and Ruth exchanged perplexed looks, while Luke and Elliott merely sat with half-suppressed grins on their faces.

"Children, Miss Naomi," Queen Olwen said, with her own smile playing on her lips. "My Lord and I hope you have enjoyed your feast." The children nodded and smiled broadly. "Not every meal will be quite so . . . sumptuous, but we hope, non the less, that you will enjoy your stay with us." At this mention of their not continuing the journey with Naomi a cloud crossed Elliott's face. "My Lord and I will now bid you a good night." The party stood as Fionn and Olwen left the hall.

When they were once again seated Claymore asked them if they required anything else, there was a general negative.

"I'm stuffed," Hannah said, with a yawn.

"Me too," Ruth sighed.

"I will leave you then," Claymore announced; and swept from the hall.

"Time for bed I think," Naomi said.

"I'm not tired," Elliot declared.

There was an edge of defiance in his tone, that ruffled Naomi.

"Tired or not," she said, "it's been a long day, and it's *time* for bed."

"Why? It's not as if we're going anywhere tomorrow. *Is it*?"

"Can you remember where your room is?" Naomi said, refusing to be drawn on the subject. "Or would you like *me* to put you to bed?"

"I don't need any help from *you*."

Storming from the room, Elliott was quickly followed by the other children. Each of whom bid Naomi a, hasty, goodnight.

There was a strained silence amongst the adults when the children had left, broken at last by Woodlan.

"The lad doesn't mean it, Little Miss, he's just full of spirit that's all."

"If you'll all excuse me. I think I'll turn in too," Naomi said, unwilling to discuss the subject of Elliott's rudeness.

They each stood and gave her a slight bow as she left the hall, tears stinging her eyes.

CHAPTER FIFTEEN
Encountering, 'True Order'

The next day, Naomi washed and dressed, slowly putting off for as long as possible her departure from the children. Finally, she sat at the ornate mirror once more and scraped her hair back into a tight ponytail. She stared at herself in the mirror. She looked pale and small, so very, very small. She swallowed hard and forced herself to stand up. Making her way to the girls' room, she knocked gently on the door. A part of her didn't want them to answer, but within a few moments Hannah had opened the door, and seeing Naomi dressed to leave began to cry.

"Oh, Miss! I'm going to miss you so much."

Hearing Hannah, Ruth rushed to the door, and then they were all hugging and crying.

"You do understand why I have to leave you here, don't you?" Naomi asked.

The girls sniffed back their tears and nodded.

They crossed the hall to the boys' room, and Luke answered the door.

"Are you coming down to see me off?" Naomi asked, a subdued looking, Luke.

"Yes, Miss."

"And, Elliott?" Naomi asked, peering over Luke's head into the room.

Luke bit his lower lip and shook his head.

"Right . . . we better go then," she said.

At the bottom of the great stairs, they were met by a serving boy, who led them to the same antechamber they had eaten in the day before. Woodlan, Lugh and Marcus were already there, sitting round the fire, conversing in hushed tones. On their arrival, Lugh greeted the children in his usual genial way.

"Good morning to you all, did you sleep well."

The children nodded their assent.

"Where's the laddie, Elliott? Is he no' coming down?" Lugh asked.

"No, he . . . no," Naomi answered.

"I see . . . well, let's get breakfast ordered, I don't know about you, but I am famished."

Lugh gave Luke's hair a good-natured ruffle, then gallantly seated Naomi and the girls at the table which, despite the sadness the girls were feeling, brought a smile to their lips.

After a good breakfast, which Naomi could hardly eat, Queen Olwen entered the antechamber. All conversation stopped as they all stood up and bowed. Luke beamed up at the queen, who returned his smile with one of her own.

"There is one missing," she said. "Where is Elliott?"

"He didn't feel like coming down, My Lady," Luke said.

The queen looked thoughtful for a moment, then turned to Marcus.

"Do you have everything you need?"

"Yes, My Lady and we wish to thank you, and King Fionn, for all your help and hospitality."

"I hope it will not be *too* long, until we see all of you again . . . Children it is time to say goodbye."

The children, startled by the queen's abrupt command, stood speechless for a moment. Luke broke the silence.

"Take care of yourself, Miss, and don't worry about us . . . we'll be good."

Naomi smiled, tears standing in her eyes, tears that she struggled to hold back, as the girls hugged her and the rest of the company; Hannah hugging Woodlan for just a little longer than everyone else.

All their goodbyes said, the children stood next to their stately hostess; Luke seeming taller somehow and the girls doing their best to look brave.

Naomi felt a wave of pride overcome her.

"I'll be back as soon as I can," she said, with a catch in her throat. Then turned and left the room, praying that she had not just made a promise that she could not keep.

On reaching the castle gates, one of the two guards handed Marcus and Lugh a bow and a small quiver full of arrows.

"We will have to make each of these count," Lugh said, examining the quiver. Then, catching sight of Naomi's troubled face, added, "Should we need to use them."

Once beyond the castle, they continued north across King Fionn's land for a day and a half, at which point, they stopped at a line of rowan trees.

"This is where the land of the elves begins, from here we must make as little noise as possible and try to make ourselves as invisible as possible," Marcus warned.

"I will wait for you on the border," Woodlan said.

"What do you mean? Aren't you coming with us?" Naomi cried.

"No, Little Miss, there is little chance of me going unnoticed. I will see you again in a few days." He said, reassuringly touching Naomi lightly on the shoulder. Then he crumbled into the earth and was gone.

Naomi immediately felt Woodlan's loss, keenly.

Lugh, resolutely straightened the bow across his chest and made to cross the line of trees, but Marcus laid a hand on his arm.

"Wait one moment, there is something we need to resolve before we can continue our journey." Lugh gave him a nod of understanding.

Naomi wondered what they could mean.

Marcus turned and looked back the way they had just come.

"Show yourself," he called out.

Nothing happened.

"You cannot follow us into elf country alone, it is too dangerous."

Still nothing.

"You will put us all in danger."

"You move across the land like an elephant," Lugh added. "The elves will have you captured and tied up before you get a mile into their land."

At Lugh's reproof a slight figure emerged, reluctantly, from behind a large thorn bush."

"Elliott!" Naomi exclaimed.

"I'm not going back."

"Oh yes you are, young man."

"If you take me back, I'll just run away again."

"It's far too dangerous, you could be killed," Naomi cried. Then, pointing at Marcus and Lugh, said, "Can't you see that they're carrying weapons? This isn't some computer game!"

"I know that!"

"Elliott, please."

"I'm not going back," Elliott insisted.

"Marcus, tell him he needs to go back," Naomi pleaded.

It was a moment before Marcus spoke; and when he did Naomi was filled with foreboding.

"Why do you want to come with us?" he asked.

"Because it's the right thing to do," Elliott declared. "My whole life, I've had one adult after another telling me they're doing the right thing for me. My parents telling me; it's right that they should split up because they don't love each other any more; and it's right that I shouldn't see my dad because he's got some things he has to sort out at the moment; then it's right that I should go into care because my mum is struggling to cope. I want to try and do something that I think is right. I haven't cared about anything in a long time, but I care about this, *this* matters."

Marcus turned to Naomi.

"I understand your feelings of responsibility towards the boy, but we don't have time to take him back, and he won't go back on his own. We will have to take him with us, and besides that . . . there is some truth in what he says."

"He's just a child . . . he doesn't know his own mind."

"Perhaps, but sometimes circumstances and experiences turn children into adults earlier than we would like."

Naomi looked at her three companions, and knew she was beaten. With great reluctance, she opened her arms in a gesture of acquiescence.

Elliott hurried to join them, and they crossed through the rowan trees into the land of the elves; the lush green beauty of which, disguised the danger it held for them.

After two, uneventful, days their path was crossed by a towering waterfall which cascaded down into a wide, rock littered river. The water caroused over the rocks at such a speed that they were not able to pick their way over them. There were, however, two giant pine tree trunks strewn across its banks. Naomi stared at the trunks apprehensively, feeling she knew what was coming next.

Marcus stood at the end of one of the trunks and said to Naomi and Elliott, in a raised voice, so as to be heard over the crashing water.

"We will have to use the trunks to cross the river." Naomi's heart sank. "Once you are on the trunk keep looking straight ahead, it is wide and the water is barely touching it, if you take it slowly and steadily there should be little chance of your falling." Naomi would have felt better if Marcus' speech of reassurance hadn't been quite so qualified.

Lugh, meanwhile, was already on the other trunk, making his way nimbly across it. Then, without warning, Elliott stepped onto the log to follow him.

"Elliott!"

"I'll be *fine, Miss.*"

Naomi watched, with her heart in her mouth, as Elliott, arms outstretched, tight-roped his way across to the other side.

Marcus was now on the trunk, waiting for Naomi to follow him. Calmed somewhat by the success of Lugh and Elliott, Naomi adjusted the pack on her back and stepped onto the trunk. She immediately had to adjust her balance and Marcus moved towards her, but she put up her hand to signal she was okay; then keeping her eyes on Marcus' feet, began to edge her way across.

They were about halfway across when Naomi felt a splash of water hit her forcefully across her calves. She staggered, but managed to right herself, but before she could take another step, she felt another splash, then another and another, each one stronger than the one before. She began to struggle to keep herself upright and called out to Marcus. Marcus reached out his hand to her, but he too was now struggling to keep his footing, as the water dashed increasingly violently over the pine trunk. Naomi reached unsteadily for Marcus' outstretched hand then stopped, terrified at the sound of a deafening roar. Hardly breathing, she turned her head in the direction of the sound. To her horror, she saw a massive wave rushing towards them. Taken aback, she slipped and fell with a thud, face down onto the trunk. Panic stricken, she managed to somehow wrap herself round it, steeling herself for what was to come.

The water smashed against her body, she gave out a cry and instinctively tightened her grip on the trunk. Once the main rush had washed over her, she managed to lift her head up to see where Marcus was. She saw him half in the water, clinging onto the log. Another wave rushed towards them, she tightened her grip again, her legs shaking under the effort. The water was now a torrent. It went up her nose, choking her; she felt her grip slip; she scrambled to stay on the precarious refuge, her face glued to the log.

Then, through the heavy spray, Naomi thought she saw a slight figure standing at the top of the fall who, to her utter shock and amazement, dived headlong into the wild water, appearing to dissolve on contact with the gushing foam. The whole scene could only have taken a few seconds, but Naomi had no time to take in what she thought she had just witnessed, as the water continued its fierce efforts to force her into its lethal depths. Just when she thought she could hold on no longer, the strength of the water began to abate. Naomi cautiously lifted her head up. Marcus was pulling himself back up onto the log. Breathing heavily, he dragged himself to a standing position and shouted out to Naomi, while moving carefully towards her.

"Quickly, take my hand, I don't know how long she will be able to hold the water back."

Desperate to get to safety, and mobilised by the urgency in his voice, Naomi took his hand and once in a standing position, carefully followed him across the sodden timber falling, shaken and exhausted, onto the river bank.

Elliot and Lugh rushed to her, kneeling close to her side, a look of anguished concern on their faces. Naomi lay under their gaze breathing heavily, too exhausted to move or speak. She felt the July sun blaze through the trees and was grateful for its warmth. Eventually, her breathing began to slow and feeling the weight of the soaked pack on her back she made a feeble attempt to remove it. Lugh moved to help her, but Elliott beat him to it. Once free from the weight of the pack, she sat up, stretching her shoulders and neck. Lugh offered her a draught of water which she refused with a shake of her head. Lugh moved away towards Marcus. Naomi followed him with her gaze and was surprised to see a woman by the edge of the river, looking pensively into the water as if she were in silent conversation with it.

"Who's that?" Naomi whispered to Elliott.

"She's the one who stopped the water, Miss," he whispered back. "She jumped from the top of the falls straight into the rushing water. I couldn't believe it. She disappeared into the water, and I thought for sure she was dead, but within a few seconds of her hitting the water, it began to slow; you and Marcus made it to the shore; and she emerged from the water unhurt and . . . what's even more strange . . . bone dry . . . *Un* . . . believable!"

The stranger continued to stare into the water. There was a quiver of arrows, and a bow hung around her tall, slight frame. Her hair was snow white and hung down her back in a waist length plait. She suddenly turned her head and met Naomi's gaze with a pair of pale blue eyes, canopied with long, chalk white lashes; her skin was almost translucent. Naomi could tell immediately that she was of Cachada's race.

Naomi blinked under the stranger's impassive scrutiny; giving her an awkward smile of gratitude which the stranger returned with continued impassivity. Naomi turned away uncomfortably and looked towards Marcus and Lugh.

Marcus was taking a long, thirsty draught from Lugh's water pouch. When he had finished, he handed the pouch back to Lugh and turned his attention to the new arrival.

"Rydanna . . . thank you for our lives."

There was a familiarity and warmth in Marcus' voice as he spoke, which Naomi had never heard before and which, for some reason, she found a little jarring. It left her feeling, perhaps not quite as grateful as she should have been towards their saviour. Pushing these unwelcome feelings to one side, however, she forced herself to say in an even voice.

"Yes, thank you."

"Indeed, you are well met," declared Lugh, coming forward and clapping Rydanna on the arms.

Rydanna's face remained impassive at Lugh's exuberant greeting, as she said:

"My Lady Cachada has sent me. News reached her that you had entered the elves' valley and, while she had made a plea for you with the many waters, she feared something like this would happen. Unfortunately, since Gaia began shaking the world, her influence over the waters has diminished. The elves' hatred of humans sits well with their belief that the time of mankind's dominance is over and all efforts should be put into aiding their demise. My Lady sent me to use what power and influence my people possess to aid you in your journey." Rydanna's voice, in stark opposition to her glacial appearance, was soft and warm.

"Your help is most welcome," Marcus said. "I am sure we will have need of it again before this journey is over."

"Your journey is already over," a hostile voice announced, from somewhere above them. "Did you really think that you could cross our border without us knowing."

Startled, by the unexpected voice they all looked up into the trees, which bordered the river, for its owner. Without warning, a body came flying from one of the trees and landed directly in front of Naomi; in the same instant Lugh moved and raised his bow to the elf's head.

"If you value your life and the life of your . . . *friends*," the elf sneered, while keeping his eyes fixed on Naomi, "you had better lower your bow." The elf's face was bending down so close to Naomi's that she could feel his hot breath on her face as he spat out his warning.

"Lugh . . . *Lugh*," Marcus called out, urgently.

Reluctantly, Lugh turned his head slightly in answer to Marcus' call, keeping one eye on the elf, and his bow unmoved. Marcus signalled with a throw of his head to the trees. Elves were appearing in the treetops, and around the tree trunks, bows raised, aimed threateningly at their little troupe. The elf who was bowing intimidatingly over Naomi, turned his head slowly to look at Lugh and smiled at him triumphantly. Lugh, with murder in his eyes, slowly lowered his bow.

"So, you are the champion of the humans," the elf said, turning his attention back to Naomi. "Seeking to make your pathetic plea to Gaia for the continued existence of your race. Well, your quest ends here . . . *human* . . . Take them." Elves rushed forward and grabbed each of them roughly.

"Where is the nymph?" the lead elf asked.

The elves looked in every direction in search of Rydanna, but she was nowhere to be seen.

"No matter, she has slunk back to her mistress. She can take the news of her failure with her and all will know that the elves have not succumbed to the imaginary fear perpetuated by humans . . . and those who bow down to them, but have done what needed to be done to save our peoples."

As they were dragged off by their captors a knowing look passed between Lugh and Marcus, at the news of Rydanna's escape.

Once they were past the tree line, the elves threw the captives together. The bowmen lowered their bows; while more elves, who had been waiting at the edge of the trees, goaded the prisoners forward with lances.

After some time, they eventually arrived at the foot of a grassy bank. The lead elf stood in front of it, muttering some words in a strange language that Naomi did not recognise. At the conclusion of his whispered oration, an opening appeared in the bank large enough for them to enter two abreast.

Each of the captives was assigned a personal gaoler who held on, firmer than was necessary, to their arms. The gap led into a narrow, dark passageway. The ground beneath Naomi's feet was soft and the air was cool and surprisingly fresh. Shortly, the passageway began to widen and become lighter. Until all at once, she was staring, open mouthed, at the most breathtaking sight of her life.

A sculpted, vaulted ceiling, encrusted with a fabulous array of jewels; and which seemed to stretch for miles; glistened and glittered above them, raining down shafts of coloured light onto a white, stone city. There were buildings, from floor to ceiling, carved out of the rock face, much like Rochan's valley, but much more elaborate. They were littered with stained glass, lancet windows, encased in ornate wrought ironwork. Luminous platforms, held up by scrolled columns and accessed by crystal stairways; which were decorated with ornate railings and balustrades; created a shining highway in the air. In the near distance a spectacular waterfall coursed magnificently down the face of a mountain and ran into the city feeding an alabaster fountain. The fountain was decorated with base reliefs of elves in various scholastic poses and dominated a communal area, which was dotted with polished stone tables and chairs; many of which were decked with sumptuous and elaborately embroidered cushions. Towering, gothic archways led off from the fountain area and completed the infrastructure of the wondrous city before her.

Elves, old and young, sat at the tables eating, or in groups talking. The elves themselves were as imposing as their city. While they looked mostly human, apart from their lanceolate shaped ears, there was a mystical air about them and, when they moved, they seemed to float, rather than walk, in their long flowing robes.

As the captives were pulled towards the shining gothic piazza, the elves stopped their various occupations and gazed at them, disgust and loathing shining in their eyes. Naomi felt that most of the revulsion was directed towards her and Elliott, and she remembered the distrustful stares of the inhabitants of Oakvale, but while then she had just felt uncomfortable now, she felt threatened.

There was a malignancy emanating from the elves that was palpable. She felt the need to check if Elliott was all right, but as she turned to see where he was, her gaoler pulled hard on her arm. She let out a cry of pain and, as she was dragged towards one of the archways, she was acutely aware of the amusement her discomfort gave to the elf onlookers.

The elves dragged them through the archway along a stone avenue. At the end of the avenue there was a set of stairs leading down, but unlike the crystal ones which led up through the city, these were plain and hewn roughly out of the stone. The elf 'escorting' Naomi let go of her arm and took a torch from just inside the stairway. He then began to make his way down, commanding her to follow him. Taking advantage of her release, Naomi turned to look for Elliott. He was standing a little way behind her, still in the grip of his gaoler. Naomi was pleased to see that he looked as defiant as ever and gave him a reassuring smile.

"Move NOW *human,* or you will be sorry."

Naomi turned towards the torch bearer and carefully followed him down the stairway to a dank corridor. The corridor was lined with heavy wooden doors, each adorned with a small grill panel near the top.

Once at the bottom of the stairs, Elliott, Marcus and Lugh were thrown into one cell, and Naomi into one next to it. The heavy cell door locked, contemptuously, behind her.

Naomi quickly took in her new surrounding which consisted of a wooden bed, covered with sparse bedding, a bowl for washing in, and a chamber pot, the last of which items Naomi eyed with foreboding. Turning from her 'accommodation' she stretched up to the metal grate in the cell door and called out.

"Elliott, Elliot, can you hear me?"

"Yes, Miss, I can hear you."

"Are you all right?"

"Well, apart from being stuck in a stinky cell, I'm fine . . . How about you, Miss, are you all right?"

"As you say, apart from being in a stinky cell . . . I'm fine."

Elliott then said something Naomi couldn't quite make out.

"What was that, what did you say, Elliott?"

"I was just asking Marcus what he thought they would do with us."

"What did he say?"

"I don't know," Marcus answered.

"Oh!"

*   *   *

Naomi sat for some time on the bed in her cell, feeling completely helpless. Now and again, she heard the hushed tones of her fellow captors in the adjoining cell and wondered if Marcus and Lugh might be coming up with some plan of escape.

At length, she heard footsteps on the stairway. The door of her cell was opened by a surly looking elf, who commanded her to get up and come with him. Outside the cell, another elf was opening the adjoining cell door.

"You . . . human child, come with me," he commanded.

Elliott emerged from the cell, and they were both herded up the stairway.

After the dimness of the dungeons, the pair squinted in the bright glow of the luminous city. Their gaolers led them to the fountain area, where their appearance once again caused a stir of disdain amongst the citizenry. They continued down through another archway until they reached a lofty, opaque glass door. The elves pushed the door open, revealing a handsome female elf sitting imposingly on a luxurious, diamond encrusted, jade throne. Pushing Naomi and Elliott forward the elves commanded them to:

"Bow before Queen Riona . . . queen of the elves."

Naomi and Elliott obeyed, stiffly.

The queen's appearance was deeply unsettling, her face was unreadable and when she spoke her voice was void of emotion.

"You have met the Queen Olwen?" she asked, directing the question to Naomi.

"Yes," Naomi answered

"Yes . . . your *Majesty*!" one of the elves corrected.

"Yes . . . your Majesty," Naomi mimicked.

"Her fault has always been her soft heart . . . You are on a quest to save humankind?"

"Yes."

"Why exactly?" But without waiting for an answer the queen continued, "You are unstable, you bring death and destruction to all you touch."

"What about earthquakes and tsunamis?" Elliott cried out, defensively. "They bring destruction and death too and Miss is going to try and stop them, and that will help everyone."

The queen rounded on Elliott with a look of contempt.

"The only things they destroy are the scars on the landscape you call cities, which cover and suffocate the earth beneath them. The natural disasters, as *you and your kind* call them, merely shift the landscape, moulding it into a new scene of beauty, leaving behind it, not devastation, but evidence of its majestic power reformed." Regaining her composure she turned back to Naomi. "We cannot allow you any chance of leniency for your people, if we do so we will all suffer. You will stay here until Gaia has finished her task."

"You have no right to keep us here!" Naomi exclaimed.

"Rights! Rights! You speak of rights. My p . . ."

"Yes!" Naomi interrupted, annoyed at the Queen's arrogance. "We have just as much right to this world as you have, and perhaps we have made mistakes, but if the present disasters continue unchecked millions of *innocent* men, women and children will die."

"There are no innocent among the humans." Although the queen's voice remained even, it was now tinged with a hint of malignancy as she fixed her gaze on Elliott. "Even their children are only despoilers in embryo." Turning back to Naomi she continued, "While my people and I find the presence of humans in the city *deeply* distasteful, you will, nonetheless, remain here until Gaia has completed the fate of your people. And then, I will allow you to leave so you may warn, what is left of your race, that their time is over and even their *ancient* link with the old ones can no longer protect them from the dominance of the elves. We will rule over them, and at last there will be the establishment of true order . . . take them away."

"Please! Let the boy go, you don't need both of us. . . He's just a child." Naomi's plea fell on deaf ears. The queen's face remaining impassive, as the elves dragged them both out of the room.

Back in her cell, Naomi paced back and forwards racking her brains trying to think of a way out of, what seemed like, a hopeless situation. Then suddenly it hit her . . . Woodlan!

"Marcus, Marcus," Naomi called through the door, softly.

"What is it?" He asked, anxiously.

"Woodlan, can't he rescue us, like he did from the caves of the mountain dwarves?"

"Perhaps he could, but I doubt he knows where we are. He will still be waiting for us on the border of the elf lands. The time for us to meet him has not yet passed and I fear, by the time he does hear of our fate, the elves will have put measures in place to detect any rescue attempt made on his part."

Naomi leaned her head on the door of the cell, feeling utterly defeated.

CHAPTER SIXTEEN
Getting Better

Naomi sat on the bunk in her cell, staring at the bare wall in front of her, feeling utterly sorry for herself. A tray, with an empty plate and a drained cup, lay at the end of the bunk. The food the elves had brought had been, though unappetising to look at, surprisingly tasty. Well at least they wouldn't starve she thought. The bed was uncomfortable though, and she wondered how many nights she would have to spend, tossing and turning, on its unforgiving slats? The thought of spending who knows how long, alone in this cell, filled her with dread. Deep in, self-pitying, contemplation she was suddenly distracted by a scratching noise. At first, she couldn't tell where it was coming from. Then, as it became a little louder, she realised it was coming from low down on the back wall of her cell. Naomi went to the door grill.

"Do you hear that?" she said.

"What did you say?" It was Marcus' voice, edged with concern, which answered her.

"I can hear scratching coming from the back wall of my cell."

"Oh!"

"What do you mean, Oh!?" Naomi didn't like his tone. It had a finality about it.

"Well, it's probably . . . a . . . rat."

"What? A rat . . .! Oh lovely, just perfect."

"Do you like rats then.?"

"*No!*"

"Rats, who could love *rats*," Lugh cried, "filthy, disgusting . . ."

"But you said," Marcus continued, ignoring Lugh's outburst, "that that was perfect,"

"It doesn't mean that I . . ." Naomi stopped, the scratching was getting louder, and one of the bricks in the cell wall was moving."

"What's wrong? Are you all right?" Marcus called out.

"*Of course*, she's not all right she has rats in her cell," Lugh said.

"Miss! . . . Miss! What's happening," Elliott cried.

"I think I'm about to meet one mighty . . . big . . . rat," Naomi answered, while searching the room, looking for something to defend herself with.

"Miss! Miss! Are you okay?" Elliott continued to call out, anxiously.

By now Naomi had grabbed the nearest object at hand and was standing, chamber pot at the ready, with her back to the door, prepared to do battle with her unwelcome visitor. The brick pushed through the wall and fell to the floor, Naomi aimed the pot at the hole and was just about to throw it when . . .

"Rydanna!" Rydanna's disembodied head appeared through the hole and, on seeing Naomi, looked questioningly at the pot in her hand.

"I thought you were a rat," Naomi said, slowly placing the chamber pot on the floor.

The voices of her companions, in the adjoining cell, were becoming more anxious.

"What's happened, Miss? Is it a rat? Are you okay?" Elliott cried.

"Naomi . . ! Naomi . . ! Naomi . . !" Lugh and Marcus called out in unison.

"Shh" It's okay. It's . . . Rydanna."

"Rydanna?" they chorused back.

"Yes . . . she's . . . she's . . ."

"Come to rescue you . . .?" Rydanna said, helpfully.

"Yes . . . of course . . . She's come to rescue us."

"Here," Rydanna's head had disappeared and now her hand was visible holding a knife, "take this and start to remove the mortar around the brick below this one. If we work from both sides, it will take less time. One more brick and you should be able to fit through."

"Right," Naomi said, and started on her task.

At length, they loosened the brick enough to remove it and Naomi squeezed through into a dark, dank cavern; lit only by the light reflecting from the bejewelled city high above. Once through, she and Rydanna began to loosen the bricks of the other cell, Naomi using the knife Rydanna had given her, and Rydanna using the tip of one of her arrows. Once they had removed one of the bricks she passed through more arrows to Marcus and Lugh. Before long they were all standing in the dripping cavern, free of their cells.

"How did you know where we were?" Marcus asked.

"I mingled with the waterfall that feeds the city and listened to the elves who passed by. Your capture is all they are talking about. Once I discovered where they had imprisoned you, I made my way down here through one of the many waterways which run through the underground caverns that surround the city. I began walking the length of the wall, trying to work out exactly where your cells were located. Just when I was about to give up, and thought I would have to return to the city to try and get more detailed information, I heard voices through the wall. I couldn't make out if they were you or not, but I took the chance that you were the only prisoners."

"Thank you, Rydanna, for . . .once again, rescuing us." The rest of the group echoed Marcus' gratitude.

"Do not thank me yet. Getting down here undetected was fairly easy for me alone, getting us all out safely . . . that will be the difficult part."

"Let us hope we can do it without going any deeper into these caverns," Lugh said. "There are stories among my people of when the elves were building the city, and how many were lost to creatures older than time. Creatures created before mankind, faerie, elf, or any other races lived on the earth."

"We have little choice but to take our chance amongst the caverns." Marcus said. "We need to get as much distance as we can between us and the city, before the elves discover we have escaped,"

"Is there no way we could pass through the fall and sneak through the city?" Lugh persisted.

"That would be impossible," Rydanna said. "The fall acts as a gateway to the city, the elves built the city in this place, centuries ago, in honour of the fall's beauty and magnificence. The fall, in return for that honour protects the city from access through its waters. I could mingle with the fall's waters because the elves, always wishing to *display* their achievements, have allowed my people to do so that they might marvel at the splendour of their kingdom. The fall did not consider one river nymph as a threat. It will never allow five strangers to merely walk through it into the city, and even if it did, I doubt greatly that we could 'sneak' through the city."

"Lugh, my friend," Marcus said, placing his hand on Lugh's shoulder. "We have no option."

Just as Lugh was about to nod a reluctant consent, Rydanna spoke up.

"There is one way, it would still mean passing through the fall, but rather than going into the city we would pass across the water and climb up the outside wall of the city."

"Is the wall not guarded?" Marcus asked.

"Not on that side, the elves have complete faith in the fall's ability to protect it."

"But that still leaves us with the problem of getting through the fall," Marcus said.

"Perhaps not!" Rydanna turned and looked directly at Naomi. Naomi quailed a little under her gaze, afraid to hear what she was about to say next. "Marcus says you possess the ancient power handed down to your people by the Timeless Ones. Is that true?"

"Yes," Naomi said, somewhat reluctantly.

"Then you can use it to help get us through the fall."

"How? I mean this is all new to me . . . I wouldn't have a clue what to do."

"Once you enter the fall, it will recognise your power, you must hold its attention while we pass through."

"Hold its attention? How do I do that?"

"You must enter the waters and join with it. It has been many years since the ancient power has been felt among the elements, the fall is bound by the ancient laws to allow you an audience. Once you have its attention, you must do all you can to keep it upon you, until we are across."

"Oh! I don't know about this . . . I mean . . . what can I say to it?"

"It is either that, or we risk facing whatever lies within the depths of these caverns."

All eyes on her, Naomi took a deep breath, and thinking of Elliott, said:

"Okay, I'll give it a try."

Rydanna didn't look convinced by Naomi's half-hearted affirmation but she turned, resolutely, and began to lead the way through the gloomy cavern back to the falls.

Water dripped from the cavern walls, its floor was soaked and riddled with rivulets, which made it slippery underfoot. The group trudged their way across the cavern until they reached a narrow passageway. It was pitch black inside, and a narrow stream ran out of its entrance.

"Stay close to the walls," Rydanna ordered.

In the pitch darkness they edged their way along the tunnels' sodden walls, images of giant rats running through Naomi's mind. As her eyes became accustomed to the dark, she could just make out Elliott's figure in front of her. She cast a wary eye across the floor, checking to see if there were any smaller shadows running at their feet but, thankfully, all she could make out was the stream trickling gently along. In a little while, they could hear gushing water, and she knew they were nearing the fall. Not for the first time on this fantastical journey Naomi's heart sank. Once again, she was walking into the unknown, without any idea of what the outcome would be.

The tunnel began to open out and gradually become lighter, the noise from the fall getting louder all the time, until they all stood facing its gushing grandeur.

Rydanna began to call out to them above the noise of the rushing water.

"Once Naomi enters the water, I will give her time to call to the fall, then I will enter to make sure it is safe. If it is, I will signal to each of you to come through. We must cross one at a time, so there is less chance of us being detected."

"What will happen when we're all through . . . I mean what will happen to Miss?"

Elliott's question gave voice to Naomi's own thoughts, but she had no desire to worry him further.

"Don't worry, Elliott, I'll be fine," she said.

Elliott was just about to query this assurance by his teacher, but Naomi didn't give him a chance, taking a deep breath she made to walk into the fall. She stopped short, however, as a thought suddenly struck her and turning back to Rydanna she asked:

"What do I say? I mean how do I call it?" she asked.

"Call it by its name, Vanora."

Naomi nodded, and with her heart beating almost out of her chest, she entered the rushing water.

The ice, cold water crashed down on her, drenching her. She shivered and her eyes closed, involuntarily. At first, she couldn't think of anything except trying to stay upright under the fall's unforgiving force. Eventually, just as she had managed to steady herself, and began to focus her mind on her task, the water suddenly stopped beating down. She opened her eyes. Blinking, she found herself looking through a crystal cascade of water at the glittering elf city. She was entranced, for a moment, by its beauty, until a thunderous voice took hold of her attention.

"What brings you here human, we have felt your presence in the land, what is it you want *here*?"

Naomi took a moment to calm herself and then began:

"Oh, mighty falls Vanora, I have come on behalf of my people to . . . ask forgiveness and . . . seek your wisdom to . . . to understand how I may save my people from Gaia's wrath." On finishing her request Naomi was at once filled with a sense of scepticism, emanating from the fall.

"Why would you come to me for such advice?"

"I have heard of your great power and . . . and wisdom and thought you could help me."

"Who has told you of me?"

Naomi was stumped for a moment, and then said:

"Cachada . . . of the river people, she has praised your strength and good judgement."

"Cachada sent you to *me*?"

"Yes, she said you could advise me how best my people could make up for the wrongs they have done and so be worthy of leniency from Gaia."

"Make up for a millennia of desecration and murder?" Naomi knew immediately she had made a mistake, her body shuddered as the fall's hatred took hold of her. "You come to me in your human arrogance and think now, when mankind is finally receiving the punishment it deserves for wreaking havoc on the earth, you can somehow replace the forests you have stripped clean, the waters you have polluted, renew the earth you have ravaged and . . ." Naomi, unable to withstand the intensity of the fall's antipathy, buckled over and its waters began crashing down on her once more, deafening her to anything else it had to say. On her knees, she held her hands to her head, in a futile attempt to protect herself from its crushing weight.

Meanwhile, Rydanna had crossed the falls safely and had signalled for Elliott to start crossing. He was almost across when there was a roar from the falls and he, like Naomi, was forced to his knees. Rydanna tried to re-enter the falls, but was thrown forcefully back, as were Lugh and Marcus, who were attempting the same feat from their side. Naomi and Elliott continued to struggle under the pummelling water. All at once, there was a loud rumbling beneath them and they were sliding, uncontrollably, down a sheer rock face. Naomi held her breath and closed her eyes. However, as she steeled herself for the inevitable impact, the rock face began to gradually curve, slowing her velocity. Next, she flew through the air for a moment, then came down with a splash, flat on her back in a sea of mud. It was pitch black. She couldn't move for a moment, surprised to still be alive, then she remembered Elliott.

"Elliott! Elliott" she called through the blackness, while trying to stand up in the muddy surface.

"Miss! Miss! It's okay I'm here." Elliott called back, wiping off the tacky mud which held him down.

Elliott's voice was near, but Naomi couldn't see him. Then she heard him, squelching through the mud.

"Stay where you are," she called. "Just move your feet up and down in the mud and I'll move towards the sound."

Elliott did as she asked and Naomi moved towards him, arms outstretched. It wasn't long before Naomi's hands had found Elliott's head and were pulling him into a relieved embrace.

"Oh! Thank heavens you're all right . . . you are all right, aren't you?"

"I think so. I can't feel any pain anywhere." Naomi continued to hold him. "I'm fine, Miss . . . you can let me go now."

"Oh! Right . . .of course," she said, letting go of him with a gentle pat on his arms. "Well . . . erm . . . our eyes should get used to the dark soon, then we should be able to get a better idea of where we are."

"I think I can already see a light, Miss."

"Where?"

"Behind you, Miss."

Naomi turned round and sure enough, in the far distance, there was something shining. Whether it was a light, or some kind of ore, there was no way of knowing. But, without any other options, they began to squelch their way cautiously towards it.

It was heavy going, the mud was deep and claggy. Eventually, they reached the shining object, which turned out to be a white ore running in seams along the walls of a tunnel

"I think it's silver, Miss . . . this must be a silver mine."

Elliott's assumption seemed to be borne out by the presence of the broken-down wheelbarrow; they almost tripped over; laying on its side just inside the entrance of the tunnel.

"If this a mine, Miss it might lead up to the surface."

"That's true," but, Naomi thought to herself, it could also lead to a dead end.

She listened in the darkness, hoping to hear one of the others fall into the murky pit. No one did.

"Okay . . . let's give it a try," she said.

They began to make their way along the tunnel, following the shining ore deposits. Inside the tunnel it was even darker than the cavern they had just left, and so close that breathing was difficult. They were soon both exhausted and breathing heavily, but they forced themselves on. After some time, Naomi decided they should rest, she could hear Elliott behind her struggling for breath. They both flopped down onto the damp floor. After a few minutes, Elliott broke their spent silence.

"Miss . . . do you think what Lugh said was true, about there being . . . ancient creatures down here?"

Naomi thought for a moment and was just about to say something reassuringly benign, but the words stuck in her throat, and she found herself saying.

"I don't know . . . I could lie to you and tell you everything is going to be fine, but I think you've seen enough to know for yourself that what Lugh said could be true. Let's hope that they are just stories, but we need to keep our wits about us, just in case."

"Thanks, Miss."

"What for?"

"For not treating me like a kid."

The tears stung Naomi's eyes, because . . . he *was* a kid, she thought.

"I'm sorry," she said.

"What for, Miss?"

"Not being able to keep the fall's attention, it's my fault you're in this mess. I should have made you go back."

"Nothing and no one could have made me go back, Miss, and as for the fall, well . . . whatever it is you can do, you've only been doing it for a short time. I mean a few of weeks ago you didn't even know you could do it. We all make mistakes when we're learning something new, I think you were really brave to try."

"Thank you," Naomi smiled.

"You're welcome, Miss."

A few weeks Naomi mused, was that all it had been since this nightmare adventure had begun. Only a few weeks since they had rambled pleasantly along, listening to Elliott's lecture on the fells.

"You know a lot about the outdoors, where did you learn it all?" Naomi asked.

"Books mainly and I was in the scouts . . . until . . . mum and dad split up and they . . . put me in the home."

"I'm sorry about that, it must have been hard on you."

"Yeah, well. Stuff happens."

"Yes . . . it does . . ." Naomi said, reflecting on her own childhood and feeling at that moment a deep affinity with Elliott; she understood his feelings of abandonment, she had felt them herself. There was no point in dwelling on the past though, right now their present was precarious enough. "Are you ready to go on?"

"Yeah."

Slowly, they got to their feet and continued on. Eventually, and all at once, they felt a gush of cool, stagnant air and the tunnel began to widen until it opened out into a dimly lit grotto. Stalagmites and stalactites were dotted about the ceiling and the floor. The walls were black, and water trickled down them, creating a thin sheet of blue liquid, which covered the floor. Elliott immediately bent down, scooping up some water into his hands to quench his overpowering thirst.

"Wait a minute," Naomi cautioned. "We don't know if it's potable."

"Potable?"

"Whether it's safe to drink or not."

Elliott put his hand to his face and smelled the water.

"It smells a bit funny, Miss, but there's no reason why it shouldn't be drinkable, it's coming from the rivers and falls above."

"Okay . . . but I'll drink it first."

The water tasted strange, sort of tinny in Naomi's mouth. After drinking, and waiting a few moments with no adverse effect, Naomi nodded to Elliott that he could drink. After they had taken their fill of water they began to survey their surroundings. Primitive, broken and rusted mining equipment was scattered everywhere and although this showed that the mine was no longer in use, the light from the dying torches suggested that it hadn't been completely abandoned and that someone may have been there fairly recently. While that was a worry, (not knowing who or what that someone may be) it also meant that there was probably a way out. And sure enough, although three sides of the grotto were closed in by the black rock, there was a wide archway leading out. Naomi and Elliott splashed their way toward it.

They had hardly made any headway when they felt the ground beneath them move. They both stopped to steady themselves and, thinking it was another earthquake, they each instinctively looked around them for falling debris. Instead of falling rocks, however, they were shocked to see the walls around them ripple and, even more disturbingly, charcoal figures begin to slide from the rock face and lumber their way towards the archway.

"I think they're going to block the exit, Miss."

"Run . . . RUN!" Naomi shouted.

They ran as fast as they could towards the exit, but it was too late. The figures were already closing together to make a solid wall, barring the way through the arch. Once the wall was complete, it began to move towards them. They turned to run the other way, only to find a duplicate wall of stone men also shifting their way towards them. Turning her head every which way, looking for a way to escape, Naomi felt a tug on her arm.

"There's a ledge, Miss," Elliott said, pointing up towards the rock face.

Looking up, Naomi could just make out, above one of the fading torches, a narrow ledge.

"If we can reach the ledge, Miss we can climb along and out."

"We need something to climb on so we can reach it," Naomi said.

They both looked around frantically at the broken mine equipment. Naomi spotted a rusted wheelbarrow.

"The barrow!" she shouted. "Quick help me move it."

They dragged the barrow until it was just underneath the torch, then turned it upside down.

"See if you can reach and pull yourself up?" Naomi said.

Elliott climbed on the barrow and reached up to the protruding brace, which was holding the torch in place. He couldn't quite reach it.

"I'll hold the barrow in place, and you jump and try and reach it," Naomi said.

"What about you, Miss?"

"I'm taller than you I'll be fine. Do it Elliott . . . NOW!"

Seeing the walls were getting closer and closer, for once, Elliott didn't argue. He jumped up and caught the brace first time, then managed to scramble up the wall and use the brace as a boost onto the ledge. Naomi gave a sigh of relief.

"Hurry up, Miss! They're nearly on top of you," Elliott warned.

Sure enough, there was only about a metre on each side between her and the malevolent barricades. Quickly, she climbed onto the barrow and grabbed hold of the brace and began her ascent. Just as the walls closed together, she felt Elliott's hand on her back helping to steady her as she clambered onto the ledge.

They both knelt on the ledge for a moment shaking, then gradually they got to their feet. Elliott took the lead as they began to edge their way along towards the archway. No sooner had they started to move than the granite figures beneath them started to shift back towards the arch. Naomi and Elliott felt their precarious perch tremor, they fastened themselves closer to the wall and cautiously continued on, trying desperately to keep ahead of the figures beneath them. At last, they reached the archway, unfortunately, there was no way to climb down.

"We'll have to jump, Miss."

"It's too far."

"It's either that . . . or get eaten by the stone people."

Naomi let out a sigh of resignation.

"Okay . . . but I'll go first."

"It's fine, Miss, it looks like the waters deeper on this side."

"Elliott, noooo!"

Elliott flew threw the air and hit the ground, not with a splash, but with a humph, as if he had landed on cushions.

"Elliott . . . Elliott," Naomi called out.

"I'm fine, Miss, it's not water it's . . . well it's . . ."

"What . . . what is it?"

"They're cobwebs, Miss."

"Oh no!" Just then, the ledge shuddered violently and feeling it give underneath her Naomi closed her eyes tightly . . . and jumped.

"Ahhhh! Yuck . . . yuck," Naomi dragged the sticky webs off her

"I don't think there's much point doing that, Miss, they're everywhere."

"Come on let's get out of here . . . before their owners come back."

Naomi and Elliott began to wade through the tacky quagmire, with each step there was an ominous crackling underfoot. More webs hung all around them, Naomi flinched every time she touched one and was so busy concentrating on trying to avoid them that she tripped over something large and awkward.

"Ow!"

"Miss . . . Miss . . .! Are you okay," Elliott cried.

"I think so . . . what is it.? she asked.

Elliott, with a surprised look on his face, was examining the object she had fallen over.

"It's Lugh, Miss."

"What . . .! Are you sure?"

"Yes, Miss."

Naomi scrambled her way towards, the lifeless, Lugh; he looked deathly pale. Naomi checked to see if he was breathing. He was, but only just. She tried to lift his head, but found he was stuck to the floor.

"We need something to break him free," she said.

Elliott, bravely Naomi thought, began to scrabble about on the floor looking for something they could use, and within a few moments presented her, unceremoniously, with a skeletal arm. She jumped at the sight of it. Elliott merely shrugged. Squeamishly, Naomi took it from him and began to hack away at the web that held Lugh fast. Elliott, further discovering what looked like a leg bone, joined in. Once they had cut Lugh free of his web prison, Naomi tried to wake him by gently shaking him and calling his name. He gave no response. Elliott leant down close to his ear and shouted his name, prodding him hard with the leg bone. Lugh remained unconscious.

"We're going to have to take him with us," Elliott said.

"How?" Naomi said, staring down at, the not unsubstantial, Lugh.

"We'll have to. . . pull him." Naomi gave him a look of incredulity. "We can't leave him here, can we? Look, you get one arm I'll get the other."

They both took one of Lugh's arms and pulled as hard as they could, straining under the weight, but managing to move him incrementally along the floor, stopping for a moment between each pull.

"This is going to take forever!" Naomi cried.

"Just keep pulling, Miss."

At Elliott's command, Naomi couldn't help thinking for a moment that she had suddenly become the child and Elliott the adult.

They huffed and puffed their way along the floor of the cavern, constantly on the lookout for a way out of the spiders' den. Until at last . . .

"Look, Miss, a doorway!" Elliott called out.

A few meters to their left there was a crudely hewn doorway, they dragged their burden towards it.

"What's that noise?" Naomi froze, listening intently.

"I can't hear anything," Elliott said.

"Shhh! Listen."

There was now a distinct scuttling noise echoing all around them. In silent understanding, they began straining to pull the immobile Lugh towards the doorway as fast as they could, the scuttling getting closer and closer.

Terrified, they pulled with all their might, and stumbled through the rough doorway, dropping Lugh, unceremoniously, the minute they were through. Once free of their burden, Naomi immediately began looking for a way to block the entrance to the now, hundreds of giant spiders they could see hastening towards them. The doorway had nothing holding it up and was cut straight out of the rock wall. If they could just somehow collapse the doorway, Naomi thought. Then, almost instinctively, she placed her hand on the side of the doorway and closing her eyes; so as not to be distracted by the awful sight coming towards them; imagined the rocks around the opening collapsing. Almost at once, she felt the rock beneath her hand begin to shudder. The sound of scuttling stopped. Encouraged by the reaction, she concentrated even harder on her goal, and feeling the rock give way in her hand jumped back, just in time, as the doorway caved in, blocking the way of their attackers.

"See, Miss . . . you're getting better all the time."

Naomi let out a short laugh at Elliott's declaration of encouragement. That was one problem solved, she thought, but now they had the problem of what to do next. The cavern they were in now was cramped and it was again difficult to breathe. There were three tunnels coming off it and Naomi had no idea which one to take, and even if she had known, there was the added problem of Lugh. There was no way they could carry on dragging him along, but how could they just leave him there. Elliott looked at her expectantly,

"I think we should rest here for a bit," she said, "see if Lugh wakes up, or starts to recover."

"Okay, Miss."

They both sat down, utterly spent, next to Lugh's still body. After some minutes of sitting Elliott broke the silence.

"Miss, can I ask you a question?"

"Of course," Naomi answered, stifling a yawn.

"You know the Magician, at the castle?"

"Yes."

"Well, I've been wondering . . . I mean . . . he gave Hannah, Ruth and Luke a gift . . . but he didn't give me anything. Why do you think that was . . . do you think it's because I'm bad?"

"Oh! Of course not!" Naomi exclaimed. Then thinking for a moment she said, "I think that he gave you what you wanted most, excitement and adventure. That's why you're here, isn't it?"

"I suppose it is . . . I never thought of it that way. Miss, do you think Luke really was moving that planet?"

"It wasn't a planet, Elliott, it was a sphere," Naomi answered, in her best teacher mode. "And I'm sure Quinn was manipulating the whole thing."

"I'm not so sure, Miss."

"Why?"

"Well . . . when we got back to our room that night, Luke was making the pla . . . sorry, sphere move up and down. Not like when the magician was there, just simple movements."

"It's probably just some clever toy." Naomi said, dismissively. She had not much liked the Magician, for all his spectacular 'tricks,' and she felt uncomfortable at the thought of Luke being influenced by him in any way.

"You're probably right, Miss," Elliott said, stretching and yawning loudly.

They both lapsed back into silence.

Naomi tried hard to think of how they were going to escape their present situation, but she was too tired. She felt Elliott's body slump onto her arm; he was fast asleep. Her own head began to droop, she shook herself awake. She had to try and keep watch, there was no telling what other dangers awaited them in the dark. It was a losing battle though and her head began to droop once more. She forced her eyes open. Then, in her state of torpor, she thought she saw several spherical lights, about the size of footballs, bobbing towards them from one of the tunnels. Closer and closer they came, until eventually the whole cavern was full of light, but it wasn't a glaring light, it was . . . magical. A soothing warmth spread through her tired, aching body, filling her with deep feeling of calm; and then she was moving, she had no idea how. Just gently floating along. She could see the walls passing by, but it was like looking through a prism, the whole world was aglow. She took a deep, soothing breath, and closed her eyes.

CHAPTER SEVENTEEN

Blue Caps

Elliott woke up with a start. "Miss . . .!" Disoriented, he shot up and looked around for Miss. The sight that met his eyes was spellbinding. He was sitting in a, gorgeously apparelled, four poster bed set in a grotto. The grotto was lit by a myriad of muted coloured lights pulsating, hypnotically through limestone structures formed into giant mushrooms. Stalactites hung from the ceiling like stone chandeliers. Stalagmites made up the grotto walls, walls which had been formed over centuries into shapes of billowing clouds, and alabaster pipes; like those of a giant church organ; all mixing together to create a truly stunning scene.

Hewn, expertly into one of the walls, was a small fountain. Water fell into its translucent, lace patterned basin from a single, silver spout fashioned into a dragon's head. The sight of the flowing water awoke Elliott to the fact that he was very thirsty.

He climbed out of the sumptuous bed on to the stone floor, which felt unexpectedly warm under his feet, and walked over to the fountain. At the back of the basin there was a stone cup. Elliott filled it and drank so quickly he almost choked.

"Be careful there is no need to rush."

Elliot swung round at the sound of the unexpected voice; cup in hand; accidentally throwing water over its owner.

"Who are you?"

"I am Gloam." A young woman of tiny proportions floated in the air, wiping herself down from her, unexpected, soaking. She was wearing a luminous lace gown, which like her surroundings pulsated with various colours, her pure white hair lay gently across her shoulders, her skin was pale but glowing, her eyes were round and brimming with inquiry.

"What do you want . . . and where did you come from?" Elliott asked.

"I am here to help you and . . . I come from here."

"Did you bring me here?"

"I was one of those who brought you, yes."

"There was a woman with me, did you bring her too?"

"Yes! The Old One, she is well."

"*Old* . . . I don't think she's that old. In her twenties maybe?"

"Twenties?"

"Yeah. Twenty-five, twenty-six maybe."

Gloam continued to look at him questioningly.

"Doesn't matter . . . There was a man with us too."

"Yes, he is with our healers. He was very sick, but we think we found him just in time."

"So, he'll recover then?"

"We are very hopeful."

"What was wrong with him, do you know?"

"Yes, he was bitten by one of the giant spiders, their bites are fatal, but their venom is slow acting. If caught in time, our healers can administer the remedy and cleanse the victim. We have had to do this many times for the elves, who see it as a rite of passage to hunt the spiders. We try to discourage them, but elves are proud. Their pride will one day be their downfall. The giant spiders are creatures from the ancient times, they mean no harm, but the elves have taught them to fear strangers, it is most unfortunate. My people do what we can to protect both elf and arachnid."

"Who are your people?"

"We are blue cap faeries."

"Oh."

"We have lived in these grottos for centuries, aiding those who share our underground home, and those who have mined it in the past. It is many years since we have seen a human. How did you find your way into the nest?"

"It's a long story."

"Oh! My people love stories," Gloam declared, and stared at Elliott expectantly.

"Err . . . I'm not very good at telling stories you'd be better off hearing it from Miss."

"Miss?"

"Yes . . . the . . . Old One."

"Very well. I look forward to it. Perhaps she could tell us at meal."

"Yeah! I'm sure she will." At the mention of a meal Elliott's ears pricked. "What time will we be eating?"

"Soon, but first you need to get dressed."

Elliott looked down at himself for the first time and was embarrassed to see that he was wearing, what looked like, a girls' nightie.

"Where are my clothes?"

Gloam gestured towards the bed where Elliott's clothes were hanging, good as new, from an ornate hook on the wall. He moved over to the wall and took them down, then looked at Gloam expecting her to leave. She showed no sign of doing so.

"I'd like to get dressed . . . If you don't mind?" he said.

"Of course," Gloam said, accommodatingly. Then, without warning, she moved quickly towards Elliott. She buzzed around him like a firefly, attempting to remove his nightshirt.

"Whoa! Whoa! What are you doing?" Elliott shouted, grappling with his would-be dresser.

"Helping you to dress of course. You really need to stay still it will be much easier."

"I can dress myself . . . *thank you*!" cried Elliott, struggling to disentangle himself from her surprisingly strong grip.

"But I am here to help you," she said, continuing her unwanted attentions.

A pantomime of struggling continued for a few moments until Elliott, afraid that his *helper* was getting the better of him, gave her one almighty push.

"Gerroff!"

Gloam flew backwards, a shocked look on her face.

"You do not wish me to help you?" The shock on her face was matched by the surprise in her voice.

"No . . .! I don't."

Gloam stood fixed to the spot, with a look that said she wasn't sure what to

R. E. BUSBY

do next. Elliott thought she might be hurt and started to feel a bit guilty about how hard he had pushed her.

"I'm sorry, I hope . . . I didn't hurt you?"

"Oh no. I am quite unharmed," she said, continuing to stay put.

After a few more awkward moments, and when Elliott was sure she wasn't going anywhere, he said:

"I want to get dressed . . . alone."

"You wish me to leave you?"

"Yes."

"You are sure?" Gloam asked, incredulously.

"Yes . . . I'm sure." Elliott answered.

"Very well," and with a deep look of scepticism Gloam turned slowly about and left the room.

"Well that was weird." Elliott said out loud. While Gloam, outside the door, was thinking much the same thing.

Elliott dressed quickly, one eye on the door just in case his would be attendant returned. Once dressed, ready to seek out the promised meal, he opened the door to his room and immediately let out a small cry as he almost ran right into Gloam, who was floating directly in the doorway.

"If you follow me, I will take you to meal."

"Thank you," Elliott said, glancing back, and wondering if blue cap faeries could see through doors.

Gloam led Elliott through a myriad of adjoining grottos, eventually stopping in one in which a square table, big enough for four, was laid with a mouthwatering meal of sausages, bacon, eggs, new potatoes and bread.

"We hope the meal is acceptable, we remember the human miners we brought here to heal; or those who got lost in the caverns and were brought here to rest, before we showed them the way to the surface; and this is the sort of fare *they* preferred."

"It's *very* acceptable, thank you," Elliott said, sitting down and tucking in hungrily, watched by a smiling, satisfied Gloam. He hadn't been eating long when Naomi joined him, led by another of the faeries.

"Hiya, Miss," Elliott said, mid chew. "The foods great."

"Well I can see you're enjoying it," Naomi smiled. Then, giving Gloam

156

a nod of acknowledgement, she sat down and began to fill her plate, while introducing her own escort. "Elliott, this is Sprink,"

"Mmmph." Elliott nodded, with a mouth full of bacon, "Zis iz Gloam."

"Pleased to meet you Gloam."

"Pleased to meet you, Miss Old One."

"Miss . . .?" Naomi left it there. She was getting used to being address by unexpected titles. "Do you know about Lugh?" she asked Elliott.

"Yes. They think he's going to be all right."

"Will we be able to see him later?" Naomi addressed her request to Sprink.

"He is sleeping, it will be some time before the remedy completes its work. When he wakes, we will tell you and you may see him then."

"Thank you. Also . . . there were two others with us, another man and a woman."

"Technically she's a river nymph, Miss."

"Yes . . . Well anyway, I wondered if you knew anything of them?"

"I will send searchers to look for them immediately," Sprink answered, and sailed off at once.

Once Sprink had gone, they both sat in silence enjoying their meal, being waited on by the ever-helpful Gloam, as if they were in some sort of bizarre, themed restaurant.

Rested and full to bursting they watched fascinated, as Gloam wafted back and forth, clearing the table and refusing any offers of help from her guests.

"Is there anything else I can get you," she asked.

"Oh no. Thank you," they answered in unison.

"Elliott has told me that you are good at storytelling, Old One, and would tell the story of your journey to the caverns."

"He did, did he?"

Elliott raised his eyebrows and smiled sheepishly.

"Yes. My people love stories and now you are rested I hoped you would tell us your story." Gloam's voice was drenched in expectation.

"You mean you want me to tell it right now?"

"Yes please. We get so few visitors you see and have not heard a new story for many years."

"Alright then . . . sure."

Gloam's eyes widened with joy, and she clapped her hands twice in quick succession. Rolling balls of light began to fly into the grotto from every direction, coming to a stop around the table where Naomi and Elliott were seated; here they hovered for moment and then transformed into a class of diminutive, floating faeries, male, female, young and old all shining expectantly towards Naomi.

Despite the extraordinary sight before her, there was something comforting in the situation, it was as if she were surrounded by her Reception Class waiting for the end of the day story. She found herself slipping easily into teacher mode, telling her story as best she could. The faeries listened intently, never interrupting, except with the occasional intake of breath. She did notice, however, that their faces became more concerned and troubled as she recounted her encounter with the falls, and when she had finished many of her listeners had tears in their eyes.

Gloam moved forward purposefully and looked searchingly at Naomi. After a moment or two others began to call out.

"The Old One has no belief in herself, how can she help us . . .?"

"Yes, how can she bring The Healing?"

"We have waited so long . . ."

"There is no time to find another . . ."

"What can . . ."

Gloam lifted her hand to silence the voices behind her, then cupped Naomi's face in her tiny hands. Naomi felt a charge surge through her body so strong that she thought it would stop her heart, Elliott made to rush to her but was held back by some of the other faeries. Naomi thought she was about to pass out, then all at once she felt a sharp explosion in her chest and a rush of warmth flooded through her.

For a few moments she felt and knew nothing then, as her mind began to refocus, everything around her had a new familiarity to it. Everything she had experienced, all the different races she had met, they were no longer strange fairy tales come to life in a grotesque dream, rather it was as if she had always known of their existence. Their past associations with mankind filled her mind. She witnessed the separation of their peoples. In the present day she saw those from the faerie world sometimes touch the fringes of the human world, where they were passed off, by those who saw them, as over-tiredness or an over active imagination; but still they watched, some with disdain and hatred, others, with faith and optimism, but all were waiting, waiting for something . . . someone . . . then all at once Naomi knew the future . . . *her* future. She met Gloam's gaze with a new understanding.

"There is hope . . ." Gloam said, smiling. Then releasing her hold on Naomi turned to the others and continued, "The knowledge of the Old Ones still exists in her, it merely needed to be reawakened." She directed this last remark to Naomi.

"I need you to show me the way out of here as soon as possible." Naomi said, her voice edged with a new determination which surprised, a somewhat bemused, Elliott. "Have your people had any luck finding our other friends?"

"I will send someone to enquire." Gloam turned and directed one of the others to find out how the search was progressing, at the same time, dismissing the group as a whole. "I will see that provisions are made up for you. While I am gone, please feel free to look round our home, I think you will find many things of beauty and interest."

"Thank you," Naomi said. "For *everything*."

Gloam beamed a smile back at them both and flew from the cavern.

Gloam was right, the grottos were beautiful, and Elliott found so many interesting fossils, minerals and ores to admire that the time flew by and almost before they knew it, Gloam had returned and she wasn't alone, a much-dishevelled Marcus was with her.

"As you see we have found your friend. He was lost in one of the many abandoned mines that exist in the level below where we found you."

"It's good to see you," Naomi said.

"And you . . . Lugh?"

"He was bitten by a spider. Our friends," Naomi nodded in Gloam's direction, "are taking care of him, and they say he should be okay. What about Rydanna?"

"I think she managed to avoid the fall into the caverns, she is probably waiting for us on the surface."

"But what if she isn't? We can't leave her down here," Elliott declared.

"Did you not say that Rydanna was a river nymph?" Gloam asked.

"Yes, I did," Elliott answered.

"Then you need not fear for her safety, there are many rivers that run through these caverns, your friend will merely have to find one and follow it to the surface. River and sea nymphs often visit us, to enjoy the beauty of our caverns, and explore the old waterways. She will be quite safe."

Gloam turned her attention to Marcus. "We will take you where you can wash and eat, and after you have had some rest, we will lead you all to the surface."

"I will thank you for the wash and food, but I do not need rest. We need to be moving on."

Gloam gave him a look tinged with reproof, but merely answered:

"Very well, follow me please."

Marcus followed Gloam from the grotto, leaving Naomi and Elliott alone once more. Having now explored the caves there was little for them to do but wait patiently for Marcus' return. While they waited, Elliott began to ruminate on the scene he had witnessed between Naomi and Gloam.

"Miss . . . what happened to you when Gloam touched your face, it looked . . . well . . . really painful."

"I'm not sure how well I can explain it. Everything suddenly became. . . real, all of this I mean."

"I could have told it was real, Miss, I have the bumps and bruises to prove it," Elliott moved uncomfortably in his chair as if to emphasise his point.

"Well I've felt like I was in some sort of bad dream, but when Gloam touched my face, it was as if . . . she passed on to me a millennia of history, the history that exists between the human race and all the races we have met here. A history that has been hidden from us all. This ability I've inherited, I felt it pass down to me through the ages, understood for the first time its potential . . . its . . ." Elliott's face was a mixture of confusion and worry. "I don't know if I'm making any sense, even as I'm telling you, a lot of what I felt is fading again . . . like a dream does when you wake up. What I do know is, that I have to go on, I have to reach Gaia, no matter what."

"You're not alone, Miss. You've got me, Marcus, Rydanna, Woodlan and Lugh . . . well maybe Lugh. What are we going to do about Lugh, Miss, I mean if he's not well enough to come with us?"

"I'm afraid we'll have to leave him behind there's . . ."

"*Leave me behind . . .* I don't think so."

A very pale looking Lugh was stumbling towards them, attempting to tie up his shirt, squeeze into one shoe, while tripping over the lace on another, all the time endeavouring not to drop his coat, which hung precariously over one arm. He had the look of a man who was on the run. Sure enough, he was quickly followed by three very distressed looking blue caps, all talking at once.

"You are not well enough to leave your room . . . the remedy has not had enough time to work . . . please you need more rest . . . let us take you back . . ."

"Really, I'm fine, I'm a strong fellah you'd be surprised . . . I can manage . . . really."

Seeing they were getting nowhere with their reluctant patient, the blue caps appealed to Naomi.

"Please, Old One, tell him he must come with us . . . look how pale he is . . . he will not listen . . ."

Trying to keep a straight face Naomi looked at the disarranged Lugh. He did look deathly pale, and he probably could do with a little more rest, but she also knew from the steel in his eyes that there was no way they were going to able to keep him there.

"I understand what you're saying but, I think you're fighting a losing battle." Seeing the deep disappointment in the blue cap's eyes she quickly added, "Couldn't you make up some of the remedy, so we could take it with us? I'd make sure he took it as often as needed, and that he rests as much as possible." The little nurses didn't look convinced but, after an exchange of glances, gave a collective nod and swept away.

"While I am very grateful for all the blue caps have done," Lugh said, looking relieved at his escape, "they are a little too up close and personal for me, if you know what I mean?" Lugh punctuated his statement with a slow wink, which Elliott returned with a look that said, 'I certainly do know.'

"You do look awful though," Elliott said.

"I will be honest with you laddie, I have felt better. Where are the others?"

"Marcus is here," Naomi answered, "and he believes Rydanna is waiting for us on the surface."

"How is Marcus?"

"He's fine. He just got lost in one of the mines, he's cleaning up and getting a meal. Once he's ready the blue caps say they'll show us the way to the surface."

As if on cue, Gloam entered with several other blue caps carrying four very old back packs, and Naomi and Elliott's coats. They placed them on the table and floated off, leaving only Gloam with their guests.

"Your supplies are ready. We have filled your flasks with water from the lake Glihean, it lies deep in the earth surface, so deep that only my people can reach it. Its water has restorative powers and should aid you on your journey, as one sip is sufficient to quench any thirst. I also have some other gifts for you." Here she clapped her hands, and two blue caps entered the grotto, each carrying a bow, and a quiver full of arrows, which they handed to Lugh and Elliott.

"We are much obliged to you I'm sure," Lugh said.

Gloam returned Lugh's words of appreciation with a look which made it clear that she had met with Lugh's 'nurses,' and agreed fully with their diagnosis. Lugh smiled uncomfortably back at her.

"Wow!" Elliott exclaimed on receipt of the weapon. "Brilliant."

"You know how to use it then?" Lugh asked, playfully.

"Well, I've had a bit of practice."

Naomi knew that Elliott was referring to the one lesson he had had on the school camping trip so added quickly.

"But I'm sure he would be grateful for a few more lessons."

"Don't worry laddie, I will teach the ways of the bow, and glad to do it."

Elliott gave Lugh a broad smile of anticipation.

Gloam, turned away from Lugh and Elliott to face Naomi.

"For you, I have this," she said, producing from inside her glowing robe, a long grey pouch with a strap attached. Then, she pulled out of the prosaic sleeve what could only be described as . . . a stick! It was about thirty centimetres long, mottled silvery grey in colour, and at one end it had a light brown tip, where the bark had been scraped off. Naomi looked at it with a furrowed brow.

"It is a rowan branch," Lugh revealed, his eyes widening.

Naomi continued to look perplexed.

"It is said," Gloam continued, "that the rowan tree was chosen by the Ancient Ones, from all the trees, to assist humankind in connecting with the natural world. The old ones, those like yourself, used it to enhance their abilities, that is why I give it to you now. It could be said to create a bridge between you, and the elements you are attempting to communicate with. It will aid you in clearing your mind and allow you to channel your power more effectively through it."

She placed the branch in Naomi's hand. Lugh and Elliott held their breath in anticipation. Naomi closed her hand slowly around the branch, and waited, expectantly . . . Nothing happened.

"You need to get to know one another," Gloam said, recognising Naomi's disappointment. "Give it time. The branch has lain dormant for many seasons you must learn to trust one another."

If Gloam had told her this just a few hours ago Naomi would have struggled to believe her, but now she just smiled and thanked her, sure in the knowledge that what she told her was true.

At this moment Marcus returned, looking clean and refreshed, he was escorted by Lugh's three, would-be carers. Each of which began to fuss once again around Lugh; telling him to put the remedy in a safe place, and to make sure he took a spoonful of it twice a day; then turning to Naomi, they made it quite clear that they held her responsible for making sure Lugh did as he had been told. Naomi nodded her assent vigorously to their commands and Lugh, in his turn, tolerated their fretting with good humour. After a few minutes, Gloam shooed them away while the group picked up their packs to make ready to leave; Naomi pulling the pouch that held the Rowan branch over her head and straightening the strap carefully across her chest.

Gloam clapped her hands once more and a blue cap brought in a leather scabbard. She handed it to Marcus who, grabbing hold of the hilt, drew out a magnificent silver sword which shone dazzlingly in the glowing grotto.

"The sword was forged by my people from the silver found in these mountains," Gloam said. "The silver is rare, and so is the sword, you will never need to sharpen it, and its strength is unparalleled. It has never been used my people have held onto it for such a time as this. We knew there would be a reckoning after the separation, the sword was forged in anticipation of this. While it may seem a symbol of war, it was made to bring peace, you must use it to protect the Old One." Marcus nodded his understanding.

The 'Old One' quailed somewhat at the thought of what danger may lie in their path that would require such a powerful weapon to protect her.

Gloam lit their way to the surface. Leading them assuredly through a maze of tunnels. Until, at last, they came to an opening in the rock face, wide enough for them all to climb through. Gloam explained that they were now on the edge of the elf country, but would still be in danger from the elves, as it would probably take them one or two days to cross over into the north lands. She wished them safe passage and hoped they would find the rest of their journey less arduous. Gloam said her goodbyes while still underground, explaining that her people very rarely came above ground during the day, as they found the natural light difficult on their eyes. Naomi was truly sorry to say goodbye, she had felt a strength and confidence in Gloam's presence that she was loath to lose.

They climbed out into a bright, sunny July morning and, despite the loss of Gloam's reassuring influence, Naomi felt a new sense of hope in their journey. The terrain before them was green and undulating, interlaced with large patches of colourful wildflowers, babbling streams and clusters of green wooded areas. For a moment, Naomi was seduced by its beauty into forgetting the possible dangers it held for them.

This feeling did not last long, however, as a caution from Marcus, 'to keep a keen look out, as the elves would have scouts out everywhere looking for them,' was a stark reminder of the despising elves who were now, in effect ... hunting them.

CHAPTER EIGHTEEN

Keeping Low

They made their way swiftly across the deceptive landscape. Naomi was pleased to discover that she was no longer struggling to keep up with Marcus, in fact she felt stronger and fitter than she had ever felt in her life. She couldn't help smiling to herself, as she remembered all those times in the staff room when she had had, 'just one more biscuit,' and said how she was going to start her fitness regime tomorrow; well, she reflected, 'now I'm on the boot camp to end all boot camps.'

Elliott, who ran close to her, was also keeping up with the rapid pace easily, a look of adventure etched on his face, a look which took the smile from Naomi's. She worried that to him it was still some sort of game. The quiver of arrows shifted easily across his back, Naomi's stomach contracted as she thought that he, an eleven-year-old boy, might have to use them to defend himself. She pushed the thought from her mind and refocused, there was no point in dwelling on what she couldn't change. Everything was different now, the world was turned upside down and if she didn't get to Gaia and make her plea, she knew that Elliott wouldn't be the only boy having to grow up before his time.

They stopped only once to eat and drink. Gloam had not exaggerated the properties of the water of Glihean, not only did it quench their thirst with one mouthful but equally held off the pangs of hunger. When they stopped for the night, Marcus said they had made good time and should make it to the border of the north lands by the end of the next day. They all breathed a little easier at this news.

They made camp without a fire because it might be seen by the elves. Luckily, the food the blue caps had filled their bags with; which was wrapped in a kind of grease proof paper and consisted of flat bread, dried meat and fruit; required no cooking. They ate with relish and after their meal Lugh gave a very pleased, and willing, Elliott some archery lessons. Elliott surprised them all with his natural ability and Naomi praised his efforts with all the enthusiasm of a proud parent. Eventually, it got too dark to see properly, so they all made their beds, Marcus taking the first watch. The blankets the blue caps had supplied them with looked, and felt, so thin Naomi prepared herself for a chilly night. However, once she had wrapped herself in it, she found it to be surprisingly warm and comfortable and was blissfully asleep within a few minutes of lying down.

She awoke, just as dawn was breaking. Sitting up and stretching, she saw that Lugh now sat in the spot where Marcus had been on lookout the night before. Elliott still slept on soundly, but there was no sign of Marcus. She stood up and walked over to Lugh.

"Good morning."

"Good morning, Miss."

"Where's Marcus?"

"He's scouting a bit ahead, checking the way is clear and seeing if he can find any sign of Rydanna."

"Do you think she's okay?"

"I do not know, we would have expected to hear from her by now, but it is likely that she is just laying low . . . Wait a minute, you could find her."

"Me?"

"Aye! With the rowan branch. I have only heard of them in stories mind, but if those stories are true, it is a powerful thing you have there, Miss."

Naomi unconsciously touched the pouch lying across her chest and felt a tingling in her hand, she examined her hand . . . nothing . . . she laid her hand on the pouch again and . . . yes, there was definitely a warmth coming from it that she had not felt when she had first put it on.

"What is it?" Lugh asked.

"I don't know . . . it . . . it . . . feels different. I can't explain it."

"Maybe you're getting to *know* each other."

"Maybe," Naomi smiled. "Here's Marcus."

Marcus was making his way rapidly towards them and when he reached them it was clear he was deeply concerned about something.

"What have you seen?" Lugh asked.

"Nothing, nothing at all. No birds, no animals . . . nothing."

"You're thinking it's too quiet?" Lugh said.

"There is something out there . . . *someone*. I could feel them watching me."

"Elves?" Lugh said.

"I would say so."

"What's up?" Elliott had woken up and was now standing next to them, yawning and rubbing his eyes.

"Elves," Lugh said.

"Where?" Elliott spun around, taking up a defensive stance which, despite the danger they were in, brought a half smile to the adults' faces.

"In the fields, I think," Marcus answered.

"What are we gonna' do?" Elliott asked.

"Make our way through the wooded areas, where there is more cover," Marcus said.

Naomi and Elliott eyes widened slightly at this suggestion.

"I know we have not had the best of experiences travelling through the woods, but travelling in the open is too dangerous, we would be easy targets for the elves," Marcus cautioned.

"But Miss has the rowan branch now," Elliott countered, confidently.

Naomi felt a pang of anxiety at the mention of the branch again and wished she shared Elliott's confidence in her ability to use it to help them.

"That is true, but it does not mean we should take any unnecessary risks," Marcus replied.

"Before you came back, I was suggesting that the branch could be used to find Rydanna," Lugh said.

"It is possible," Marcus agreed. "But I think Rydanna will find *us* when *she* is ready."

"Well, if anyone would know what Rydanna might do, you would. So, I bow to your greater knowledge."

For some reason Naomi felt a slight tension in her stomach at Lugh's reference to Marcus' 'knowledge' of Rydanna, there was a playfulness in his tone that suggested a relationship between the two that went beyond mere friendship, Marcus' face remained passive.

"I think it best that we eat breakfast quickly and get on our way," Marcus said.

In less than half an hour they were beneath the shade of a narrow wood that curved a sinuous path along the edges of the flat land. Marcus took the lead; Naomi was directly behind him and thought that she had never seen

167

him so on edge before. His worry transferred itself to her. She kept looking back at Elliott to check that he was okay until she realised that this, was in turn, worrying Elliott. She forced herself to stop looking back and content herself with listening for anything that could signal danger. After a couple of hours, they came to the edge of the wood. There was an expanse of open countryside for about fifty meters, before the wooded path began again. Marcus stopped and said nothing for some time, lost in thought, staring out at a seemingly harmless flower strewn meadow. The others stood behind him waiting patiently for his orders. Naomi found herself musing on how any other day the sight before her would have caused her to stop in admiration of its beauty, but now she saw only the possible threat posed to them by crossing its exposed expanse. The little group continued to wait on Marcus, but he was not the first to speak.

"Why don't we crawl across it, commando style?" Elliott's whispered suggestion turned all faces towards him, and while Naomi knew what he meant, Marcus and Lugh answered him with quizzical expressions. "Flat on our stomachs, using our arms to pull us along," Elliott explained, with accompanying gestures.

"That isn't a bad idea the laddie has there," Lugh said. "It would certainly make us less of a target, Marcus."

"It would also mean that we would struggle to see anyone coming towards us, they could overpower us before we knew it," Marcus countered. Elliott looked crestfallen. "But, staying low *is* a good idea," Marcus added quickly, much to Elliott's delight. "We need to spread out, we don't want to make one easy target for whoever may be out there. We'll all go at once, moving as fast as we can. Ready?" They all nodded their assent. "Now!"

At Marcus' command, they all took off, running low, spread out across the meadow; Naomi keeping Elliott in her sights, as he zig-zagged towards the wood. The pack swung awkwardly on her back, and she had to work hard at not falling over. To her relief, they made it to the wood without incident. But no sooner had she followed Elliott into the wood when she felt a sharp pang in her side causing her to cry out in pain. Marcus and Elliott looked back at her. Lugh was already firing arrows at their assailants.

Naomi felt sick to her stomach, and everything began to go out of focus. Blinking hard, she saw the shimmer of Marcus' sword, as he pulled it from its sheath, and then, to her horror, she saw Elliott trying to load his bow, while having to dodge arrows coming at him from all sides. She grabbed at her stomach and felt the rowan branch. She tried to take it from its pouch, but couldn't get a grip on it, then the world began to spin and everything went black.

CHAPTER NINETEEN

Bonding

Naomi opened her eyes to a distorted shape leaning over her, which gradually formed itself into the familiar shape of Rydanna.

"Here take this." Rydanna lifted Naomi up effortlessly with one arm and held a cup to her lips with the other. Naomi opened her mouth obediently and Rydanna tipped the contents of the cup into her mouth. Naomi gagged almost immediately at the taste, Rydanna held her still in her strong grip.

"You must swallow it; it will help with the pain and healing."

Naomi forced herself to swallow and retched violently when the vile concoction hit her stomach, covering her mouth in an effort to stop herself from bringing it straight back up again.

"Wader . . . please . . . some wader."

Marcus appeared above her and passed his flask to Rydanna, who administered the soothing power of the Glihean water to her, very grateful, patient.

"Thank you," Naomi breathed, as the water washed away the worst part of the taste of her medicine. "What happened?"

"The elves were lying in dens under the floor of the wood, waiting to ambush you as soon as you entered," Rydanna answered, laying Naomi back down.

"Elliott!" Naomi cried, springing back up. "Elliott! What hap. . ."

"I'm here, Miss." Elliott's face appeared in front of her, beaming. "I'm fine."

"He's more than fine," Lugh added with pride in his voice. "Those elves were no match for his bow or his nimbleness. He outmanoeuvred them at every turn."

Elliott shrugged his shoulders and smiled modestly. Then declared, excitedly, "You should have seen Rydanna, Miss, she stormed in like some sort of Ninja, knocking elves everywhere, and Lugh was taking one down with every arrow, then Marcus with his sword sweeping them right left and centre it was like . . ."

"Was anyone killed?" Naomi interrupted. The thought of Elliott seeing anyone killed at such a young age, and seeming to glory in it, filled her with horror.

"Oh no, Miss, we wounded a few before they ran off, but no one was killed, and we have a couple gagged and tied up over there." Elliott signalled with his head behind him. Naomi straightened up and saw two, very miserable, and angry looking elves gagged and tied up back-to-back. "So they don't shout for help, Miss." Elliott said, with a hint of condescension. "Also, they wouldn't shut up about how sorry we were all going to be, and how we would pay *dearly* for what we had done. So Lugh gagged them."

"Well," Naomi said, turning to Lugh, "it looks like you didn't need my help after all."

"Not this time perhaps," Rydanna said, "but if we are to make it to the border of the north lands it will be through your use of the rowan branch."

"In what way?" Naomi asked.

"You are tired, we will discuss it after you have rested," Rydanna said.

It was true, she was tired, not sleepy tired, but bodily tired. She was aware of a dull ache in her left side, just above her hip.

"What happened to me?" she asked. "I mean, I presume I got hit by an arrow, but why did it make me so *ill*?"

"The arrow that hit you had been dipped in the venom of the spiders that live in the blue cap caves," Lugh answered. "A good dose it was too." Naomi's stomach contracted again as she took in the full meaning of Lugh's words; they had meant to kill her.

"What they *didn't* know," Lugh continued, "was that we had the blue cap's remedy."

"What you gave me to drink . . . *that* was the remedy the blue caps gave you?"

"Aye."

"But it tastes disgusting, how is it you can take it so easily?"

"I don't know, I did not think it tasted that bad."

Naomi gave him a look of complete incredulity.

"Having tasted some of your home-made brews over the years," Marcus interjected, "I can well believe that."

"Aye," Lugh said, patting Marcus, heartily on the back. "We've had some good times, with some good brews." The two friends smiled at one another, good naturedly.

"You need to rest," Rydanna's insistent voice broke in. "It won't be long before the elves come back, with reinforcements, and you are going to need all your strength for the task ahead."

Naomi wanted to ask her about 'the task ahead', but the mixture of the venom and the cure had left her feeling so sick she knew Rydanna was right, so she lay back obediently, and was soon asleep again.

When she woke up, she felt little better than when she had fallen asleep.

"How are you feeling?" Lugh asked, helping her to sit up.

"Awful."

"You're going to have to take another dose of the remedy."

The very thought made her sick.

"What about you, don't you need to keep taking it too?"

"Do not worry, the blue caps made up plenty, there is enough for both of us. I have already had my dose."

She knew there was no avoiding it, the blue caps had made it very clear that without the remedy Lugh would have died, so she took a deep breath and swallowed down the vile tasting concoction. She was prepared for it this time, so it wasn't such a shock to her system, and although her stomach turned over a few times she managed to keep it down more easily. Rydanna was crouching over a small fire cooking fish; seeing that Naomi was awake she offered her some, Naomi refused, but Rydanna insisted, saying again 'that she would need all her strength for the coming task.' Naomi swallowed reluctantly but was pleased to discover that the fish actually helped to settle her stomach. As she ate, she looked around her. Marcus was on guard and Elliott was practising his archery skills; the two captured elves were watching him with murder in their eyes. After she had finished her meal Rydanna came to take her plate, and Naomi took the opportunity to ask her what they were going to do next. Rydanna looked furtively back at the two elves, then moved closer to Naomi and in a whisper began to speak to her.

"We must travel the rest of our journey by water, the elves will be waiting ahead for us. There will be too many of them for us to have any chance of avoiding them on land, but there is a river about five miles from here. To reach it we must go back somewhat the way you came, but once there, we will be able to stay ahead of the elves and ride its waters to the border into the north lands."

"What is it that you need me to do?"

"The river is wild at the best of times, but as soon as we begin to make our way over it, it will do all it can to stop us. *You* must use the Rowan branch to make it possible for us to ride the river."

"I see."

Naomi wasn't sure exactly how she was going to achieve this task, but as she felt the branch glow once more, she instinctively knew there would be a way.

Fed and watered once more they packed up their things, leaving the elves to be rescued by their companions, and set off, slightly west of the way they had come, towards the mountains. Naomi felt incredibly shaky on her feet, but refusing Lugh's help, and ignoring the pain in her side, she forced herself on.

* * *

Naomi's progress was slow, she was constantly struggling with waves of nausea and the pain in her side seemed to increase with every step. She was aware that she was slowing the group down and every minute she expected the elves to overtake them. The tension they all felt was tangible. Naomi was also aware that the others were surrounding her like sentinels, protecting her on all sides, she felt a rush of gratitude towards them, but also a deep anguish that she might be the cause of their being caught. Thankfully, after several anxious hours they reached the foot of the mountain range, where a wide river lay rushing and bubbling its way northward.

Rydanna approached a pile of leafy branches, strewn near the edge of the river, and lifted them up to reveal two dug-out canoes.

"Naomi, Marcus and I will take the lead," she said. "Lugh, you and Elliott will follow in our wake."

Then without another word, Rydanna led the others in pushing the canoes onto the water.

Rydanna signalled for Naomi to take the bow, Marcus sat in the middle and Rydanna took the stern, while Lugh took the bow and Elliott the stern in the other canoe. At first, Naomi was relieved to be sitting down, but her relief didn't last long. Almost as soon as Marcus and Rydanna began to paddle into the river the water underneath them began to swell, lifting the canoe high in the water as if it was trying to throw it back onto the shore. Naomi looked back at the canoe holding Elliott and Lugh; the pair were struggling already to keep upright. Naomi felt a rush of panic. Then, Rydanna's voice called through the noise and spray.

"Use the rowan branch."

Naomi scrambled for the branch pulling it from its pouch then instinctively put it in the water. A warm glow tingled through her body; she gripped the branch tightly as the water rushed wildly over it trying to force it from her hand. Feeling a new connection with the branch Naomi, without speaking, called to the waters for calm. At first, they resisted, but she focused her will through the branch and slowly the turbulent water around the two boats began to abate. Naomi kept her eyes closed in order to keep her focus. This meant that she didn't see the incredible sight which surrounded the two vessels.

The water immediately surrounding the boats was calm and smooth, however, no more than a couple of meters on every side of them the river stormed, rising and falling angrily, like a caged animal desperate to pounce on its prey.

On they went. Naomi had no idea of time; how long she had been holding off the angry tide; eventually though, she began to tire and found herself struggling to remain focused. Her arm began to shake under the constant pressure of the water as it continued to fight to free the branch from her grip. Her eyes snapped open, shocked by the scene which surrounded her, she almost pulled the branch from the water. Her strength beginning to fail her, she called back to her companions:

"We're going to have to stop. I need to rest. I can't hold on for much longer."

Rydanna signalled to Lugh and Elliott to make for the shore. Once Naomi could see they were close enough to ground the boats she pulled the branch from the water and, sighing with gratitude, began to massage her quaking arm. The trembling spread through her whole body and for a few moments she couldn't stop shaking. Marcus quickly removed his coat and covered her with it.

"I'm . . . not . . . cold . . . just exhausted," Naomi breathed, heavily.

"We have made good time, and are well ahead of our pursuers, some rest will be good for all of us," Rydanna said.

Naomi felt herself teeter forward and found herself in Marcus' arms. He carried her further up the bank of the river, wrapping his coat more firmly around her and sitting her down up against a large, flat rock. Then, retrieving his pack from the canoe, he removed his blue cap blanket and made a pillow of it behind her head. Taking out his flask he held it to her lips. Somewhat revived by the Glihean water Naomi smiled at him. Marcus returned her smile with a look of deep concern. Finally, checking she was as comfortable as she could be under the circumstances, he left her to join the others who were discussing setting up watches.

The air was warm, and Naomi lifted her face towards the glistening sun, breathing in its strengthening rays. She stayed like this for some time, half awake, half asleep, until Lugh came and administered the remedy to her. She took the dose obediently, like a sick child, then quickly followed it with a sip of the Glihean water and something to eat. Eventually, as the sun began to drop in the sky, she felt well enough to stand. As she did so, Elliott, who had been keeping a close eye on her, rushed to help her up. She thanked him, and the others alerted by her voice turned from their watches towards her.

"I think I'm well enough to go on now," she said.

The others left their sentries and came towards her and Elliott.

"Good," Rydanna said. "If we go now, we have a chance of making the border before nightfall."

Just then Naomi felt the rowan branch quiver and she found herself calling out . . .

"Elves."

The others looked all around, and a volley of arrows suddenly flew amongst them. They all grabbed what they could and ran for the boats; Marcus sweeping up Naomi in his arms and placing her in the boat. The others jumped into the canoes and started rowing frantically. The elves were now visible and running towards them, firing arrows as they ran. The river, in its turn, reacted violently to their return. Naomi plunged the rowan branch into the water, with an assurance which surprised her. The raging waters cowered before her silent call, like a censured dog, her bond with the rowan branch, was complete.

Naomi's power over the water remained firm, her focus was less intense and more natural. She no longer struggled against the river's resistance and so they were able to make it to the border without having to stop again.

It was almost dark when Lugh called out that they had reached Bodach; a giant, round-topped, mountain that marked the border. They paddled towards the nearest bank, pushed the canoes onto its shore and gratefully stood on dry ground again. They all began to make camp. Naomi made a feeble attempt to gather some wood for the fire but was quickly stopped by Lugh. Lugh took a blanket from one of the packs and laid it over Naomi's shoulders and sat her up against a large boulder. Naomi was grateful for the chance to rest for, despite her newfound relationship with the rowan branch, she was exhausted from her exertions on the river and was soon nodding off into a welcome stupor.

"Someone's coming . . .! Someone's coming!" Elliott called out.

On hearing Elliott's cry Naomi lifted her head and looked stupidly around her. The others, weapons in hands, were looking in the direction of Elliott's call. Their alarm didn't last long, however, as they all recognised the large figure striding towards them.

"It's Woodlan!" Elliott cried, happily.

Woodlan's steel, blue eyes beamed on them like a ray of hope. They quickly lost some of their shine, however, on seeing the enfeebled Naomi.

"What happened to, Little Miss?" Woodlan cried out.

"It's a long story," Lugh replied.

"And one I'm waiting to hear," Woodlan said, accusingly.

"Woodlan, I'm okay . . . really," Naomi said.

"Excuse me, Little Miss but you look like you've been to hell and back."

"Oh!" Naomi breathed, somewhat abashed.

"She hasn't had her remedy yet, that will buck her up," Lugh said.

"Remedy? What does she need a remedy for?"

"For the poison," Elliott said.

"Poison!" Woodlan exclaimed. "What have you been doing to the lass?"

"It wasn't us . . . it was the Elves," Elliott protested.

"Well it looks like I'm back just in time," Woodlan said, grabbing the remedy from Lugh, with a look of deep disapproval, and administering it to Naomi as if she were a baby.

Lugh was right, the remedy did go some way to reviving Naomi, some of the colour came back into her cheeks and restored some brightness to her eyes; so much so that Woodlan's look of anxiety softened.

"Some food and a good night's sleep and we'll have you right as rain," he said.

Naomi submitted to Woodlan's nursing, smiling softly as he gently remonstrated with her because of her lack of appetite; eventually lying down to sleep at his command.

CHAPTER TWENTY

Scouting Out Danger

The next day the pain in Naomi's side was reduced to a dull ache and another dose of the remedy, after the usual initial shock to her system, had left her feeling revitalised. While the now constant warmth of the rowan branch next to her chest also filled her with a new found strength and confidence. Woodlan, however, continued to throw anxious glances in her direction as they made their way through the mountains, never letting her get too far from his side.

They continued travelling northward, the wind was north westerly, and Naomi was just thinking how much easier the cooler air made the relentless trekking when she heard a familiar, but unexpected sound.

"A helicopter," she said to herself, and then more loudly. "A helicopter!"

The others heard her call and turned to her, following her upward searching gaze.

"Can you hear it, it's a helicopter?"

The wub, wub, of the helicopter could now be heard distinctly overhead.

"There it is, Miss . . . over there." Elliott said, pointing west of them.

They all looked in the direction Elliott was pointing and saw a rescue helicopter flying towards them. As it got closer, it occurred to Naomi how much faster a helicopter could get them to Gaia, but then she thought, would they believe her, although surely the sight of Woodlan and Rydanna would give credence to her claims. Just as she was debating whether to try and signal to them or not, the helicopter began to change direction. She felt her heart sink as the helicopter moved away from them and realised how, for a moment, she had felt the relief that might have come from sharing her burden with others . . . others of *her* kind. Quickly, however, her feelings of disappointment were replaced by ones of concern. The helicopter was flying erratically, it looked as if the pilot was struggling to keep it on a straight course. The reason for this became clear quite soon; following in its wake was a small cyclone.

The ominous, swirling predator drew closer and closer to its prey, drawing the rotating blades into its menacing black funnel; until its helpless, gyrating quarry was enveloped and hidden from view. The cyclone, continuing its own furious rotation, drew up to the near cliff face and hurled its prey on to it, where it smashed and splintered like a child's toy. Naomi let out a cry of shock and stared on as the cyclone sailed, impassively, out of sight. She jumped slightly as a hand lightly touched her arm. Elliott stood beside her, a look of shock and confusion on his face which matched her own. She covered his hand with hers, and for a moment they were locked together by an understanding of their grief and shared humanity. No one spoke. Eventually, Naomi squeezed Elliott's hand before slowly releasing it and moving on.

They continued journeying north. Naomi traversed the rugged terrain almost blindly; as the helicopter crash played over and over again in her head. After all she had seen and heard, this one single act of seeming random violence affected her the most. It was so merciless and brutal. Mercy. Wasn't that the very thing she was going to Gaia to plead for, mercy for her people. She went cold as she thought of what would happen if Gaia wouldn't listen, or if she didn't even get the chance to ask. She was all at once filled with an urgency she had not felt on the whole journey.

For the next two days she pushed herself to her limit, walking until it was dark, stopping only when she thought that Elliott needed to rest. Unable to sleep, she insisted on taking a turn at watch. Lugh and Woodlan, concerned for her health, tried to slow her down and dissuade her from taking watch. She thanked them for their concern, but she was not to be held back.

On the fourth day there was a change in the weather, which up until now had been cool but dry. Grey clouds intermittently covered the bright, August sun. By mid-afternoon it had begun to rain, just a sprinkling at first, but gradually the sky blackened, and the rain came in torrents. They carried on for as long as they could but eventually, they were forced to take shelter in a cave. Soaked and shivering Naomi watched as the heavens rampaged above. Thunder roared through the cave and lightening tore across the sky, again and again, forcing Naomi and the others back from the cave entrance. Only Rydanna and Woodlan stayed close to the entrance. The rain fell heavily on an ever-impassive Rydanna, Elliott watched on fascinated, as the water touched her then melted, leaving her completely dry. Woodlan stood close to Rydanna, the rain turning his grey figure darker, and causing the peacock feather in his hat to droop dejectedly against his pensive face. At last, the storm began to move away, and the clouds cleared, revealing once more a beautiful clear blue sky, adorned with a warm benevolent sun. They left their shelter; the storm seemed to have done no harm to the rugged terrain surrounding them, but Naomi remembered a similar storm and a blue, sodden ribbon attached to a teddy bear, and quickened her pace.

That night, around the campfire, as the adults sat lost in their own thoughts; Elliott having eaten little and fallen into an exhausted sleep;

Marcus began to reveal the last part of their journey.

"Tomorrow we will reach Lake Doruis, in the middle of the lake lies a small island, that is where we will find access to Gaia. I cannot imagine, after all the resistance we have met, that those who wish to stop us will not make some kind of attempt to prevent us from reaching the island or even getting as far as the lake. There is a faerie settlement not far from here. Lugh, you go there and see if you can find out anything from the locals. Rydanna and I will scout out the surrounding area. Woodlan will stay here to protect Naomi and Elliott."

They all nodded their assent and set off.

*   *   *

Lugh entered the small settlement just before nine o'clock. While it consisted of mostly humble, simply constructed, wattle and daub dwellings, there were a few with some stone structure to them. Predominantly the Inn which, in this primitive place, looked practically palatial with is heavy stone walls and glass windows. Lugh made straight for this well-lit structure.

On opening the door, he was greeted by a low hum of voices, which stopped almost immediately on his entrance. Lugh made his way to the bar, watched closely by the curious patrons.

"I'll have a pint of your best ale," he said.

The woman behind the bar, an unusually heavy-set woman and taller than average for her race, looked Lugh's tall figure up and down with a clinical eye. Then, seemed to decide that he was acceptable.

"We have one ale, and if that's no' good enough for you, you'll have to go elsewhere," she said.

"I'm sure any pint *you* pull will be perfection itself," Lugh smiled.

The woman's demeanour softened; but not for long, as the sound of a snort of derision from somewhere in the bar swiftly returned her to her usual stoic bearing. Lugh, ignoring the disparagement, sat down on one of the bar stools, (which almost gave way under his weight) and continued his charm offensive.

"Are you the owner of this lovely establishment?"

"I am."

"It seems to have stood up well to the recent storm."

Before the owner could answer, a voice called out from behind Lugh.

"Aye that was a rare one, not seen the like in many a year."

Lugh turned towards the voice, which belonged to a man who was sitting leisurely by a blazing fire. He was smoking a pipe, a mug of ale, half drunk, on a small, round table sat in front of him.

"No' rare enough to damage this house, it's been standin' for three hundred years, and it will stand for at least three hundred more," declared the stout landlady.

"It was a rare one nonetheless," the man by the fire concluded. Taking a long, slow puff of his pipe as if to emphasis his pronouncement.

"It must be a mighty strong, well-built building to have also withstood the recent earth shaking without sustaining any damage," Lugh continued, keen to keep the conversation going in the direction that might furnish him with any useful information for what lay ahead of them.

"Earth shaking! There has been no earth shaking here."

This declaration came from man seated at a table close to the bar, with two other men.

"You have been lucky then; the quakes have brought about quite a change in the landscape around you." All the patrons looked keenly at Lugh. "I'm surprised you've no' felt any of their effects."

"Do you think we might get them here then?"

The question came from a young boy, who was collecting glasses and cleaning the tables. His voice was brimming with excitement at the prospect of hearing something that might possibly break the monotony of his life.

"I don't know. I only know that I have seen some of the devastation they have wreaked elsewhere and have come through more than one *rare* storm recently myself. Have you experienced nothing unusual recently then, apart from the storm I mean?"

"Come to think of it," another voice piped up. "I heard a rumour the other day that wolves were seen gatherin' in the Lowlands."

"No!" said the man near the fire. "What would bring them down out of the mountains? They are too feared of man to show their faces."

"There may be one reason," said the young boy apprehensively; aware that most of what he said was usually dismissed as childish nonsense by his more *mature* customers.

"And what might that be?" another patron asked, in a voice laced with scepticism.

The boy, somewhat rankled by his listeners obvious disdain, straightened up to his full height and said, with more confidence than he actually felt.

"The Quest."

"Quest! What quest be you on about?" the patron questioned.

"The quest I heard of. About a human girl and one of our kind, the son of a wood nymph, making a journey to see Gaia."

"And for why would they be doing that?"

"It's to do with the calamities the gentleman here is talking about," said the boy, warming to his subject. "The story is, that they are nature's way of paying the humans back for all the cutting down of trees and pollution they've been doing all these years, and Gaia won't intervene because the humans have gone too far in stealin' and harmin' the lands and waters."

"Well, that's true enough," said the sage by the fire.

But the young man's nemesis was still unconvinced.

"Where did you hear this here story?"

At this direct question as to his source of his information, the young man suddenly seemed to lose his new-found confidence.

"Well?" his nemesis insisted.

"Hermit Mamdrid," he said, softly. His eyes firmly planted towards the floor.

The whole place instantly erupted with laughter.

"Hermit Mamdrid. Why everyone knows he's mad as they come."

"Wait! Wait!" Lugh shouted, feeling sorry for the boy, and coming to his defence. "Before you dismiss the lad completely. I have to say, I have heard the same rumours myself. All across the land they are saying the same kind of things."

The laughing customers quickly curbed their amusement at the stranger's affirmation of the boy's story.

"Well, if it be true they have brought it on themselves," said the fireside oracle.

"What do a human girl, and the offspring of a wood nymph hope to achieve by going to Gaia?"
another of the curious patrons asked.

"They say she means to plead for mercy for the humans, that she has the power of the Old Ones running through her veins," Lugh answered.

"And Hermit Mamdrid says," the boy began again, his confidence renewed by the support of his new ally, "that she will have to use all her power, because the time of the humans is over and the coming calamities will all but wipe them out."

The bar fell quiet for a moment at this stark revelation.

"I've no love for the humans mysel'," one of the other men at the table near the bar said, "but they have wives and husbands and bairns the same as we do, they're no' *all* responsible for what's happened. The girl should be allowed to plead for some mercy for her own kind,"

"The wolves, I think, won't agree with you. If it hadn't been for Gaia they would have been hunted to extinction from this land by the humans. If the wolves *have* come down from the mountains to stop them, this girl will indeed have to use all the *power* she has to overcome them. They have felt the hate and bloodthirsty arrogance of the humans keenly and have waited a long time to repay them for it," the young boy's nemesis added.

"Aye well, if this all be true, there be little we can do about it," the landlady interrupted. "Let's have a cheerier note. Fingal give us a song to lift our spirits."

A general cry for the good Fingal to grace them with his talent broke out. Fingal, who was one of the bar-side table trio, knitted his brow in thought, and then began in deep round, tenor tones to sing about a lad from MacMoray, who left his home to seek his fortune and had all sorts of riotous adventures, before he returned home a wiser, but no richer man.

*   *   *

Naomi and Woodlan had sat for hours by the campfire, saying little. Naomi dozing now and again, Woodland checking the perimeter, and both, consciously and unconsciously, aware of every sound that came from the surrounding terrain. Naomi was in mid doze when her eyes snapped open at a scuffling sound, someone was crossing the rocks and coming towards them. Woodlan was already standing guard towards the direction of the unseen visitor. Eventually, the pair became aware in the gloom, of a large figure moving unsteadily towards them. They quickly realised it was Lugh, and Naomi let out a breath of relief. Lugh entered the camp calling out to them, unrestrainedly.

"Hullo all . . . I'm back."

"Shhh! Elliott's asleep," Naomi cautioned him, with a smile in her voice.

"Oh Aye! The laddie," Lugh apologised, pursing his lips in an exaggerated fashion and putting a finger to his mouth in a mute shushing gesture.

"You found the village then?" Naomi said.

"Oh Aye," Lugh said, warming his hands by the fire.

"And it was big enough to have a pub I see."

"There was a . . . small . . . establishment . . . yes," Lugh answered, sheepishly.

"Did you manage to find out anything useful?" Woodlan asked him, smiling genially at the merry looking Lugh.

Lugh blinked at this question and furrowed his brow, as if trying to clear his mind. All at once, his cheerful countenance was replaced by a more sober expression.

"There are rumours that the wolves have left their mountain hideaways and are gathering in the Lowlands."

"Did you hear if they were heading for Lake Doruis?" Woodlan asked.

"No . . . But can you think of any other reason they would be putting themselves in danger. Why not wait the end out and come down when it is all over. I can only think, they plan to make *sure* the end goes in their favour by doing all they can to prevent us making it across the lake to Gaia."

"How many of them are there do you think?" Naomi asked.

"Enough to make a fight of it. A fight I'm not sure we could win without help."

This was devastating news. Naomi looked at the sleeping Elliott, and thought how could she take him into such danger, but equally how could she stop him from going with them. She was now more than resigned to the fact that *she* may have to give up her life, but she was once again riddled with feelings of guilt at the thought of anything happening to Elliott. There was little time to dwell on this dilemma though, as Marcus and Rydanna returned in quick succession and confirmed Lugh's report. Marcus informing them that if they were to have any chance of making it to the lake before the wolves they would have to leave immediately.

Naomi gently woke Elliott who; once he had gotten over the initial surprise of being woken when the moon was still high in the sky; was full of questions. Naomi did her best to answer them, without alarming him. She need not have worried though because, as usual, Elliott saw the whole thing as only another part of one big adventure and had only one question.

"How can there be wolves Miss? Wolves in Britain were hunted to extinction hundreds of years ago."

"To be honest, I'm not sure," Naomi answered.

"When it became obvious what the men of these islands intended,"

Rydanna broke in, "Amorok called to Gaia. Pleading for her to save the few wolves who were left, and hide them with the faerie folk from the view of mankind." Rydanna's, soft spoken, answer was tinged with reproach.

Elliott, oblivious to any reproach, continued his questioning with childish enthusiasm.

"Who's Amorok?"

"He is the voice of the beasts."

Rydanna's simple answer did not satisfy Elliott.

"What does that mean?"

"There is no more time for questions we must get moving," Marcus interrupted.

Elliott began packing his backpack with a deeply unsatisfied expression on his face.

Naomi reflected on the imposing creature she had met in the Link and was filled with dread at the thought of having to do battle with him; and who knew how many others like him.

CHAPTER TWENTY-ONE

Gaia

Carefully but swiftly, they picked their way across the rocks until, just as the sun began to rise, Marcus signalled for them all to stop.

"Just over that ridge we will get our first sight of Lake Doruis," he said, "and we will be able to see if the wolves have reached the lake before us. However, even if we cannot see them, it does not mean that they are not near; or in fact that any other dangers are not close by. We must stay close together, and if we are attacked, we must protect Naomi at all costs."

At this last comment of Marcus', Naomi caught sight of Elliot gripping the string of his bow that lay tight across his chest, and she couldn't help, despite the danger, being moved by the determined look on his face.

At the top of the ridge Naomi got her first sight of the lake.

Surrounded by prodigious mountain ranges it looked surprisingly unimpressive. Its water looked dark and murky, and a small island sat in its centre. The island was almost devoid of vegetation except for two giant Scotts pine trees, which looked out of place on the otherwise barren landscape. They could see no sign of the wolves and so began their descent towards the lake. There was a tangible tension within the little group, as they did their best to make their way down while forming a protective ring around Naomi. They went on this way until suddenly the rowan branch began to burn, halting Naomi in her tracks.

"Stop!" she shouted. "There's something wrong." She stood for a moment, her hand holding firmly to the burning branch. The rest of the group looked on anxiously. Then, all at once, she knew. She turned her head back up the mountainside, just in time to see the rock face begin to crumble. "Run!" she cried.

Woodlan made to sweep her up, but before he could, a huge boulder knocked him off his feet and Naomi fell as the arms that had been extended to save her, knocked her over. She found herself tumbling uncontrollably down towards the lake, eventually crashing, almost senseless, face down on the shore. Bruised and battered, she began to push herself up; stopping short, her heart skipped a beat at the sight of two enormous paws, claws extended, right in front of her.

For a moment, she was paralysed by fear. Then, swallowing hard, she forced herself to her knees and found herself looking up at the, ominous, figure of . . . Amorok. Eyes fixed on hers, he covered her right hand with one huge paw, digging his claws mercilessly into her wrist. Naomi cried out in pain, simultaneously her head was filled with the deep bass of Amorok's voice.

"Your journey ends here human!" Amorok declared, digging his claws deeper into Naomi's wrist.

Blood dripped copiously from her wound and seeped into the sandy earth beneath them. Naomi, wincing in pain, felt Amorok lift his free paw ready to strike her down. At that same moment, the rowan branch glowed hot and before either of them knew what was happening roots were rising up from where Amorok stood, entrapping his back legs and pulling him down. He jerked his claws out of Naomi's wrist; surprise in his eyes; trying to release himself from the pernicious roots which circuitously wrapped around him. Naomi, free from Amorok's clamp, fell back and watched as a writhing Amorok was swiftly entwined and eventually tethered to the ground. Once immobile, Amorok let out a piercing howl and within moments wolves began appearing out of every nook and cranny on the mountainside, rapidly galloping towards their leader.

Naomi scrambled to her feet as the lithe figure of Rydanna leapt in front of her, bow and arrow in her hands, poised and ready for battle. In an instant she was joined by Lugh and Elliott, likewise poised. Next, Woodlan came crashing down the mountainside, flinging aside, like rag dolls, any wolves that got in his way. Lastly, Marcus came running along the shore, sword held up menacingly in both hands, reaching them swiftly, to complete the protective wall around Naomi.

The wolves, undaunted by the sight of the little 'army', continued their advance; snarling and growling threateningly as they came.

Within moments, a few were close enough to begin an attack. Forming themselves into a small pack, they stood still, eyes fixed on their enemy, lips curled. Suddenly, in rapid succession two of the pack were in the air, leaping towards them, and just as swiftly falling to the ground; felled by arrows flying from the bows of Rydanna and Lugh . . . The battle had begun.

Arrows began flying everywhere, trying to keep the wolves at bay. Any that got too close were either brought down by Marcus' sword or thrown and heaved back by Woodlan who, immune to their sharp teeth and slashing claws, could take on two or three at a time. It was not long though, before the wolves began to look as if they were going to get the upper hand by their sheer force of numbers.

Woodlan was overcome and forced to the ground by several wolves working together. The rest of the group closed ranks around Naomi, in an effort to fill the gap created by the loss of Woodlan.

They continued to fight on, arrows and sword flying and slashing at the growing enemy, in what was now, every minute, looking more and more like a futile attempt to keep them at bay. Just as their plight seemed hopeless, a volley of arrows came flying over the wolves from another direction. The two opposing groups, equally surprised by this new offensive, ceased battle and looked in the direction from which the arrows had flown. Running along the shore was Lixell, accompanied by a small party of satyrs, about ten in number. Taking advantage of the wolves' momentary surprise at their entrance, the satyrs managed to weave their way through them and take up positions with the other combatants, adding to the protective wall around Naomi.

"We come to aid the quest of Naomi the human," Lixell declared, bows pointed decidedly in the direction of the wolves. The wolves answered with derisive snarls, obviously unimpressed by this small company of reinforcements, "and we do not come alone."

The blast of a horn echoed around the lake. They all looked around them for the source of the sound. Another blast filled the air, and then . . . Naomi saw him, standing on the ridge of a mountain, a lone centaur, horn to his lips; its sound resonated once more. As the reverberation dissipated across the hills, he raised the horn in the air.

A herd of about thirty centaurs appeared on both sides of him. They remained still, looking down on the scene below them then, all at once, began a thunderous descent towards the battlefield; led by a steely eyed Guthran. The wolves took *this* threat more seriously. Recovering from the initial surprise of these new arrivals, the wolves set about reorganising themselves and prepared to begin the battle again; on two fronts.

Naomi knelt near the tethered Amorok, cradling her wounded arm, as the battle began to rage around her once more.

Arrows flew, swiftly and accurately, from the bows of the newly arrived satyrs and centaurs. Elliott, with a maturity beyond his years, was picking his targets carefully, and more often than not, hitting them. Marcus deftly wielded his sword as three wolves snapped and growled at him, trying to manoeuvre their way past his defences and bring him down. Woodlan, having managed to release himself from his attackers during the unexpected arrival of Lixell and Guthran, was once again keeping the wolves at bay with the threat of his enormous bulk; swatting them like flies if they got too close.

Lugh and Rydanna were in a standoff with several wolves, who were pacing back and forth waiting for a chance to strike. This standoff lasted sometime until, all at once, two of the wolves leapt towards Rydanna. Lugh started firing arrows with unimaginable speed at the rest of the pack who simultaneously made a rush at him. Rydanna, meanwhile, had managed to hit one of her assailants square in the chest with her arrow. Naomi; who was watching the whole scene in horror; let out a cry as Rydanna was caught on her shoulder and thrust to the ground by her second, flying assailant. Rydanna dropped her bow as she fell, but managed to roll away before the wolf could secure her with its lethal claws.

Jumping to her feet, Rydanna dodged and weaved avoiding the wolf's savage assault and snapping teeth. Naomi took a sharp intake of breath as another wolf, seeing that Rydanna was unarmed, joined in the attack. Rydanna pulled an arrow from her quiver and began to wave and poke it threateningly towards her attackers. Her attackers merely sneered at her feeble attempt to hold them off and, leaning down on their haunches, made to go in for the kill. Hardly aware of what she was doing, Naomi took the rowan branch from its pouch and, holding it tightly in her bloodied hand, focused on the lake. Within a moment, just as the wolves began to leap, a wave reared up onto the shore where Rydanna and the wolves were sparring and engulfed them all, pulling them into the water, where they disappeared out of sight.

Naomi held the rowan branch in a death grip, staring at the lake, almost afraid to breathe. An age seemed to pass before, without warning, the water broke and Rydanna's head appeared. Naomi let out a sigh of relief. Rydanna was bleeding above her right eye but otherwise seemed unhurt. Swimming back on the shore she redeemed her bow and resumed her place in the battle.

The wolves fought savagely and intelligently and, while they still outnumbered their opponents two to one, they were ultimately no match for the lethal, well-placed arrows which soared towards them, cutting them down until their numbers were almost halved. The wolves, caught up in the heat of battle, seemed heedless of the danger and continued their fearless offensive. Until, a piercing howl punctuated the air and brought to a halt the snarling and snapping and swooshing of arrows.

The combatants remained in a wary cease fire as Amorok's howling continued to fill the air. Finally, he let out a long, plaintive cry and slowly and deliberately the wolves began to back away. Many of the wolves eyed Amorok with resentful gazes, obviously reluctant to give up the fight in spite of their losses. Marcus and the others remained battle ready until the wolves had disappeared into the surrounding terrain, and only Amorok, and the dead or dying bodies of his pack remained. Only then did they lower their guard and weapons.

Amorok strained in his bonds, indicating for Naomi to touch his right paw. Naomi, still smarting from her last encounter with the wolf's claws, hesitated for a moment. Then cautiously she laid her, still bleeding, hand on his restrained paw. Amorok's deep bass tones filled Naomi's head.

"You have won the battle here today . . . *with help.*" Naomi felt the force of Amorok's anger directed towards Gurthran and Lixell and shuddered. "There will be no such help when you make your plea to Gaia, and she will hear the cries of those who have fallen today. Their sacrifice will not be in vain, it will be a testament against your plea. She will remember the state of the heart of those who can hunt another creature to extinction; their blood competes with your blood *now* for the attention of Gaia."

When he had finished speaking, Amorok struggled to remove his paw from under Naomi's hand. Naomi lifted her hand. She remained still for a moment, recovering from the strength of Amorok's contempt towards her. At last, she forced herself to look him directly in the eye and, tightening her grip on the rowan branch once more, she released him from his bonds. Once free, Amorok perused the scene of his losses, then gave one last plaintive howl and bounded away.

"What did he say?" Guthran asked.

"Nothing good," Naomi said.

She had no desire to relive Amorok's admonition, she just wanted to move on before something else happened to stop her; or her strength failed her. She looked around at those who had come to help her. Many of them were bruised and bleeding, but thankfully none had fatal wounds.

"I'm deeply grateful for your help," she said. "I know it could not have been an easy decision for any of you, and I will never forget that you were willing to risk your lives for me . . . and my people, thank you." The satyrs and centaurs all bowed in acknowledgement of her thanks. Naomi returned their bow and then turned to Marcus and asked, "What now?"

"We need to get across to the island. You must use the branch," he said.

Naomi stared across the water and then squatted down by the lake's edge and plunged the branch into its icy depths, concentrating on her desire to cross the lake . . . nothing happened. Naomi closed her eyes and with a furrowed brow made her silent plea once more. Still nothing happened. Naomi turned a hopeless face towards the many faces which stood expectantly on the shore.

"Maybe you need to ask out loud," Elliott suggested.

Naomi turned back to the water.

"I wish to cross the lake and speak with Gaia," she said.

Almost immediately, a path of white steppingstones appeared, glimmering just below the surface of the water. Naomi smiled over her shoulder at Elliott. Then rising to her feet, she stepped onto the first stone. Breaking the surface of the water, she felt the stone stay firm under her weight. Elliott was the first to move forward to follow her but as he got near to the water's edge Naomi put up her hand to stop him.

"Elliott, I want you to stay here," she said, and before he could protest at being left behind, she added. "With Woodlan, Lugh and Rydanna. I think it might be best if only Marcus and I go the rest of the way."

Woodlan came forward and placed his heavy hand gently on Elliott's shoulder, nodding his agreement. Elliott acquiesced, reluctantly. Naomi started to make her way across the stones, Marcus made to follow her, only to find that the first stone gave way under him. Naomi looked back as she heard him splash into the water. Marcus tried his foot on the next stone but once again it sank into the lake.

"Well . . . I guess this means I'm going alone," she said.

"If you wish, I will attempt the crossing," Rydanna said.

At the sound of Rydanna composed voice Naomi stopped in mid-step.

"What makes you think you will be able to cross?" she asked.

"My people's affinity with the waters may allow me passage," Rydanna answered.

Naomi stood perplexed for a moment. She was somewhat intimidated by, the ever-composed, Rydanna and wasn't overly anxious for her personal companionship.

"Then . . . please . . . yes . . . I'd like you to try." Naomi said at last. Coming to the conclusion, that she would rather have Rydanna's company than none at all as she stepped into the unknown.

Without another word, Rydanna waded into the water and disappeared into its depths. Naomi waited a few moments and, when Rydanna did not resurface, continued across the steppingstones. She had almost reached the island when she saw, with some relief, Rydanna emerge from the lake and stand waiting for her on the shore. On joining her, Naomi looked back at the opposite shore and waved. Elliott waved back, eagerly.

Turning her attention to the island, she was once again surprised at how strangely bare it looked. Just a few bushes and large boulders, along with the two tall Scotts pines. The pines stood a few meters apart; their top branches mingling close together. Naomi felt somewhat perplexed, she had expected more. What was she to do now? She threw a questioning glance towards Rydanna and was struck by the look on her face, she was almost smiling, and her eyes were alive with interest. Naomi searched the landscape for whatever it was which had so wholly captured Rydanna's attention. She could see nothing that could cause such a reaction in her usually impassive companion. Turning once again to the fascinated Rydanna, Naomi touched her lightly on the arm, awaking her from her reverie.

"Shall we continue?" Rydanna said.

"Continue, to where?"

A flicker of puzzlement crossed Rydanna's face, quickly followed by a look of comprehension. Rydanna raised her hand as a signal for Naomi to make her way forward, towards the gap between the Scotts pines.

Naomi obeyed Rydanna's signal and passed though the informal archway, created by the majestic pines. Instantly, she let out a breath of astonishment; it was as if she had stepped into an enchanted painting. There were trees, flowers, leaves and grass, all around her shimmering and glistening; butterflies in glorious colours, bees, birds and all manner of insects, fluttered, buzzed and sang in one harmonious chorus. She suddenly felt a tingle in her right hand, and looking down saw that her wound was completely healed. Speechless, she walked on for some time in a dreamlike state with, the equally silent, Rydanna by her side. At length, almost imperceptibly, the shimmer around them began to transform into a thin mist that clung to them like silver cobwebs, gradually thickening, until it began to envelop the chimerical spectacle which had greeted them. Naomi's heart beat a little faster with the growing opacity. Then, just when the mist was about to completely engulf them, a storm of insects materialised out of the gloom, flying and fussing around Rydanna. It quickly became clear that they were attempting to block her way.

"I can go no further with you," she said. Then, much to Naomi's surprise, she placed her hand reassuringly on Naomi's arm and said, "I will wait in the forest, until you return."

Naomi, fearing her courage would fail her if she spoke, made no answer except a short nod. She turned, continuing through the now impenetrable mist. On and on she went, becoming more disoriented with each step, while at the same time pushing down a growing feeling of panic by concentrating, with arms now outstretched, on groping her way through the mist. Slowly and deliberately, she placed one foot in front of the other, expecting every moment to trip or fall. It seemed an age before, much to her relief, the mist began to dissipate, and she could just make out the earth beneath her feet. Eventually, the mist cleared completely, and she found herself standing in a dimly lit grove before a giant oak tree. The trunk of the tree was split almost perfectly down the middle; its heavy branches stretched out and bent low, lightly caressing the woodland floor around it.

"Ow!" Naomi cried out, suddenly.

The rowan branch was burning at her chest, she quickly pulled it from its pouch, wincing at the sudden surge of heat which burned her hand, and dropping it hastily on the ground, watched as it melted into the earth.

Where the branch had fallen, the earth began to glow. A bolt of light shot across the ground towards the oak, transforming into a marble aisle leading directly to the fissure of the blasted tree. Naomi, heart pounding, felt an irresistible urge to step onto the pathway. Tentatively, she stepped onto the glowing marble, as she did so everything around her disappeared; only the path and the tree remained. She walked steadily down the alabaster aisle until she reached the base of the mighty oak, where she felt another compulsion overcome her. This time, it was to place her hand into the gaping fissure. Shaking slightly, she put her hand into the yawning cleft . . .

A woman, almost transparent to look at, immediately appeared before Naomi. She was colourless, with long flowing hair, which danced lightly around her. Her neutral eyes and mouth smiled down benevolently on Naomi and when she spoke her voice, soft and soothing, filled Naomi's whole being with a feeling of peace and light.

"Welcome, child. You have brought the rowan branch. The healing process will now be completed."

Naomi, slightly confused at this assertion of Gaia's, (for she knew, without doubt, that that was whose presence she was in) asked, "I don't understand . . . I don't know . . . what do you mean?"

"What is your name, child?"

"Naomi."

"Did you not bring the rowan branch to the island?"

"Yes . . . I did. I mean the blue cap faeries gave it to me. They told me that it would help me to . . . communicate with the natural elements and more effectively channel the power of the Old Ones."

"They spoke the truth. Are you saying, child that you did not bring the branch here willingly to me, to fulfil its true purpose?"

"I don't understand what you mean. I came because I was told that if I made a plea to you that I might be able to save my people . . . and the faerie folk, and stop what's happening, the branch was only supposed to help me reach you."

Gaia's glacial countenance continued to shine down benevolently on Naomi. Then a look of searching filled her eyes, followed by an attitude of sad comprehension.

"I see I was right," she said. "You did not bring the branch to me of your own free will, another placed it in your way . . . you have been deceived as to its true purpose."

"What is it's true purpose?" Naomi asked, her stomach tightening.

"In the ancient days, a human came here to me to receive the power and take it with them into the human world. I gave that human a rowan branch to act as a conduit between humankind and the earth. I told the bearer of the branch that if at any time one holding that power should return the branch to me, the earth would be released from the restraints of the old links. It is the final element necessary to complete the healing the earth cries out for; the old links will be cleared away and new ones made."

Naomi's thoughts began to race in every direction; a growing fear and comprehension gripping her heart.

"Who was it who knew its true purpose . . .? Who was it who deceived me?"

"Marcus MacFreya."

Tears filled Naomi's eyes.

"He lied to me!" she cried. "But why. . .? I've just made things worse coming here . . . haven't I?"

"I am sorry my child, but the branch is here and what is . . . is . . . I must use it to finish the call against your people. The healing time cannot be stopped now."

"You keep calling it a healing, but all I've seen so far is devastation and death,"

Filled with a newfound confidence; fuelled by her anger towards Marcus; Naomi stood undaunted before Gaia's imposing figure.

"I have seen billions die . . . and billions be born, since the Ancient Ones left me here and I have cared for each one of them," Gaia answered, unmoved by Naomi's outburst. "This *must* be. I understand your grief, child, but not all will be lost, and for the sake of the deception I will, if you wish it, allow you to join me in The Healing."

"Join you . . . How?"

"By linking with me . . . I warn you, child that you may not survive the experience, but I sense you know this already. If you truly wish to help your people, this is the only way now that you can do so. Through the tumult, that *must* come with the change, you can use the power the Ancients have blessed you with to reach out and save a portion of your people."

Tears filled Naomi's eyes and rushed down her cheeks at the full realisation of how she had been duped by Marcus, and probably all those with him, into helping bring about the death of billions of people. Panic gripped her at the thought of the children she had left in their care, and she knew that if there was anything she could do to ameliorate the devastation her stupidity was going to cause, she had to do it.

"I will link with you," she said, shaking off her grief.

"Very well."

Closing her pale eyes Gaia stretched her arms out wide, enveloping Naomi in a blinding white light and calling to her.

"Touch as many as you can."

Then . . . there was nothing . . . it was as if everything had stopped . . .

Naomi took a sharp intake of breath and opened her eyes. She was surrounded by thousands of images, a cacophony of noise deafened her, she covered her ears, her breath quickened. Mountain ranges, rivers, valleys, cities, towns, villages; people running, shouting, screaming through rains, tsunamis, earthquakes, floods and gales.

Naomi felt sick, but forced herself to search through the turmoil, trying hard to focus on just one image. Catching sight of a small child on a swing, she did all she could to block out all the other sounds and images. Gradually, the flashing images began to slow down, and she was standing in a large garden watching the child swinging happily, on a swing which hung from a tree branch. All at once, the wind began to strengthen and before either Naomi or the child knew it, a gale was blowing, and the child was crying and gripping onto the swing. The wind violently tossed the child back and forth. A woman ran from the house towards the little girl, but the strength of the wind was holding her back from reaching her. Naomi ran towards the child; the wind having no effect on her; lifted the child from the swing and placed her in the hands of her mother. The mother thanked Naomi profusely and offered her a place in her underground shelter.

"Thank you but I'll be fine. Hurry," Naomi said, touching the women lightly on the arm.

The woman, reluctant to leave her child's rescuer but compelled by the raging wind around them ran towards the open door of the shelter. When the door was safely closed and bolted Naomi found herself, once again, cloaked in the flashing images.

She focused once more and was suddenly standing in a kitchen where everything was shaking, uncontrollably. From underneath the table she heard whimpering. One side of the house crashed to the ground and the whimpering from under the table turned into screaming. Naomi bent down, three children, a teenage girl and two young boys, sat huddled terrified under their precarious shield. Surprised by their sudden visitor they stopped crying.

Naomi touched each of them and found herself saying, "Rester ici jusqu'à ce que le tremblement de terre se termine."

The earthquake continued to wreak havoc around the three forlorn figures, but they remained unharmed. Naomi moved on.

Now, she was standing on a beach, hundreds of people were running towards her, a massive wave following in their wake. Naomi watched helplessly as it began to engulf everyone in its path. She ran forward, catching hold of the people nearest to her, a young couple, who were just about to be lost under its might. As she touched them the water, instead of covering them, held them up and they found themselves safely surfing the mighty swell.

"How . . .?" The young man said, opened mouthed.

"You'll be safe now," was all Naomi said, and moved on.

Through the window of a small cabin on the side of a snow-capped mountain, an avalanche hurtling towards it, a family sat holding hands round a table praying. Naomi placed her hand on the frozen windowpane, the snow slide swerved past the cabin; merely brushing it with a smattering of snow. Naomi moved on.

On and on, experiencing one devastating scene after another, reaching out to everyone within her grasp, answering as many of the desperate calls for help that she could and trying, without success, to shut out the screaming. The constant screaming. Just when she thought she would start screaming herself, her body began to convulse uncontrollably, and at last . . . the screaming stopped.

Naomi lay, lifeless, curled up in the base of the oak; the immense branches of which, lifted up gently from the earth and slowly closed the giant fissure around the, still, foetal figure.

The glow of the forest, where Rydanna remained; a silent immovable sentinel; fell into a solemn gloom and the island submerged, reverentially, beneath the lake.

*   *   *

"What's that light?" Elliott called out.

A blaze of light was emanating from the centre of the island, shooting straight up to the now glowering evening sky.

"It is Gaia," Guthran answered. "The Old One has succeeded in reaching her, all we can do now is continue . . ."

Guthran was interrupted by an ear-splitting bang, which was quickly followed by a thunderous roar, and before any of them knew what was happening the mountains and ground surrounding the lake, began splitting and collapsing in on themselves. Several of the centaurs and satyrs were hit and felled by falling rocks. Others reared up, or ran to and fro, looking for a way to escape the falling debris only to disappear into the giant crevasses which were ripping through the shoreline. Marcus grabbed Elliott pulling him clear of a massive rock bounding towards him.

"Quickly into the lake." Woodlan's booming voice could just be heard, calling above the almost deafening noise around them.

Marcus, still holding on fast to the stunned Elliott dragged him into the water with him. Many of the others followed as they came to the realisation, as Woodlan had already, that the lake, despite all the uproar around it, remained still and untouched; the debris and fissures stopping short at the edge of its waters. Lugh ran towards Marcus and Elliott. Just making it in time into the calm water ahead of a pursuing rock which, stopping on the edge of the lake, appeared to almost brood at the loss of its prey. Those who remained, of the centaurs and satyrs, were now also in the water watching the terrain transform before their astounded eyes.

Unremittingly, the landscape heaved and roared all around the lake, while the onlookers watched anxiously from their anomalous sanctuary. Elliott stayed close to Marcus' side, half-terrified half- fascinated by the dreadful display of havoc. Marcus stood with his arm lightly around Elliott's shoulder, wearing a countenance of awe and astonishment. Eventually, he turned his head slowly towards the island, at the sight of which he lowered his eyes, and for a fleeting moment, a look of regret crossed his brow. Then, turning his gaze back towards the continuing cataclysm, his face hardened and he became as cold and as calm as the lake beneath him.

At last, the shuddering and rumbling slowed, then stopped. The clamour and commotion was replaced by an eerie silence. Elliott was the first to speak.

"Do you think it's stopped?"

"I hope so," Lugh said. "That was . . ."

Before Lugh could finish, Elliott was calling out.

"Marcus look! The island . . . it's sinking." Elliott's terrified voice arrested all their attentions. "Miss! Miss! We have to save Miss!" Elliott began to wade further into the water as he shouted. Marcus grabbed him and pulled him back.

"It is too late," he said, his voice barely above a whisper.

"What do you mean it's *too* late . . .? We have to try, we can't just leave her to drown . . . Lugh, Woodlan . . . *please!*"

Unable to meet the child's gaze, Woodlan and Lugh lowered their eyes to the water.

Elliott was about to appeal to the centaurs and satyrs, but they merely turned to face the island and bowed their heads in a silent display of homage.

"Then I'll go by myself," he said, struggling against Marcus' firm grip.

"No, boy . . . it is no use," Marcus said.

"You don't *know* that."

Taking the boy firmly by the shoulders and leaning down, so his face was close to his, he said:

"Yes . . . *I do.*"

There was something in the finality of Marcus' voice that convinced Elliott that what he said was true and overcome by the starkness of the reality of the loss of the teacher he had come to love, he crumbled, crying, into Marcus' arms. Marcus held the boy close and raising his eyes to the disappearing lake said solemnly . . .

IT IS OVER . . .

Printed in Great Britain
by Amazon

62291084R00112